BRONXWOOD

COE BOOTH

Go There.
Other titles available from

PUSH

Copyright © 2011 by Coe Booth

All rights reserved. Published by PUSH, an imprint of Scholastic Inc., *Publishers since 1920*.

SCHOLASTIC and associated logos are trademarks and/or registered trademarks of Scholastic Inc.

Library of Congress Cataloging-in-Publication Data available

ISBN 978-0-439-92534-1

10 9 8 7 6 5 4 3 2 1   11 12 13 14 15 16 17/0

Printed in the U.S.A. 23

First edition, September 2011

The text was set in Alisal Regular.

Book design by Elizabeth B. Parisi

For Lisa and Rashid

ACKNOWLEDGMENTS

Special thanks to Mom, Mike, Haadiyah, Micayla, Alyssa, Hamza, Hasan, and Halima — you're all a constant source of inspiration; Holly Black, thanks for all your help with this book; Jodi Reamer, thanks so much for being in my corner; and, as always, thank you, David Levithan, for your endless support!

ONE

I been driving for hours, got the radio blastin', and I'm flying up the New Jersey Turnpike like I be doing this shit all the time. Like it ain't no thing. Regg is 'sleep with the passenger seat pushed all the way back, and I know it's just 'cause he tired from being up all night doing whatever he do, but still, it feel good that he trust me with his brand-new Escalade when I don't even got no kinda license and don't really know how to drive for shit.

It's, like, four in the afternoon when I get back to Bronxwood. I pull the truck up in front of Building A, and the only reason Regg wake up is 'cause I hit the brake too hard to keep from slamming into the car parked in front of me. When the truck stop, he look 'round, not knowing where the fuck he at, and I just crack up 'cause he missed the whole drive back from DC. "You get enough sleep?" I ask him. "'Cause I could drive 'round some more if you need more time."

"Nobody could sleep, the way you was driving."

"Nigga, you was snoring and drooling and shit."

"You dreaming, man," Regg say. "My eyes was closed 'cause I was praying for my life." He open the door and say under his breath, "Musta been crazy giving you the keys to my truck."

Regg is my pops friend, the only one that's alright, you ask me. He mad cool, the kinda guy you know got your back no matter what. And he the size of a linebacker, so that help too, 'specially in the kinda places we was hanging out at for the last twelve days. First we drove down to Atlanta and stood there for more than a week, then, on the way back, we went to Baltimore and DC for a couple days. The whole time was mad fun even though we was working. I played two parties in Atlanta, and one in Baltimore. Made some good money, for me. Regg was doing his business too, but he don't want me knowing what he do. He don't want me going down for whatever shit he doing.

I cut the engine and get out the truck. Regg come 'round to the driver side and, before I see it coming, he grab me up in one of them guy hugs and say, "Remember what we talked about, man."

"Yeah, I remember," I say, and he let me go.

"Call me if you need me, Ty."

I reach in and grab my heavy-ass duffel bag and back-pack from the backseat. Then I watch Regg try to squeeze his ass in the driver seat, get out and push the seat back, like, a foot and a half, then get in and drive away. I just stand there for a second, watching him go. Hanging with him was cool, but ain't nothing like being back in the Bronx.

It's the first day of August and it's real nice outside, sunny and hot, but not Atlanta hot. It feel good walking into my building, like I'm home or something.

But that feeling don't last too long. Just 'til I get to the fifth floor, open the door to the apartment I'm staying at, and see the way the place look, like fucking animals was living here while I was away.

I go inside and Greg is 'sleep on the couch. The whole living room is jacked. They got them white boxes half full of Chinese food all over the table and on the floor, cans of beer and bags of chips and shit on the floor and chairs. I knock a empty thing of Pringles off one of the chairs and put my duffel bag down on it, but there ain't even no other place to put my backpack on, that's how fucked up they got the apartment. I go in the kitchen and it ain't no better. I mean, I been living with these dudes for, like, seven months, and I know they some nasty niggas when they wanna be, but this shit don't make no kinda sense.

My friend Cal come from down the hall in sweatpants and no shirt. "You back," he say, like I don't know I'm back. "You make money?"

"Course." I don't tell him, yeah, I made money, but I'm coming home with a duffel bag full of new clothes, shit they be selling down south that I ain't seen in the Bronx yet. "Made a lot," I tell him.

3

Made it. Spent it. Still damn-near broke.

Cal wipe some Oreo cookie crumbs off the chair before he sit down at the kitchen table and start rubbing the crust outta his eyes. "Last night was crazy," he say, laughing. "We had a party that was wild. I got with this girl and she —"

"What 'bout Tina?" I can tell when Cal 'bout to go into one of his stories 'bout all the females he getting, and the best thing to do is shut that noise down fast.

"Me and her had a fight."

Nothing new 'bout that.

"She coming by on Sunday so I could babysit CJ."

"It ain't babysitting when it's your kid," I say.

"Whatever." That's when he finally look 'round the kitchen. "Shit." He turn and look 'round at the living room. "Fuck."

"Just so you know, I ain't cleaning none of this up," I tell him. "And I ain't chipping in for Keisha to clean this shit up neither."

Cal look back over at me. "What your problem?"

"I ain't got no problems."

"Good, then," he say, standing up and getting the milk out the refrigerator. Then he go up in the cabinet and get down the Cocoa Puffs, and when he try to find a clean bowl, there ain't one 'cause all the dishes is in the sink, dirty. But he do find a measuring cup and one of them big spoons and he sit down and start eating, like that's a normal way to eat cereal.

"I ain't playin'," I tell him. "Y'all gonna need to do something 'bout this shit 'cause —"

"Your pops getting out today, right?" Cal ask, even though he already know the answer.

I swear, I ain't in the mood for Cal today. It's like the whole time I was with Regg is through and now I'm back to this shit, only today it's pissing me off more than it normally do.

"I'ma be back," I say and, just like that, I up and leave the apartment before Cal can say something else to me.

Outside, I walk 'cross the street, over to Kenny candy truck that's out in front of Building G. Kenny sister Adonna is leaning up against the truck with her arms folded in front of her like she got a attitude 'bout something. But that's the way she always act. She fine as hell though, so even when she mad she still look good. And she wearing shorts and a tank top, showing off all that skin. Damn.

I been knowing Adonna from back in the day when me and my family used to live here at Bronxwood. Before we got stupid and moved outta the projects like we had it like that. Then, when my pops got locked up, they threw us outta that new apartment and we ain't had no place to go. The city put my family through a lot of shit. 'Til I decided to come back here and live with my boy Cal. And be on my own.

Now that I'm back, me and Adonna be seeing each other all the time. She real nice, but something 'bout her, 'bout all them girls like her, that just stop me from trying to get with her. I can tell by looking at her that she one of them females that's more trouble than I need in my life. She know she hot, and she know niggas would break they neck to get with her, but I don't know. I hook up with her and I can tell it's gonna be all 'bout me buying her stuff. I don't need that.

Only thing, the last couple times she seen me, I know she been checking me out. Now that I be spending money on clothes and shit and lookin' good, she definitely on it now. When she see me, she smile but not all sexy like she usually do 'cause she probably don't wanna act like that in front of Kenny.

"Hey, Adonna," I say.

She look me up and down real fast, trying to be slick 'bout it, and go, "Hi, Tyrell."

Kenny hand her a Sprite and say, "I'm gonna put that on your bill."

"Yeah, yeah," she say, and roll her eyes.

"What up, Ty?" Kenny ask me.

"Chillin'," I say. "Let me get a loose."

Next to me, Adonna is still standing there opening her can of soda and taking a sip. After Kenny hand me the cigarette, I'm like, "What you doing today, Adonna?"

She shrug. "Nothing. It's so boring around here. I saw you driving that Escalade and I thought it was yours at first."

I shake my head and go, "Yeah, right. Wish I could roll like that."

Adonna look me up and down again and stop at my sneakers. "You must be making good money DJing, right?" She try to hide her smile.

"I'm doin' a'ight."

Even though I don't mind talking to her, I could probably get to Southern Boulevard in time if I go fast. So I tell Adonna I gotta go, light up my cigarette, and smoke while I walk away from her. This my first cigarette in, like, four, five days. I thought I was through with them, but it don't look that way. Least not today.

I'm walking fast down the block, on my way to the train station, not really thinking 'bout nothing. The second I turn the corner near the bodega, that's when I see them. My ex, Novisha, and some dude. Some pretty boy. They walking right in my direction too. And they holding hands.

TWO

Novisha don't see me at first. She too busy smiling and talking to that guy, and anyway, it ain't like I don't see her all the time 'round here. See her, yeah, but I don't never say nothing to her. But this the first time I'm seeing her with another dude and, straight up, my mind go right there, thinking 'bout the two of them together, her doing to him what she used to do to me, and him getting to see all of her, and I can feel my jaw get tight and my blood start pounding 'cause, yeah, I'm mad. And not that she with no other guy, 'cause me and her ain't even together no more. But 'cause it bring back all that shit that happened in January when me and her broke up.

'Cause, the truth is, the way she treated me was fucked up. She told me she loved me and all that, and put me on hold, saying she wanted to wait to have sex 'til she got married. And I believed that shit too. 'Til it came out that she wasn't even no virgin, that she was lying to me the whole fuckin' time we was together.

Yeah, she called me a lot of times after all her lies came out and tried to tell me she was sorry and crying to me on the phone, but I wasn't hearing it. I was through. She musta finally got the hint 'cause after a while she stopped calling and I stopped caring.

So now I just walk past them on the street, 'cause whoever he is can have her for all I care. Her and her lies is his problem now.

I smoke the rest of my cigarette for the next block, then stop at the pizza shop to get a slice, and 'cause I got a little money now I get extra cheese and pepperoni on it and start eating it on my way to the train station. It's already almost 4:30 and I need to get to Troy camp by 5:00 or I'm not gonna get no time to see him. His foster mother be coming for him between 5:30 and 6:00 and I don't want her seeing me there with him.

When I get a block from the train station, I try to finish my slice fast. Just eat and not think 'bout nothing. Not that nasty-ass apartment. Not Novisha and whatever guy she wanna get with. Not even Troy, but that's hard. I can't help thinking 'bout him 'cause everything 'bout his situation still piss me off.

When ACS took him away from my moms and put him in foster care, he got lucky in the beginning 'cause the lady he was living with was real nice to him and treated him good, like he was one of her own two kids. She even let Troy call me every night after dinner if he was good that day, and after a while, after she knew she could trust me, she let me bring him to school and pick him up a couple days a week.

Me and Troy used to go to McDonald's when it was cold outside and he would play on them slides and shit. And when it got hot out, me and him would go to this park over by Crotona and I would let him run 'round for a while before he had to go back to that foster home. I just wanted to spend time with him. Not that a couple hours a couple times a week was gonna make up for the fact that me and him was split up, but least it was something.

Him being in foster care is the thing I never wanted to happen in the first place. But I fucked up and it happened anyway. The real messed-up thing is, I can't do nothing to change none of it. My moms coulda did something all this time, but she never did nothing. And now, the only one that can get Troy back is my pops.

I finish my pizza and throw away the bag and napkins on the ground in front of a garbage can that's so full, more stuff is 'round it than in it. I hear the train coming, so I gotta run in, swipe my MetroCard, and fly up the stairs like I don't care. I'm not tryin' to waste no more time today. Good thing I do run too, 'cause I make it into the train right before the doors close. But, damn, running up the stairs like that kinda mess with my stomach. It feel like the pizza is trying to come back up, which would be mad embarrassing in front of all these people on this train.

So I sit down and try and get my stomach to settle back down. But my mind is still running wild. I gotta find a way to fix Troy situation. Yeah, my pops is getting out, or already out for all I know, and I know he gonna find a way to get Troy out the system, but it ain't gonna happen tomorrow. The city never do nothing fast. For now, he stuck where he at.

If Troy was still at that first foster home, it wouldn't be all that bad, but he ain't there no more. I shoulda knew it wasn't gonna last. At the end of June everything changed. Troy foster mother sent her kids down south to they family, and she probably ain't wanna be stuck with Troy, not after getting rid of her own kids for the summer, so she told the agency she wanted to give Troy back. Just like that. Like that wasn't gonna fuck him up. So the agency had to move him to this other home over on Simpson Street where they got two other foster kids that both is babies, and now Troy don't got nobody to play with or nothing.

The only good thing is the agency paid for him to go to camp all summer, and he be out the house from 8:00 in the morning 'til something like 6:00 at night, so least he got to be 'round kids his own age all summer 'cept on the weekends.

While the train go from stop to stop, what I'm thinking 'bout is trying to find a way for Troy to get back with that first foster mother again, and if she even wanna take him back when her own kids come back home. 'Cause she was always cool with me, and school starting next month and no way is his new foster mother gonna let me pick him up from school like the first one used to.

A couple minutes later, just when the train pull outta the Gun Hill Road stop, my cell ring and it take me a second to make myself even reach in my backpack to look and see who it is. 'Cause if it's my pops, I don't know. I mean, like, what he gonna say? And what I'm s'posed to say back to him? And why I ain't think 'bout none of this the whole time he was locked up?

After three rings I pull my cell out and it ain't my pops calling me. Jasmine name on the screen. I click the talk button and hardly get the word hi out my mouth before she start talking my ear off.

"You back?" she ask, and don't wait for no kinda answer. "I know you are because I can hear you on the train. Where you going?"

I can't help but smile 'cause it's like she don't care that she all up in my business. "I'm going to see Troy at that ghetto camp they got him at."

"Hey, I used to go to camps like that and look how good I turned out."

"Damn," I say, kinda under my breath, and me and her both laugh. Then we talk for a while 'bout what she been up to the whole time I was gone, which she say was just working and going home and being bored. Jasmine work at this Spanish restaurant over by Hunts Point, not all that far from Bennett, this real nasty motel the city made us stay at back in January when we was homeless. That's where me and her first met and got close, which is what happen when they got you living in a fucked-up place like that with all kinda roaches and shit.

And Jasmine fine too, which don't hurt none.

Jasmine start telling me 'bout how the air conditioner at the restaurant broke down a couple days ago and how hot it was in there, but that still ain't stop people from coming there to eat. "All these construction worker guys came there for lunch and I was sweating on their plates," she say, laughing. "And they still came back the next day!"

"That's 'cause you hot when you hot."

She laugh again. "Yeah, right. I probably looked as bad as I smelled!"

Jasmine don't know. She could never look nothing but sexy as hell. The lady she work for don't hardly pay her nothing, and she don't need to. Jasmine make decent enough money just from tips.

The train pull up at the Allerton station, and this bum get on that smell like he been pissing on hisself for a month. Dude got the whole car hummin' in, like, three seconds. "Hold on, Jasmine." I get up and walk through the train to the next car 'cause I don't need none of that funk on me, smelling like that the rest of the day. I sit down and say, "A'ight. I'm back."

"So, talk to me. Is your father out yet? You seen him?"

Damn.

"Ty?"

"I don't really know nothing right now." I don't know what else to tell her. Jasmine know how I feel 'bout my pops.

Matter of fact, her and Cal the only ones that know that I actually thought 'bout going to see the man when he was at some halfway house back in March. And 'bout how I changed my mind at the last minute. After that, I never went to see him even though he was right there in Queens.

Then in April, Regg told me my pops got sent back to Rikers 'cause he did something he wasn't s'posed to. I never found out what it was, just that it was enough for his ass to be sent back up to finish out the rest of his time. Which was alright with me 'cause then I ain't hafta think 'bout if I was gonna go see him or not. 'Cause one thing I don't do is go to no jail to see nobody.

Jasmine know all that. Me and her is tight like that.

"Well, let me know the second you hear from him, okay?"

"Yeah, a'ight," I say, then go, "I can't hardly hear you no more. This signal getting weak or something. I'ma call you back after I get off the train."

"Okay. But don't forget because I have to talk to you about the party."

"I ain't gonna forget. Bye." I end the call, kinda mad. I don't get it. Why everybody keep talkin' 'bout my pops today?

THREE

I don't call Jasmine back after I get off the train at 174th. I just wanna walk and not deal with nothing or nobody. I just wanna get to that camp and see Troy and let him know I ain't forget 'bout him or nothing. I told him when I was leaving and how long I was gonna be gone for, but still, twelve days is a long time for a kid. And even though I know the money I made DJing them parties is gonna help me buy him some new clothes and shit for school, he ain't gonna understand that 'cause he only eight.

Course, Troy new foster mother s'posed to be the one to buy him clothes, but she ain't gonna get him nothing good. She only do what the city pay her to do and that's it. That's why I gotta keep looking out for him myself, make sure he alright.

That's how my pops raised me.

Not that my pops used to go 'round telling me "do this" or "do that." He ain't hafta. I knew what to do by watching him, seeing how he handled his shit, and then doing what he did. That's how come I knew what I had to do when he was sent up last year. 'Cause I seen how he did it.

I ain't saying I did it all that good or nothing, 'cause I know I fucked up. And that's the thing. I know he gonna be the first person to tell me that when me and him come face-to-face. And I don't wanna hear it. I don't need to hear it. I been telling myself the same thing since Troy got tooken away by ACS and put in the system. Nothing my pops say could make me feel worse.

By the time I get to Southern Boulevard it's after five, but them kids is still running 'round buckwild in the yard outside the community center where the camp is at. They all wearing they red camp T-shirts so they musta went on some trip or something. I'm walking by the gate trying to find Troy, but he ain't running 'round with them other kids. He standing by hisself on the side of the building, playing in the dirt. And I'm like, what's up with that?

I come into the yard, and when he see me, he run over to me, going, "Ty! Ty!" He fast too. He get to me in two seconds and wrap his arms 'round my waist real tight. And he don't let go neither.

I start laughing. "You killin' me, Troy."

"You back!" He mad happy and I ain't gonna front. Me and him is feeling the same way.

"You like a boa constrictor," I tell him. "You trying to squeeze me 'til my eyeballs pop out and I can't breath no more?"

That get him to let go, only to start laughing. "I'm a snake!" he say. "I wanna get me a tattoo that got a snake on it and it's gonna be big and right here." He point to his arm. "Ty, can you make me a tattoo?"

"Nah," I say, "but I'ma call you Snake. But only if you cool enough to be called Snake."

"I am cool!" He walk 'round in a circle flexing what he think is biceps, like he a man. Tough. All I know is he lookin' crazy stupid.

'Cross the yard, one of Troy counselors, this dude James, call out to me, "What up, Ty?" like me and him is friends or something.

"Chillin'," I say back. He alright. He let me come by the camp and see Troy when I wanna, even though he know Troy foster mother don't want me spending no time with him. She only want me seeing him at the agency, but I can't stand going to them visits.

"Why you ain't playing with them other kids?" I ask Troy. He shrug.

"You s'posed to be having fun at camp."

"I am." But he don't look like he is.

"What's up?" I ask him. "How you doing?"

He shrug again. "I don't know."

"How Ms. Woods treating you?"

Instead of answering me, he just pull on my shirt and say, "Come here."

He bring me over by this cardboard box that got all

kinda balls and shit in there. He take out a football and me and him go over to the other side of the yard, away from them other kids, and throw the ball back and forth for a while. I try to call out plays, tell him where to run and where to stop and turn for the ball, but he don't be paying me no attention. He just runnin' 'round outta control, yelling, "Right here, right here," but he don't never stop moving long enough to catch the ball.

After a while I tell him I'm tired just so I can get him to talk and find out what he got on his mind. Troy like that. He get too hyper sometimes and you gotta play with him, burn off some of his energy, before he can slow down and tell you what he wanna say. Me and him go over to a bench and I spin the football in my hand, waiting for him to talk. When he do, he say, "I don't wanna be at Ms. Woods house no more. It's too boring. I wanna go back to Ms. Reed house and play with Tiffany and Brian again."

"Yeah, I know, Troy, but —"

"I don't like Ms. Woods," he say, kinda whispering now. "She make me go to church with her and it take all day. It's not fair."

"They don't do nothing fun for the kids at that church?"

He shake his head. "I said it's boring, right? I wanna go back home. Now."

"I know," I tell him. "But it's gonna take a while. You gotta be a big man, okay?"

He look down at the ground and nod his head. "Okay."

Every time me and him have this conversation I know I ain't telling him what he wanna hear. He want me to say that we gonna get to go back home and everything gonna be the way it was before our pops got locked up. But I ain't gonna lie to the kid.

Truth is, we don't got no home for him to go back to. My moms is living in this little studio apartment on top of a Mexican take-out place on 136th Street, and I been staying with Cal and them. Our whole family is all over the place. And Troy stuck where he at.

Matter of fact, I ain't even telling him that our pops is out, 'cause Troy gonna start thinking he getting outta foster care tomorrow, and it don't work like that. I don't want him thinking our pops gonna be the one to come back and fix everything for him when I been the one by his side this whole time.

Troy look so sad, I stand up and grab him 'round the waist and snatch him up off the bench like I'm a wrestler or something. Then I act like I'm slamming him on the hard ground, but don't hurt him or nothing. He start laughing. "I'm a snake," he say, wrapping his legs 'round my ankles, trying to trip me.

After a while I let him bring me down, and he go, "The boa constrictor wins!" I laugh with him, and I can tell he ain't thinking 'bout his situation no more. A couple kids from the camp come over to see what's going on and Troy tell them, "I'm a snake. Wanna bet I am?"

It's 5:25 now and I'ma hafta leave before Ms. Woods get here. Before I go, I put my arms 'round Troy shoulder and tell him, "You gonna be a'ight 'cause I'ma make sure you are. You know that, right?"

He nod, and I know he upset I'm leaving, but he used to it now.

"You be good," I tell him. "Don't worry 'bout nothing."

"Okay."

"Now go play with them other kids." I don't move 'til I see him run over to the other side of the yard where some kids is chasing each other 'round. It don't take him long to get into the action neither.

I'm on my way back to the train when my cell beep. It's Jasmine texting me. u didnt call me back where r u?

Damn. Forgot 'bout her. I text her back and next thing I know we gonna meet at McDonald's over by Tremont in twenty minutes. She said she wanna see me, and no matter what, I can never say no to that girl. And she know it.

FOUR

I get to the McDonald's first. Even though I ain't really hungry after the pizza, I buy two fries and two sodas anyway. Dollar Menu all the way. Then I grab a table and wait for Jasmine to get here.

When she walk in the door, damn, she look good. For a couple seconds, I just watch her looking 'round the place for me, then I stand up so she can see me. She smile and practically run over to my table, and a second later, we hugging. Real close. I know for a fact that all the guys up in here, and probably a couple of the females, is jealous that a girl like Jasmine is here for me. Make me feel good.

She smile up at me. "Notice anything different about me?"

I look at her body first 'cause that's the kinda guy I am, and 'cause she got a body that's slamming and I like looking at it. She Puerto Rican, but she got a ass bigger than most sistahs I know. It ain't no joke. I mean, no guy could look at it without they mind thinking up the most nastiest thoughts. And she got big titties and everything.

Everything look the way it always did. Good. Then I look at her face. Jasmine pretty with long hair. Back when we first met, she used to have acne and shit, but her skin ain't even that bad no more. I shake my head. "Nah, what's different 'bout you?"

"I can't believe you don't see it."

She smile bigger, and now I get it. "Your braces. When you get them off?"

"Wednesday."

"Cool." Okay, I gotta admit, my mind start thinking them thoughts again. Ever since I knew Jasmine, she had all that metal shit in her mouth, but now she look even sexier than before, if that's possible. And now she could do things she couldn't before. For real. But, nah, it ain't like me and her is together or nothing. I gotta get them thoughts outta my head. "Why you get them off so fast?"

She shrug. "I thought I was going to the orthodontist for just like a regular appointment, but Emiliano went in the doctor's office and talked to him for a while, and next thing I knew I was getting them off. I think Emil wanted to surprise me and have them off before my party."

"You look good," I tell her.

We sit down, so close our bodies is touching. Jasmine drink some of the Coke I got for her, then she lean over and kiss me on the lips. "I missed you," she say.

"Missed you too." I kiss her again, and it feel different now without them things on her teeth. Better.

Me and her been talking on the phone and texting a lot this summer, but I ain't seen her for 'bout three, four weeks. She been real busy at the restaurant, and I been trying to make money myself. The last time I seen her, she asked me to DJ at her Sweet Sixteen party and course I said yeah.

We keep kissing, but they only them friend kinda kisses. I ain't gonna lie though, I got my hand on her thigh. I can't help it. It's hard to keep my hands to myself 'round her.

When I'm with Jasmine I always feel good. She wasn't never my girl, but we spent a lot of time together when we was both living at that shelter. Yeah, we did a lot of stuff, but we never took it all the way, even though I coulda. But she was going through a lot of shit back then, and I ain't wanna be another dude that was only looking to screw her and that's it. I don't know. Maybe we just wasn't s'posed to be together or something.

Anyway, back then I was only thinking 'bout Novisha. Couldn't get her out my mind. I ain't had no place for nobody else. I ain't know she was playin' me the whole time.

Jasmine take a bite outta a fry and feed me the other half. We do this for a while, just eating, but she ain't saying nothing. Which is weird, 'specially when she the one that was like, I wanna talk to you.

"How you doing?" I ask her, putting my arm 'round her.

She lean her head on my shoulder, her long hair falling all over me. "Better," she say, but it don't sound all that believable.

"You sure? 'Cause the last time I seen you, you was —"

"I know. But I'm better now. Still sad and pissed off 'bout what happened to Joanny, but —" She shake her head.

"Me too."

A couple days before the end of school in June, Jasmine friend was shot and killed by some bullet that wasn't even meant for her. Crazy thing is Jasmine was right there when it happened, right in front of this gyro place 'round the corner from our school. That bullet coulda ended up in Jasmine, and she know it.

I put my arm 'round her tighter.

"I missed you," she say again. "Don't go nowhere no more."

"Nah. I ain't."

I hear what she saying, but I can tell when she got something on her mind, something she ain't all that happy 'bout. First Troy, now Jasmine. It's like everybody got problems today or something. "Talk to me," I say. "What's the matter?"

She sigh. "It's Reyna. I want her to come to my party, but every time I call her cell, there's no answer and she never calls me back. I think something's wrong, but I'm not sure. The last time I seen her was in April and she only came by to get her summer clothes. I know she wouldn't miss my birthday, but how do I know something didn't happen to her?"

Reyna is Jasmine big sister. She, like, twenty or twenty-two or something. "You know where she live at?"

"I'm not sure. I got an address for her in New Jersey, but how do I even know if she still lives there when she won't call me back?"

"She know how to take care of herself," I say. "She pro'ly a'ight. Maybe she busy or got a new man that's taking up all her time. You know how that go." I'm trying to cheer her up, but it ain't working. "She pro'ly all in love and not even thinking to call you back."

"I just wanna make sure she's at my party. If she's not there . . ." She shake her head. "I don't understand her or what she's doing. All she does is party and hang out all the time. It's stupid."

"She still young though. Wait. She gonna get it together after a while."

Personally, I don't know why I'm defending Reyna when she was the one that left Jasmine alone at the shelter with no money in the first place. I don't even get why Jasmine want her sister at her party. But I don't be forgiving people all that easy. Probably got that from my pops too.

While Jasmine finish her fries and mines, I start thinking 'bout her party and how much I hafta do before it. I been using my pops DJ equipment to make money while he was locked up, but he out now and he probably ain't gonna want me using his shit no more. Only thing is, that equipment is mad expensive, and I ain't got the kinda money to go out and buy everything I need. And I only got two weeks to try and put the rest of the money together or I don't know what I'ma do.

Truth is, all this time I been living with Cal and them, I coulda been using my money to buy my own equipment so I could keep making money after my pops take back his shit. I coulda had everything I need by now, no problem. But, nah, instead, all I was doing was buying stupid shit and having fun.

After a while, Jasmine look up at me. "So, your father got out today? When you think he's gonna call you?"

"Pro'ly when he feel like it."

"You happy he's out? I can't tell what you feeling."

"I don't know," I tell her. "What I'm s'posed to be feeling?"

She shake her head. "Why don't guys ever know what they feel?"

I don't got no answer to that one.

We don't say nothing for a couple seconds. Then she go, "Sooo, you ready for school to start? You read any of those books from the list?"

Damn, talk 'bout changing the subject. She ain't even good at it. "Nah, I ain't trying to think 'bout school right now." Jasmine don't know that she the only reason I even went to that school. I was thinking she needed me to look out for her 'specially 'cause she had just moved in with Emiliano, this forty-something-year-old man that used to go out with her sister before they broke up.

Emiliano told Jasmine if she moved into his place, he would take care of her, but meanwhile, he into her, like it don't matter how old he is compared to her. Every couple of days at school I would ask her if he tried anything with her, and she kept on saying no, no, but still the whole situation pissed me the fuck off. Still do.

Yeah, Emiliano do a good job making sure Jasmine going to school and doing what she gotta do. She don't got no moms or pops, and Reyna somewhere doing her own thing, but still, I know Emil just using Jasmine fucked-up situation to get what he want, even if he do be taking his time getting it.

"Emil keeps getting on my case," Jasmine say, "telling me not to wait 'til the last minute to start reading, but those books are so long."

"I ain't even look at that list."

"You have to. We're gonna get a test the first week of school." She shake her head. "This summer was so boring and slow. I can't wait for school to start."

That's 'cause when she there, everybody know and like her. It's a alternative school, and I gotta admit, it's way better than the last school I went to. Still, I ain't go to school every day and fucked up most of them classes. I had too much on my mind to think 'bout school.

Jasmine still talking. "Did I tell you that me and Emil went to Connecticut? He got a brother that lives there and he's married and they got a daughter that's seventeen. Me and her had so much fun. I invited her to my party. Oh, speaking of my party, Emil wants you to come over one night this week so he can go over all the details with you and we can give you a list of the songs you have to play. Like, *have to* play. Come any day around seven thirty or eight, when Emil gets home from the gym."

I like how she don't even wait for me to say if I'm free one night or not. "A'ight," I say. I don't know what it is 'bout this girl, but most of the time I end up doing what she want. Good thing me and her never hooked up 'cause if we did, I would be one whipped nigga right 'bout now. That's for damn sure.

FIVE

Cal already outside in front of our building working hard by the time I get back uptown. Just seeing him make me mad. I still ain't in no mood for him. So I just go up the path, past him leaning up against the building, and I'm just 'bout at the lobby door when he go, "You been walkin' around with your face like that all day? 'Cause, dude, no disrespect, but you lookin' jacked." And he start laughing.

And even though there ain't no way I'ma laugh with him, nigga always did know what to say to least get me to stop, even when I'm mad. "You snappin' now?"

"Nah, just speaking the truth. Look at yourself, man. How long it's been since your ugly ass got some?"

"Least I ain't damn-near married." I drop my backpack on the ground and lean up against the wall on the other side of the door. "How your wife and kid doing? How 'bout your mother-in-law?"

He shake his head. "A'ight, you got me. Damn. That's some messed-up shit." Then he laugh.

And that get me to smile 'cause me and him both know his situation is fucked up. He sixteen and already got a kid, and a baby mother that think it's her job to make his life hard. And her moms is worse than her, calling him all the time, demanding more money. Cal working out here more hours than he used to just to try and keep everybody happy and off his back. And it still ain't working.

I stand outside with him for a while talking. It's still light out, but the sun gonna go down soon. Then shit at Bronxwood gonna start getting crazy. So for now, I'm just chillin', telling Cal 'bout my trip and all the fine girls they got in Atlanta, and that funny way they talk down south. Then Cal tell me 'bout the party they had last night, and how fast everything got outta control, not that nobody cared 'cause they was all fucked up anyway. Nothing new 'bout none of this. Me, Cal, and Greg been having parties like that since I moved in with them. We been having some crazy fun. For real.

Cal working while we talk. He been selling weed so long, he real smooth 'bout it. We don't even gotta stop talking when he get a customer. Now that he sixteen and could get some real jail time if he get busted, he don't never keep no drugs on him. Only thing the police gonna find in his pockets is a wad of cash. He got this thirteen-year-old kid, Keith, from Building B working for him. Kid crack me up 'cause he real little for his age, but he doing everything he can to look hard and tough when he working. Shit's funny as hell. 'Specially 'cause Keith the one that hold all the weed. He leaning on the fence 'cross the street waiting for the signs from Cal. The whole thing is going on right out in the open. Everybody know that. But it's the projects, and the truth is, don't nobody seem to care what we do up in here.

Anyway, all the weed that get sold in Bronxwood go through Cal and his brothers. His oldest brother, Andre, run they whole business, and the middle brother, Greg, is in charge of the stash, where they keep all the drugs at. And they don't only sell here, neither. Back in February, Andre moved over to the Eastchester projects over by Allerton to live with his girlfriend, and he just took over that place too, like one building at a time, and from what I know, them dealers that was there before wasn't all that happy 'bout it. Matter of fact, 'bout three, four months ago, Andre was shot in the leg by somebody over there at Eastchester and he still limping from that shit.

Not that he let that bullet stop him. If anything, he more determined now. Couple months ago, he started spreading out even more, and now he got dudes selling for him in the South Bronx, Harlem, and even Brooklyn.

Smartest thing I did was to stay the fuck out they business, which ain't as easy as I thought it was gonna be, 'cause dudes is making money. Living with them all this time and always being the broke nigga, it's hard.

After 'bout a half hour of us standing there bullshitting, Cal say, "Look, I gotta tell you something, but I don't know if you gonna wanna hear this."

"What?"

"About a hour ago, when I first came out here, I seen Novisha across the street, coming outta her building and walking to the bus stop. And she was with some dude."

"I know," I say. "I seen them 'fore I left."

"Ty, this ain't the first time I seen her with that dude. While you was gone, she was with him a couple times, walking up and down the block, and they was —"

"I don't care," I tell him.

"You okay with it?"

I shrug. "I'm through, that's all."

Cal look at me, like, am I serious? But he should know by now I am. He was there. He know what that girl put me through. "A'ight," he go. "Whatever you say."

Then just 'cause he keep on staring at me and I don't wanna look at him, I look over his shoulder, 'cross the street over by Novisha building. Not that I think I'ma see her or nothing. It's not like she be hanging out in front of her building. I been back living here since the end of January, and I ain't hardly ever seen her outside, 'cept when she be going to school and coming home. And this summer she been away most of the time, being some kinda volunteer counselor at this Bible camp thing her church run, and the only reason I know that is 'cause I heard her moms telling somebody 'bout it one day.

And now I'm standing here and I don't know why I cut Cal off. I shoulda least found out what they was doing, if he seen Novisha kissing that guy or something. But how I'ma ask him now and not get him thinking Novisha still mean something to me when she don't?

Then I see Adonna. She coming out her building with this girl Asia and they walking and laughing and shit. Adonna still got on them little shorts, and Asia wearing these tight white pants. For real, both them girls looking good.

I keep my eyes on them for a while, then tell Cal, "I been getting vibes from her all summer."

"Asia?"

"Nah, Adonna."

Cal bust out laughing. "You crazy, dude. Adonna don't give guys 'round here no play. Never did. Can't even see her messing with no project nigga."

"I know when a girl like me, and I'm telling you, she on it."

"Tell me one dude she ever got with 'round here."

"I'ma be the first," I tell him. Then before he can say anything else, I pick my backpack up off the ground and go down the path, heading straight 'cross the street to catch up with them girls. And 'cause I know Cal watching me, I walk with a little extra swagger. I need to be smooth if I'ma try and step to Adonna.

The girls slow down when they see me coming, and I get in the middle of them and start walking down the street with them. "Where y'all beautiful ladies going?"

"The store," Asia say. "For my mom. For the third time today." She look pissed off too. "Can't wait for school to start so I don't gotta be her slave all day no more."

"Don't even say that," Adonna say. "I don't wanna think about school starting. *Summer* didn't even start for me yet."

"Why?" I say. "You not having no fun?"

Adonna roll her eyes. "None. I thought this was gonna be the best summer, with me going to parties and hanging out and meeting people. Only, I got stuck at stupid summer school, and —" Asia cut her off by busting out laughing, and Adonna look at her like she wanna kill her or something. "As I was saying, I'm in summer school, and by the time it's over, I'm gonna miss half the summer without doing anything except hanging around here. I didn't get to the beach once, and that's not the kinda summer I was made for. I was made for fun!" She laugh at her own self.

She so cute. Damn. I can't even think what it would be like if she was my girl. A female like that, she could make me feel real good.

We turn the corner and cut through the shopping center parking lot. A couple times I let them go ahead of me, just enough so I can get a good look at them asses. And they nice ones too. Both of them. I'm sweating and shit, and it don't got nothing to do with the heat neither.

When we get near the store, I ask Asia how much stuff she gotta buy for her moms. She say, "All she needs is a couple of potatoes and some garlic salt. Of course she couldn't think of those things two hours ago, the last time she made me come here."

To be honest, something 'bout girls with bad attitudes that I like. But it ain't Asia I'm trying to talk to.

Right before we go into the store, I make my move. I grab Adonna hand and say, "Stay out here and talk to me."

Asia look back over her shoulder at us, but she keep going inside. And that's all good 'cause now I get Adonna to myself for a while. Me and her stand there for a second, then this Puerto Rican lady come up behind us and practically knock us out the way 'cause we blocking the door, so I keep holding Adonna hand and bring her over by the side of the store. I lean up against the wall and she stand in front of me, and it look like she waiting for me to say something. So I go, "The summer only half over. You could still go to the beach. And I'ma take you."

"Yeah?" she ask, smiling, being all sexy and whatnot.

"Yeah. I can see me and you there on the beach. And you gonna be in one of them red bikinis. No, black. And you gonna be looking mad sexy in that black bikini."

She look me right in the eye. "You couldn't handle seeing me in a black bikini."

"For real?" I'm staring right back at her. "You look that good?"

She laugh. "Me, I know how to work it!" And she start shaking her hips and being all funny.

I laugh with her, and I'm getting excited, but I don't want her seeing it. So I try and change the subject and get my mind off it. "What you girls doin' tonight? Y'all should hang out at my place, have some fun. It's Friday night."

"I don't know," she say. "Depends on what Asia wants to do." But something 'bout the way she say it, I can tell she wanna spend some time with me. I mean, least she thinking 'bout it.

"A'ight, but if she don't wanna, just you come. Me and you can watch TV and stuff."

"I don't know, " she say again.

Adonna probably don't wanna dump her friend for a guy. Some girls is like that. And I get it. It's cool.

Me and Adonna talk a little more 'til Asia come out the store, and then we all walk back 'cross the parking lot and, I ain't gonna lie, I'm thinkin' 'bout what I would hafta do to get both them girls upstairs with me, in my bed, 'cause that shit would be wild.

Yeah, I know it's a fantasy. I ain't crazy. It ain't never gonna happen. Not only that, but I know I gotta be smart. If I make a move to get them both, I'ma end up fucking up things with Adonna even before they get started. She still the one I want. Just her. A brotha can't be greedy.

■　■　■

While Asia go upstairs and drop off the stuff for her moms, me and Adonna stay downstairs in front of her building, talking. Well, trying to. Some guy with a Navigator is pumping music for the whole fucking projects to hear, and it ain't easy talking over it.

By the time Asia come back outside, my throat hurt from yelling, but I still talk them both into coming over to my place. I ain't really sure how I do it, but I guess they just as bored as me. And there ain't nothing else to do 'round here.

When Cal see me going in the building with both them girls, me and him look at each other, and his face look like he wanna know how the fuck I made this happen. He just mad that he gotta be outside working on a Friday night, not having no fun like me.

Cal my boy, but his problems ain't mines. Shit, I'm looking out for me. Anyway, I got more important things on my mind right now. Like what I'ma do with these two females when I get them upstairs.

SIX

A hour later, me and the girls is having a good time, but not as good as I was hoping we was gonna have. We got the place to ourself, and I got a mix CD playing, one I put together at one of the parties I played in Atlanta. Shit is dope, if I do say so myself. Which I do. The girls is busy pouring vodka in cans of Pepsi and giggling and shit like they out they mind. Which don't make no sense 'cause the little bit of vodka they drinking wouldn't get a roach drunk, you ask me.

I'm on the couch with a forty in my hand, watching them. I ain't drunk or nothing, but I'm definitely working on a nice buzz.

Only good thing is the apartment is actually clean now. Cal and Greg too lazy to do shit 'round here, so I know they got Keisha, this girl on the second floor, to come and clean up after them. She a nice girl that go to college and always need extra money. She do a good job too, and she don't never steal nothing. Matter of fact, she been washing my clothes for me since I got here. Girl do pickup, wash, dry, fold, and drop-off, all for like fifteen dollars a load.

And she braid my hair for me for thirty.

Asia put her Pepsi down and start dancing, or what she think is dancing anyway. All she doing is shaking her ass and laughing at herself. But even while she dancing, she keep looking at the time on the cable box. Her moms don't play, and she told her to get her ass home by ten. It ain't even nine yet, but she getting paranoid. And we ain't even smoking no weed.

Not that we couldn't. That's the one thing we always got, living here. Might not got no bread or chopped meat or nothing we actually need, but we always got a little weed.

"Stop looking at that clock," I tell Asia as Adonna come over to the couch and sit next to me — close, but not close enough.

She laugh. "Y'all don't know my mom. That woman got a little craziness in her. She would go off if she found out I'm over here." She still dancing 'round like a crack-head. "How'd you end up living here with these dealers anyway?"

"Long story," I say, not sure how much to tell the girls. "Me and my moms wasn't getting along, so I came here."

None of the girls say anything, but they look like they feeling sorry for me or something, and I don't want none of that. So I say, "When I first got here, man, it was bad. Cal had me sleeping in his room on the top bunk bed. I couldn't even sit up without cracking my skull on the ceiling."

The girls laugh.

"Me and him living in one room, man, that got old fast. We was fighting, like, every day and I thought he was 'bout to throw me outta here. Then when his brother — y'all know Andre, right?" They both nod 'cause who don't know Andre, the biggest weed dealer we ever had at Bronxwood? "When Andre moved out, it got better here 'cause me and Cal don't gotta be sleeping in the same room no more, and I don't hafta listen to no more of his snoring and farting. And I don't gotta climb up no ladder no more just to get some sleep."

The girls laugh again, and I laugh with them even though there wasn't nothing funny 'bout it back then.

"You're not selling drugs, are you?" Adonna ask, turning her body in my direction and looking at me serious. And I take that as a good sign, that maybe she care 'bout me or something.

"Nah," I say. "You know I'm a DJ, not no drug dealer."

"You were good at the block party," she say. "Everybody around here was talking about how the music this year was so much better than it used to be."

"Yeah, that was fun," I say, smiling. "'Specially when I seen Ms. Lucas from Building D coming down the street, and I put on the oldest record my pops had, something from, like, the seventies or something, and that woman got in the middle of the street and started doing this crazy dance. And everybody was clapping and that just got her goin'. Man, I thought she was gonna break her hip or something. I been laughing 'bout that all summer."

"I can't believe I missed that," Adonna say, getting up to get another Pepsi. She open the can and pour a couple drops of vodka in it, and I wish she would put a little more 'cause maybe then she would loosen up and we could start having some fun already.

Before Adonna could come back and sit next to me again, Asia grab her hand and make Adonna start dancing with her. They both dancing with soda cans in they hands. After a minute they try to get me up to dance with them, but that ain't gonna happen. I can just see Cal face now if he walk in and see us dancing like three assholes with nothing better to do with ourself. But while I'm watching them, my mind go back there, and maybe it's the buzz I got, but first thing out my mouth is, "Y'all should kiss."

They bust out laughing. Both of them.

"Yeah, right," Asia say, putting her hands on her hips and giving me one of them looks like she think I'm outta my mind for even saying that. Even though I was just asking. I mean, they can't blame a guy for trying, right?

"Me and Asia don't go that way," Adonna say. "We're friends. *Friends.*"

They start giggling again.

"I just want y'all to kiss like friends. But on the lips. That's all."

"Hell, no," Asia say to me, then turn to Adonna and go, "No offense."

Adonna pout. "You didn't have to say it like that!"

I ain't think she could get no cuter, but man, she just did.

Asia look up at the cable box again, and this time I do too. It's something after nine and I don't know what make me think this, but I'm like, damn, my pops been out a whole fucking day practically and he ain't even call me to see if I'm alive or nothing. That just tell me how much he think 'bout me.

I put the forty to my mouth and down the rest of the bottle while the girls dance and laugh and do everything 'cept kiss. For a couple minutes it's like I'm not even still here with them. I mean, it's not like I thought my pops was gonna call me the second they let his ass outta jail, but fuck, he ain't seen me in a year. Think he would wanna see how his own kid is doing.

But guess not.

Forty-five minutes later, the girls is acting even drunker. *Acting*. 'Cause, my opinion, that bottle of vodka is just as full as it was when they got here. They probably just don't get out all that much and they happy to be anywhere 'cept they own apartments.

I'm starting to feel kinda good myself. Not only 'cause I ain't sitting here by myself, but 'cause maybe it's a good thing I ain't heard from my pops. Maybe that mean he ain't gonna come 'round here and try and take control of my life. Maybe he know I'm on my own and being my own man now, and I don't need him the way I used to back when I was little, back when I used to think everything he did was right.

"I better go home," Asia say. "But let me pee first." She leave the living room and go down the hall.

The second she gone, I stand up and grab Adonna hand. "Why don't you stay for a while? You don't gotta be home now, right?"

"No, but —"

"Then stay." I know it sound like I'm begging, but I can't help it. Ain't nothing I want more right now than for her to stay and maybe gimme some.

"What's this?" Adonna ask, acting like she just notice this chain I got 'round my neck. She touch it and get this little smile on her face. "It's nice and heavy."

I don't say nothing 'cause this is just Adonna being herself.

"Can I wear it, just 'til I see you next time?"

"Nah. It's my pops." For a second, I think 'bout telling her that he got out today and he gonna want it back, but then she probably gonna ask questions 'bout him, and that's only gonna fuck up the whole mood I'm trying to get going here.

"You sure I can't borrow it?" She acting even more sexier than normal, smiling up at me and showing off them long eyelashes.

And it's starting to work on me. "I, I don't know," I say.

"Just for a few days. I'll take good care of it. Promise." She already turning the chain 'round, and next thing I know she unhooking it and taking it off, like I already told her it was alright or something. When she get the chain off me, she hand it to me and turn 'round. "Put it on for me."

Damn, she good. I put my pops chain 'round her neck and she turn back and face me.

"How does it look? Good, right?"

"Yeah, but don't get too used to it 'cause it ain't mines."

"I know, I know."

It do look good on her too. I grab hold of both her hands and say, "Stay here for a little while." I lower my voice and stare into her eyes. "C'mon, I wanna spend some time with you."

She kinda smile. "You do?"

"Course, you know I'm into you."

"Yeah? Well, what about Novisha?" The way she say it, it's like she challenging me or something.

I look down for a half a second, then look in her eyes again so she won't think I'm trying to hide something. "Me and Novisha is through," I say. And that ain't a lie neither. "That girl is my past. Me and you could be the future, you know what I'm sayin'?"

We both looking into each other eyes now and from what I see, she look like she wanna believe me, but she ain't sure. A lot of girls don't be trusting dudes, and I can't blame them really 'cause most of the time we be flat-out lying. But I'm for real this time. I mean, yeah, everything I just said 'bout the future was bullshit, but if the future is just for now, maybe me and her could hook up.

We still holding hands when Asia come back to the living room. "Walk us home, Tyrell," she say. It ain't no question, the way she say it, so I grab my keys out my backpack and we go.

Outside, in front of the building, I'm glad Cal standing by some woman car, too busy talking to her to see me leaving with the girls. I been knowing Cal so long, no doubt he could just take one look at me and know nothing happened with me and them.

We cross the street and walk down the path to Building G. Asia walking mad fast like if she one minute late, her moms is gonna put her foot up her ass. Which might be true if what they say 'bout her moms 'round here is true.

The second I step foot in the lobby it hit me that this the first time I been in this building since when me and Novisha was together. Back then, I was over here all the time, like it was my second home. Matter of fact, when I was living in that shelter, Novisha apartment was the only place that felt like home to me.

The elevator come and while we inside I figure it's my last chance to try again 'cause I ain't one to give up easy. "C'mon," I say to them. "Kiss."

And this time, I don't know if it's the ounce of vodka they split between them or what, but this time Asia lean over and give Adonna a kiss on the lips, and even though it don't last more than a second, it's hot. And damn, it get me so excited I think I'ma catch fire or something.

I'm smiling so big my face hurt. "Yeah, that's what I'm talking 'bout." And we all bust out laughing like we crazy.

When the elevator pass the ninth floor, Novisha floor, it don't even faze me 'cause I'm having too much fun with these girls to even think 'bout Novisha. Things is different now. Shit change.

We get to Asia floor, and me and Adonna stay in the elevator, holding the doors open while she go down the hall, waiting for her to get in her apartment. Gotta do my job and make sure these girls is safe. Not that Bronxwood is the worse projects in the Bronx or nothing, 'cause they got way worse places. But still, there do be some scary dudes living here, violent motherfuckers that don't need to be up in here.

Asia live all the way at the end of the hall, so before she get to her door, the elevator alarm start going off. But, still, I wait 'til she inside her apartment before letting the doors close. Then Adonna press 19, and as soon as we moving up again, I make my move. I put my arms 'round her waist and pull her close to me and bring my lips on hers. And this ain't no kinda kiss that two girls give each other when they think they drunk. We kissing for real. I got my tongue practically down her throat and we breathing on each other all hot and shit. Damn, it feel good.

So good we don't stop when we get to 19. I hear the doors open and close and for a minute the elevator don't move off that floor. But then we on our way down again and all I'm thinking is that I'm kissing Adonna Singleton. And she kissing me back.

This is what I need. I need someone new, somebody to be into, that could make me feel this way. 'Cause it's been a while. "Come back to my place," I say to her. "Don't think 'bout it. Just do it."

Her lips is like a inch away from mines. "I can't," she say. "I —"

I kiss her again, just to remind her what she thinkin' 'bout giving up on tonight.

But right after I move my lips off hers, she say again, "I can't." Only thing, she sound like maybe she getting weaker now. She want me. I don't got no doubts 'bout that. "I'm not like that," she tell me.

"Like what?"

Before she can answer me, the elevator get back down to the lobby and the doors open up. And damn if it ain't Adonna brother Kenny, wheeling boxes of them icees and sodas and shit from his truck into the elevator on a hand truck.

Dude got the worst fucking timing I ever seen.

"Where y'all going?" he ask Adonna.

"Nowhere," she say. "Not that it's any of your business anyway."

Kenny look at me all suspicious and whatnot. "You leaving, Tyrell?"

"Yeah," I go. "I was gonna make sure Adonna got home safe first."

Kenny stop the doors before they close behind him. "Good. But you don't need to no more. I'm here now."

Damn. Kenny is such a asshole. It's like he know I was trying to get some from his sister and he making hisself her personal bodyguard or something. What, he don't think she old enough to make up her own mind 'bout what she do?

Adonna look kinda mad, but instead of telling her brother to go fuck hisself, she shrug at me and tell me she gonna see me tomorrow if I'm 'round. She say it like me and her wasn't kissing just now. Like I'm just some dude she only know by hi and bye. I mean, I know she probably don't want her brother to know what she was just doing, but she don't gotta be like this neither.

"A'ight," I tell her. "See ya 'round." And I walk out the elevator and out the building, not really knowing what just happened and how my night got so fucked up so fast.

'Cause this whole night coulda turned out way better. I coulda been walking Adonna back 'cross the street, holding hands with her, knowin' me and her was 'bout to have ourself some fun. Instead I'm walking 'cross the street by myself. Back to Building A.

The second Cal see me, he get half a smile on his face and go, "Told you."

And I can't help myself. I shake my head and start cracking up with him, like we used to do back in, like, seventh grade. Just being stupid. 'Cause I shoulda knew better than to think getting with a girl like Adonna was gonna be easy. Girls like that, that look like her, it's like they born knowing how to make guys work to get them.

I lean against the building and stay outside for a couple more hours, hanging with Cal while he work, laughing with him 'bout all kinda shit. It feel good being out here, 'cause the truth is, I don't know how much longer this kinda freedom gonna last.

Shit, knowing my pops, this whole thing might be over for me tomorrow.

SEVEN

It's mad early when my cell ring and wake me up. It feel like I only been 'sleep 'bout a hour, but the ringing so loud ain't no way I can sleep through it. I grab the cell and see the time. 5:14. In the morning. What I wanna know is, who I know gonna call me this early? I hit the talk button. "Hello?" My voice come out all rough and shit.

"Be downstairs in a half hour and bring the key for the storage room."

It's my pops. And that's all he say. Before I can even think of what to say back, he hang up.

For a while I don't move. I just stay in bed thinking 'bout what he said and how he said it. Weird thing is, I can't tell what kinda mood he was in, like, is he mad 'bout something? I used to could tell a whole lot by the way he sounded, but I ain't heard his voice in so long I don't know no more.

A half hour later, I don't know why, but I'm standing outside in front of the building like a fuckin' asshole. Ain't nobody out here at this time 'cept some guy pushing two shopping carts full of empty cans and bottles down the street. The carts is tied together and he probably got a couple hundred cans in there, plus he got a whole lot more in the two garbage bags hanging off the sides. Dude musta been up all night to pick up all them cans by hisself by this time in the morning. It look like he ready to cash out, and the sun just coming up now.

After a couple minutes of me standing there, a black van pull up to the curb in front of me and stop. To be honest, I don't even hardly recognize the driver at first. I look in the window and first thing I see is some dude with a goatee. Then, when the guy in the van turn to look at me, I see it's my pops and I'm like, damn. How I ain't recognize him?

Still, for a couple seconds I just stand there on the curb 'cause I don't know what I'm s'posed to do, get in the van or just wait for him to get out and come get the storage room key? 'Cause that's probably all he want anyway.

Before I can do anything, my pops get out and come over to me. I'm getting the key from my pocket when he grab me up in a big hug and laugh and say, "You just gonna stand there when you ain't seen your pops in damn near a year?" He hug me the way he used to, 'cept even harder now and he don't let go as fast.

But I ain't looking for this shit from him. I pull away and, 'cause I don't got nothing else to say, ask him, "Where you get the van from?"

"Borrowed it," he go.

I don't know what else to say, so I just hold out the key. "Here." Now that I seen him, all I wanna do is get back in my bed.

My pops take the key from me and say, "Come on." Then he just go back 'round to the driver side and get in like he know I'ma do what he say.

Part of me wanna just turn 'round and go back in the building and not care what he think. But that ain't gonna work with him. He don't play that, 'specially not from me. So I end up getting in the van and as soon as I close the door, he make a U-turn real fast and we outta Bronxwood.

While he drive, my pops is just smiling and talking, saying shit like, "Ty, man, you don't know. You don't know how good it feel to be out, know'm saying? When they take away your freedom, shit, man, you don't know how it feel to get it back."

He go on and on, and I just stare at him, trying to think what look different 'bout him. Most of the time people be telling me I look like him, but I never seen it. He a little taller than me and he used to be bigger than me, but he ain't hardly bigger no more. Somebody ain't spent no time in the prison gym, that's for sure. And his goatee got some gray hairs in it now, and the hair on his head is turning gray too, and that make him look mad old. He need to get up on that Just For Men shit.

When he stop talking for a second, I say, "What time they let you out yesterday?"

"Supposed to be nine o'clock in the morning, but by the time I got out it was more like ten thirty. They be taking they time letting niggas go." He laugh.

But I'm serious. "You go see Troy?"

"Not yet," he say, making a left turn and merging onto 95, which is practically empty at this time a day 'cept for some trucks.

"If you woulda called me yesterday, I coulda took you over to see him at his camp."

"I was in jail for a long fuckin' time, Ty," he say. "Going to see Troy at camp wasn't the first thing I had on my mind, know'm mean?" He laugh again all loud and shit, like I even wanna hear this. Like I need to know anything 'bout what him and my moms do.

He go back to talking 'bout all the shit he wanna do now that he out, and I go back to not listening. I mean, I know he happy he out, but I ain't feeling the same way. Now that he back he gonna start wanting to change everything and make me move back home, wherever that's gonna be. He gonna expect me to go back to doing what he want. But I ain't the same no more, and he gotta know that.

I'm looking out the window, thinking, and the sun really coming out now, but when we get to the exit we s'posed to get off at, the one for the storage place, my pops drive right past it. "Where we going?" I ask him 'cause, really, it's too early and I'm too tired to have him just taking me places I don't wanna go.

"Wait and see," he say. Then he turn on the radio and start talking 'bout how much music he missed out on and how I'ma hafta tell him 'bout all the new stuff 'cause he gotta be up on it. Like he ever was. Dude don't never play nothing but old skool.

It ain't 'til he pull off the highway that I figure out where he taking me — the Black Rock Diner over by Castle Hill, this twenty-four-hour spot me and him used to end up at all the time on the weekends after his parties. We would get there 'bout four, five in the morning, not really drunk or high, but still kinda buzzed, and me and him used to eat and talk 'bout the party and all the crazy shit that just happened, and laugh like we was stupid or something. Then we would go home and either stay up some more out on the balcony, getting high, or we would pass out, all tired and full.

He park the van in the parking lot and get out, but I take my time 'cause I ain't in the mood for the Black Rock today. I don't even know why he doing this, bringing me here. Them days is over.

But I get out anyway and say to him, "You woke me up for this?" But he already walking 'cross the parking lot and probably don't hear me.

I follow him in the diner. The way I see it, I ain't really got no other choice. What I'm s'posed to do? Stand out here in the parking lot the whole time he in there eating?

The thing 'bout the Black Rock is that it ain't never empty, no matter what time you get there. My pops go right to a table in the middle of the place, sit down, and start looking 'round like he expecting to run into some friends or something up in here. He, like, always ready to party. No matter where he at.

I sit down 'cross from him and don't say nothing. While we wait for one of the two waitresses to even see that we there, my pops go, "This place ain't change none. Shit, it look like they ain't even do no cleaning up in here since the last time I was here." He laugh.

I shrug.

Finally, a waitress come over to our table, and when she see my pops she smile real big and go, "Oh, my God, Tyrone! Where have you been? We missed you around here."

My pops go right into his smooth act and tell her right out that he was locked up and just got out yesterday.

She hit him on the shoulder real light. "Oh, I always knew you were a bad boy." And she still smiling at him, like what he told her don't matter to her at all.

My pops don't wait a second before he go, "You like bad boys?"

"Can't help myself," she say, and wink at him. And the two of them go back and forth, laughing and flirting like I ain't even sitting here. I'm just watching him, the way he acting all cool and shit. Telling everybody his business, all proud that he was in jail or something.

When they stop talking long enough for the waitress to ask what we wanna order, we don't gotta look at no menu or nothing 'cause we always get the same thing when we come here. They got this thing here they call the Breakfast Beast. It's ham, sausage, eggs, hash browns, and cheese in a French toast sandwich. It got some kinda sauce in it too, but I can't never figure out what it's made outta. The thing look real nasty, but shit is slammin'. I ain't lying. Me and my pops get it with a side order of grits and cheese, and it's on. Make you so full you can't even move for like a hour. But it's that good kinda full, where you in pain but you still happy and satisfied and shit.

When the waitress leave the table, my pops is still smiling, checking out her ass as she walk away. And me, I just can't take it no more. "Can I ask you a question?" I don't wait for him to say nothing. "Why you bring me here for?"

The smile on his face go away real fast. He lock his eyes on mines hard and go, "You got a problem, Tyrell?"

I don't like the way he looking at me. "It ain't no problem," I say, keeping my eyes on his. "I just wanna know why I'm here. Why you wake me up for? To come and eat with you? 'Cause if that's what you was —"

"You gonna shut the fuck up long enough for me to answer you?" He don't raise his voice none, but he still looking me dead in the eye and I can tell he starting to get mad. Like I care. He stare at me some more, and take his time before he say, "I woke you up 'cause I need your help with something. Tonight."

I sit back against the pleather on the chair, fold my arms in front of me, and say, "What you need help with?"

Then he tell me 'bout this party he throwing and how much he need to do between now and ten o'clock tonight when the party s'posed to start. "This ain't gonna be one of my regular parties. I'm only gonna have, like, a hundred people. Folks that got money and ain't afraid to spend none of it to come to one of my parties and have themselfs a good time. A real good time."

I can't believe this shit. He ain't learn nothing in prison.

"I need you to help me DJ," he say. "Give me more time to spend with folks and give everybody that personal touch. And we gonna have some backroom shit going on too, you know'm saying, right?" He laugh.

But I don't laugh with him. "You remember why they locked you up, right?" The words is out my mouth before I think, but I ain't gonna back down from what I'm saying.

"Yeah, I remember." He shoot me another hard look. "You remember who is the father and who is the son, right?"

"I remember," I tell him.

"Good, then."

Me and him don't say another word, not in the whole time it take for the waitress to come back with our food. My pops talk to her again while she put the plates and bowls down in front of us, but me, all I'm thinking 'bout is the smell of the food. I mean, by the time I get the first bite of that sandwich, with all them flavors in my mouth, just like that, I ain't all that mad no more that my pops brung me here.

My pops go, "Good, right?"

I don't say nothing. I just keep eating.

"I been dreaming about this breakfast for a year," he say, food all in his mouth and shit.

Funny, but I ain't think 'bout this place once since the last time me and him was here.

Something happen to my pops when we 'bout halfway through with our food. He start talking 'bout everything, telling me more 'bout the party he throwing tonight. All the details. "I'm gonna charge seventy-five this time, but I'm gonna give folks a open bar for the first hour. They gonna like that. Then, to make up for it, for the rest of the party, I'm gonna be overcharging like a motherfucka." He laugh again.

I'm hardly listening to the man. I'm too busy eating. It's a good thing he keep talking so I can get started on them grits and cheese.

After a while, he tell me 'bout this apartment Regg hooked him up with. "It's over by Mosholu Parkway," he say, "not far from the reservoir. It's nice over there." Then he tell me that him and my moms is moving in on Monday and he wanna make enough money tonight to give Regg back all the money he laid out for the apartment, the first and last month rent. "I gotta get your moms out that place she living at now, Ty. Apartment is smaller than the fucking cell I just got outta."

Damn. What he saying is messed up. When ACS took Troy away from us and I left outta that shelter we was staying at, my moms ain't had nowhere to go. First she went to stay with one of my pops friends, but I knew for a fact my pops wasn't gonna want her living there. So I'm the one that found that little studio apartment for her. I seen a sign in the front of the building saying they was renting studios, no credit check. It was me that helped move her in there and me that paid her rent all this time. Almost seven months. Me. So why he gotta criticize instead of telling me I did alright taking care of his wife while he was sitting on his ass doing nothing for none of us all this time?

But I don't say none of this to him, 'cause, at the same time, I know there's a lot of shit he can blame me for too. 'Specially what happened to Troy. I know he probably thinking I fucked up 'cause I ain't made sure my moms was doing the right thing and taking care of Troy the way she was s'posed to. I shoulda stepped up and ran the family the way he woulda did if he was 'round. And even though I tried, I wasn't good enough. And I don't wanna hear that from him right now.

So I stop talking and keep eating. Meanwhile, my pops is talking and eating at the same time. You ask me, he just rambling though. The man musta been in solitary or something, 'cause he acting like he ain't had nobody to talk to for a while.

A cell phone ring and I know that ain't my ringtone. My pops reach into his pocket and pull a cell, a new one. He ain't even been outta jail twenty-four hours. How he get a cell already? And why his phone better than mines?

My pops start talking. I can tell it's my moms and it sound like she ain't know he left her place and wanna know where he at. He smiling big when he talk to her too. He saying, "I ain't wanna wake you up. After last night, I knew you needed to rest." He laugh. "And I'ma be back in about a hour for more."

Me, I swear, I'm sitting here hoping some terrorists or somebody will roll up in this diner and shoot all of us so I don't hafta listen to none of this shit no more.

It don't stop neither. They talk for another couple minutes and I gotta say, it sound like they both real happy. Probably happier than they was before he went away.

Finally, my pops tell her he gotta go 'cause his food getting cold. But before he hang up, he go, "Lisa, you know I ain't forget 'bout that. I'ma work hard too." More laughing. Then he hang up.

No way I'ma ask what him and my moms is talking 'bout, what he working hard for. I ain't sure I even wanna know. 'Cause I know him and the only kinda work I ever seen him doing was illegal shit.

Anyway, I shoulda knew he wasn't gonna be no different this time. This the third time he been to prison, and it's always for the same shit. The thing that piss me off is, every time he sitting in a jail cell chillin', his family be going through some hard times. But he don't never get to see that part.

When me and Regg went down south, he tried to talk to me 'bout my pops. He said he knew how I felt but that I should try not to be too hard on him. He was like, give the man another chance. Regg made it sound easy, but now that me and my pops is face-to-face, I know for a fact me and him can't start over. Too much shit happened in the past.

So I get through the rest of breakfast, not really talking to him, not really listening. Least the food is good.

Before my pops pay the bill, he lean 'cross the table closer to me and go, "Let me ask you a question, Ty."

I take a deep breath, trying to figure out what he want from me now.

"You got my gold chain? Your moms say she don't got it."

Damn. "Um, I, I don't know. I mighta put it someplace, to keep it safe."

"Good. Good. Find it and bring it to the party tonight."

I nod. "I'ma look for it." Now I'ma hafta try and get that chain back from Adonna. Hope she ain't get too attached to it.

EIGHT

My pops still doing all the talking on the way to the storage place, telling me who he invited to the party tonight, like I care. "All I know is this party better make me a lot of money," he say, pulling the van into a parking spot and cutting the engine. "I got some things I'm working on."

He open the van door, but it take him a couple seconds to move. "Man," he go. "My body ain't used to that much food no more. I need to go to sleep. *Itis* is setting in hard and fast."

Finally, he get out and so do I. We go 'round to the back of the van and take out the hand truck and a dolly and some rope and shit. When we get to our storage room and unlock it, my pops look 'round and go, "Shit." Only, the way he drag out the word, it sound more like "sheeeeet."

I know what he thinking 'cause every time I come here I'm thinking the same thing, that it's messed up all our stuff is here. When we got evicted, the marshals brung everything we had in our apartment here. Our furniture is here, my pops clothes, and all Troy toys. Everything. This place always make me feel mad, 'cause we been living without none of this stuff for a long time, and it ain't right.

At the same time, I'm feeling good that my pops is seeing all this now. He need to start understanding the changes we had to go through for the past year, see how we been living. I don't think he get it.

Inside the room, my pops go over to the big-screen TV first and start talking 'bout remember this movie we watched and remember that video game we used to play, but he might as well be talking to hisself. 'Cause I'm shitting bricks, hoping he don't notice that I been using his DJ equipment without asking him first. He ain't gonna stand for that, 'specially from me.

The equipment is up against the wall, right by the door where I put it 'cause I had to get it in and out easy. Truth is, I been using it every three, four weeks. The way I see it, I ain't had no choice. We was living in a shelter and his equipment was just sitting here. So I used it, threw my own kinda parties, and made some decent cash doing it. I ain't gonna apologize to no one for that.

Still, the man uptight 'bout his shit. He had them Technics turntables, I think, since before I was born. He always talking 'bout how good they made shit back then, so you never had to buy them again. I know I ain't break none of it, but something tell me he gonna have some way of knowing I been using it.

And it don't take him more than a minute neither. "What's this?" he ask. I turn 'round and see him holding this little stash of my own vinyl I kept right in the front of one of the crates, just so it won't get mixed up with his shit. I'm so fucking stupid it ain't even real. I knew his ass was getting out. I shoulda moved them records before I went away with Regg. "You been using my equipment?"

"A couple times," I say. "To make money to take care of everybody."

He stare at me, cold.

"We ain't had no money. We was in a shelter."

Still staring. The man looking at me like he wanna kill me or something.

"Look, I know how you feel 'bout your shit, but what you expect me to do? You ain't leave no money or nothing for us to —"

I barely get them words out my mouth before he on me, grabbing me by the throat and slamming the back of my head against the wall hard. For a couple seconds I don't see nothing. Then I see my pops face all up in mines. "I ain't gonna say this again," he say, so close he spitting in my face. "You need to remember who is the father here. Do you need help?" His eyes is hard and mad. I can't even talk my head hurt so much, so I just kinda nod so he can let me go, and he do. Then he say, "Help me get this equipment outta here. I need to go home and take a shit."

It take me a second to move, but then I do and, man, I'm way past pissed off. So pissed, I can't even hardly think straight. I help him lift one of the speakers on the dolly and stack some of the crates of records on the hand truck.

It take us three trips to get what we need outta there, and we don't say nothing to each other the whole time. When we done and back outside, I ain't looking for him to drive me home or nothing so I just start walking away, 'cross the parking lot.

"Get in the van," my pops say. He don't yell or nothing, but the way he say it, I know he don't like me walking away from him.

I keep walking though. I don't gotta listen to his ass. I don't look back, but I hear him start up the engine and drive up on the side of me. I know he gonna try and get me in that van, but I don't care. I don't need him to get back home.

He drive real slow and yell out the window, "Be in front of your building by eight." Then he just take off like I'm s'posed to care.

I keep walking, out the parking lot and down the street to the train station, but I can't even lie to myself. My head hurt. I could kill that man. For real.

NINE

When I get back to Bronxwood, all I wanna do is get upstairs and lay down. Not only is my head killing me, but now the Beast is startin' to feel like I got a wet towel sitting in my stomach. I'm walking all slow into the building, probably looking like I'm fifty years old or something.

It's early and Cal probably still 'sleep. For a second I think 'bout knocking on his door and waking him up to tell him that I seen my pops and what he did, but, nah, it's too early to get into that with him. I don't know where the fuck Greg at. He must got a new girl or something 'cause he ain't hardly ever here no more. It's like me and Cal is living by ourself.

I go in my room and close the door. All I wanna do is sleep, but I can't even calm myself down. I can't believe that man went and slammed me like that. He only been out a day and already he putting his hands on people. Treating me like I'm still a child, not a man.

My pops wasn't never like that. He wasn't never the type to go 'round really beating me or Troy or nothing like that, but he definitely used to hit us when he thought we was outta line 'bout something. That's the way he always been, demanding respect, 'specially from his kids. That ain't never gonna change. But I'm sixteen. Why he think he still got that kinda right?

Actually, only person I ever seen him give a real beatdown to was my moms. It only happened a couple times that I know 'bout, and the fact that I was standing right there when it happened ain't stop him from beating the shit outta her neither. The whole thing was mad violent too.

I take my sneakers and jeans off and get in bed. All I wanna do is go back to sleep, but it ain't easy trying to stop myself from thinking. It don't take me long to figure out why my pops hit me. He trying to get me in line and get his control back. He probably know I'm my own man now and he don't like it.

But what really fuck with my head is that I took that shit from him. Why I ain't hit him back or something? Kick his ass? I mean, what the fuck is wrong with me?

I don't come outside 'til, like, ten after eight, and my pops is already down there waiting. Not that I care. Only reason I'm even doing this is for whatever cash he gonna pay me.

I'm looking good though, wearing jeans and this shirt I got down in Atlanta. The shirt is all black with a design that make it look like somebody that be wearing, like, a size 14 sneaker stepped in red paint and walked 'cross the bottom of it. It was mad expensive, I ain't gonna lie, but nobody got no shirt like it 'round here. And course I got my headphones hooked 'round the straps of my backpack 'cause I don't be using nobody headphones but mines.

I get in the van, waiting for him to say something 'bout me being late, but he don't. Actually, I was taking my time getting my music together. My friend Patrick that live on the twelfth floor was putting some new songs on a flash drive for me so I could load it in my pops deck when we get to the party. My pops don't know it, but I got most of my music already stored on his deck. And I don't only play the new music Patrick downloaded for me. I play a lot of old shit too.

I used to help my pops DJ all the time, so I know 'bout all kinds of music that kids my age ain't up on. When I play some of them old songs at my parties, they be like, "Damn. Where you get that shit from?" They don't know. I been listening to that music my whole life. Some of that music been 'round since my moms and pops was my age.

When I play, I like to mix some of my pops old music with some new beats and raps. New mixed with old. That's kinda my style. And my DJ skills is tight now. I'm better than my pops is. He gonna see.

I'm still pissed at him for what he did, so I don't say nothing in the van. Not a word the whole way. He got the radio on again, so it don't matter. Back in the day when I used to go to his parties with him, shit used to be mad fun.

I started going with him when I was, like, thirteen and it used to feel good getting to leave home with him at night 'specially 'cause my moms and Troy had to stay home by theyself. I felt like I was grown, getting to stay up late, helping my pops set up the parties and all that. Them parties was wild too, probably not the kinda thing a kid shoulda even been at, but back then, I ain't really see everything that was going on, or least I ain't understand what was really going on 'round me. Everything. The drug dealing, gambling, pimping hos. All that. Took me a while, but now I get it.

So, yeah, I'ma go and help him make this party dope, but I'm only here for one thing. Money. So I can buy my own equipment and not need his shit no more. Or him.

The party is gonna be in the basement of a pool hall. Regg know the guy that own the place and got him to rent out the basement. The space kinda small for one of my pops parties, but this ain't gonna be like all the other ones he throw.

Regg is already there, going over the room, making sure all the windows and doors is locked and the only way folks can get in is through the side door off the alley, the one where they gotta pay to get in.

And they got some other guys there too, my pops friends that always be working his parties. This dude Bones is setting up the bar, but I know he be selling drugs on the side too. In another corner, this guy Jay is setting up the poker tables. Then there's this dude Leon by this door that must go to a back room or something. Leon a straight-up pimp that probably brung a bunch of hot girls with him to work the guys at the party for every dollar they got.

Thing is, my pops get a piece of all they action.

This how my pops parties go. Folks pay to get in, but they don't only come out to hear the music. They come for everything.

Me and my pops go straight to where the DJ table need to be set up. The way we work, it's like ain't no time went by from the last time he threw a party to now. We both know what we gotta do and we just go through it, no problem, which is good 'cause it mean we don't gotta say nothing to each other. While my pops set up the turntables and mixer, it always been my job to run the speaker wires, burn the ends, and make sure they connected right. Then I gotta tape them wires down to the floor with duct tape.

When I get all that done and everything's hooked up, my pops put on one of his old-skool records to test out the sound, and he just let it play while we stand next to each other, not saying nothing, just stacking the crates of records and making sure everything in the right order, 'cause with my pops there's definitely a order, and I know in the back of his mind he checking to make sure I ain't fuck up his system while he was gone, which I ain't. Matter of fact, when I DJ, I keep everything in the same order he use.

The way he plan his parties is always the same. First, he start out with whatever R&B dance music that's hot right now, just to get folks in the door and let them know what kinda party they gonna be havin'. Then, when the place get full, he crank the party up to high and put on old shit like the Fatback Band, which always get folks they age up on the floor dancing and getting theyself thirsty so they hafta buy drinks. After a long time, he bring the beat down and throw on some slow reggae, get people in the mood for slow dancing and grinding. Sometimes he even pick out a girl to dance with hisself, a girl that ain't got no guy with her, make her feel good even if she ain't the best-looking girl there. When he dancing, I play a couple more reggae jams and, when we done with the slow music, that's when I really take over and play some new stuff, so the folks in they twenties can hear something they into too, keep them coming to the parties and maybe bring new people with them. Then, when my pops take back over, he end off the night by playing some more old music from back in the day, stuff like Shalamar and The Whispers, and while some of the younger people start leaving, most of the people stay and dance 'til the end of the party. My pops always end his parties with the same song, "Before I Let Go" by Frankie Beverly and Maze. Folks lose they mind with that song. And they leave happy. All the time.

"You see this," my pops say. He holding up a Brothers Johnson record in my face.

"What?" I go, even though I know I was playing "Strawberry Letter 23" at my last party.

"This ain't supposed to be here. This look like rap to you?"

Damn. Fuck.

"I ask a question, I want a answer." He staring at me now.

"I don't know. You musta put that in the wrong place 'fore you — 'fore you went on your trip, 'cause I don't even play that kinda music at my parties." I'm lying out the left side of my neck, and me and him both know it. But damn, it's only one fuckin' album. Why he gotta make a big deal 'bout everything?

He stare at me for a couple more seconds. "Where my chain at?" he ask me.

"I forgot it." Fuck him. Like he in a rush to get that chain back.

I don't wait for him to say nothing back. I just walk away and go over to the other side of the room to the bar. No doubt I'ma need something to get me through the night with that man.

I ask Bones for a couple beers and he like, "You old enough to drink, man?"

"Yeah," I go.

Dude used to give me beers when I was still in middle school.

He hand me the bottles. "Something wrong, Ty? Your pops is back, man." He say it like that's s'posed to mean something to me.

"Yeah, I see that."

"You lucky. Some men, they go in and never get out."

I nod my head, take my beers, and walk away. I ain't in the mood tonight. I just wanna get this party over with.

After we done setting up, it's, like, practically ten o'clock and folks is gonna start showing up in a while. I plug in the microphone and turn the lights on over the DJ table, and we good.

"Tyrone!" Regg call out from the other side of the room. Even though he calling my pops, for a second I think he callin' my name. "You ready to open the doors?" He in charge of the money, and keeping out anybody who he think gonna start something.

"Born ready," my pops say, and him and Regg laugh. Then my pops crank the music up.

Me, when I throw my parties, this is when my mind start running, thinking maybe nobody gonna show up and I ain't gonna make no money. It never happened like that for me, but still. My pops though, he chillin', drinking a beer, and moving his head to the beat of the music, just knowing the word is out that he outta prison and people is gonna pay to come and see him.

And they do. The second Regg open the door, there's, like, ten, twelve people coming in, like they was standing out there waiting. My pops don't say nothing to me, but he line up a couple more records for me to play, then he leave the DJ table and go over to where everyone standing at. All the females is giving him hugs, and all the dudes is smiling and shaking his hand. I put on the records and try to get into the music, feel it.

My pops come back and start DJing, and I step to the side and let him try and show off for his friends. I hand him the records he need and keep drinking. It's after two o'clock when my pops finally let me play some of my music. I'm up there jamming, feeling good. The music pumping in my headphones and in my body, and I got a buzz from the beers I been drinking. I got everybody out there dancing, young people and even them forty-year-olds like my pops. He out there looking like a old fool, dancing with two young girls. But with the way I'm playing and the way everybody happy, everything is good 'til I look up and see this dude Dante coming into the party and walking 'cross the floor toward my pops.

Dante one of my pops friends, but he ain't cool like Regg. I don't even know why my pops even deal with that asshole. Dante walk over to my pops and they hug like they best friends. Course I can't hear nothing they saying, but he cheesing in my pops face, telling him something and both of them is laughing and shit. And I ain't even hardly hearing the music no more 'cause I'm just watching him, pissed that he treating my pops like a chump or something.

A second later, I'm like, fuck my pops. Let his ass get played by his friend.

After a while my pops come over to the DJ table and just take back over. He don't say nothing 'bout how good I was doing, probably 'cause he know I'm better than him now. The little bit of skills he used to have is gone. He lost it in jail. Knowing him, he probably don't want me playing too long 'cause his guests gonna know they don't need to be coming to his parties when mines is probably better.

I walk away and out the corner of my eye I see Dante looking at me. I stop walking and stare back, just to let him know I know what he doing, trying to fuck with me, and I ain't scared to say nothing to my pops 'cause both us know what would happen to Dante if I did say something.

After a couple seconds of me and him staring at each other, he the first one to take his eyes off mines. Asshole. I keep walking 'cross the room, over by Regg to see if he need anything from the bar.

Regg is standing in the doorway, and he so big he just 'bout fill the whole thing up. When I get there, he lean over close to me so I can hear him and go, "What up? You look like you 'bout to choke that nigga."

Regg is cool. I can tell him everything. When we was driving down south, I told him 'bout me and Novisha and all that bullshit that happened between us, but for some reason I ain't never told him 'bout Dante. And now, I ain't sure I wanna get into it. So I just go, "Nah, it ain't nothing. Don't worry 'bout it."

But Regg just stand there like he waiting for me to say more, fill him in. It ain't easy to get nothing past him.

So I ask him to come outside with me for a second, and when we out there, I say, "A'ight. I'ma tell you. In the winter, back when we was living in that shelter, Dante was coming 'round all the time and buying my moms food and clothes for Troy and shit. Actin' like he was lookin' out for us, just 'cause."

I look over my shoulder and make sure nobody coming up behind me. In a way I wish someone was, so I wouldn't hafta even talk 'bout none of this.

"One night," I say, "the same night ACS came and snatched up Troy, my moms ain't come home at all. And that's when I found out that her and Dante . . ." I don't even gotta say it.

"Damn," Regg say, shaking his head. "I thought something like that mighta went down. That's some fucked-up shit."

"True that," I go. "She even went to live with him for, like, a couple days after I left outta the shelter. She said it was 'cause Bennett is a family shelter and they wouldn't let her stay there if she ain't had no kids living with her, but I don't know, man." I stop talking 'cause just thinking 'bout everything again make me wanna kill Dante.

Regg get close to me and he look real serious when he say, "If I was you, Ty, I wouldn't say shit to your father. He —"

"What? I'm s'posed to let Dante stand in there and act like he his friend when —?"

"Ty, your pops just got out." He look 'round real quick. "You tell him any of this shit and he gonna end up right back in there 'fore the end of the night. You understand what —"

"I could kick Dante ass for showin' up here, smiling in my pops face." I feel heat moving up through my body. "It would feel so fuckin' good to stomp on Dante face and make him pay for —"

"I'm telling you, Ty, don't tell your pops. A man hear that and he ain't never gonna get it out his mind. He gonna be picturing that shit forever. Him and your moms is doing good now. He hear what she did behind his back, he ain't never gonna forget that. Trust me."

I stand there, feeling my head getting hot. This whole thing is pissing me the fuck off. Why I even gotta deal with this? All this should be between my moms and pops. Why I even gotta know who they messing with?

"I'm serious, Ty. Keep this shit to yourself."

I'm tired of hearing Regg too, like it's up to me to keep my moms and pops together or something. "Whatever you say," I tell him, and open the door and go back inside. And right away I see Dante 'cross the room. I walk in his direction, staring him down the whole time, and when we close enough that he can hear me over the music, I say, "Stay the fuck away from my moms."

He get this little smile on his face, but he don't say nothing back. He just walk to the other side of the room where he got some friends. After he outta my way, I turn back and, course, Regg seen the whole thing. He shake his head, like he warning me again, but I just turn 'round and head back over to the DJ table so I can finish helping the man and get my money. Yeah, I'ma listen to Regg. I ain't gonna say nothing. But this whole situation getting me more tired and more pissed than I need to be.

TEN

When the party over, my pops and all the guys sit 'round getting high and relaxing. Course I get some of they weed too. After a while we break down the equipment and clean up the room the best we can so Regg friend that own the place don't get mad. Me, I just wanna get paid and bounce, but my pops wanna go back to the diner like we always do after his parties. I don't know why he dragging this thing out, but it don't matter. I'm cool with going and eating another one of them Beasts. 'Til I hear Dante tell my pops he coming too.

I gotta go in the van with my pops to help him bring the equipment back to the storage place, but we don't hafta talk 'cause on the way he call my moms and they talk for the whole ride. Then, when we get there, he tell her to get in a cab and meet us at the diner. I know she was 'sleep 'cause it's only something after five in the morning and she hate getting up early, but my pops tell her he miss her and all that shit, and next thing I know he hanging up and telling me, "She coming."

I don't care one way or another. The whole time I was down south, the only time she called me was when she wanted to complain 'bout something. She would say shit like, "I don't know why you out there in Atlanta having fun and you got me here with no money or nothing." Them calls pissed me off, but they wasn't nothing new. I mean, I been taking care of my moms for a year and she been acting like that the whole time. The one good thing 'bout my pops being back is, least that's over with now.

When we get to the diner, all the other guys is already there, sitting at a big table in the back of the place. I sit next to Regg, on the other side of the table from Dante. Regg too busy to say anything to me. He on his BlackBerry, typing some shit, probably handling his business, but I'm like, it's five in the morning. Who he doing business with now?

Being that we all still kinda high, everybody start getting loud, talking and laughing 'bout some of the shit that happened at the party. I gotta say, for one of my pops parties, this one wasn't all that wild.

We order our breakfast and for a while we sit there having a good time, but every time I look over at the other end of the table, Dante staring right at me. I'm like, what he want from me? 'Cause if he looking for a fight, I'm ready.

Then my moms get there, and I ain't lying, soon as she see Dante, the look on her face is like, oh, shit.

A second later, she try and play it off, and smile like it don't matter. I gotta say though, my moms is looking kinda okay, 'specially for somebody that just got theyself outta bed. She ain't wearing them cutoff shorts she been running a lot this summer, or one of them tank tops that she probably too old to be wearing anyway. She got on jeans and a red T-shirt, but she musta put makeup on or something 'cause her face look good. Either that or it's 'cause she smiling. Ain't seen her do that since they sent my pops up.

My moms go over and sit down next to my pops, and they start hugging and kissing, acting like they ain't seen each other for years instead of just, like, a couple hours. Kinda embarrassing, you ask me, but okay, least they happy. When I look over at Dante, he staring at them, mad. But what he got to be pissed off 'bout? He the one that used the situation we was in to get my moms in bed with him. He knew my moms since she was, like, my age. He know she don't know how to act when her man ain't 'round.

Not that she ain't responsible for what she did. She fucked up, and I ain't never gonna forget it. Wish I could.

Our food come, and all through breakfast my moms and pops sit so close they practically on top of each other. They eating but still kissing and shit. And I can see Dante getting madder and madder. Regg must see it too, 'cause he get up from the table and go over to Dante and say he wanna talk to him 'bout something outside. Dante look kinda scared, which make sense with the way Regg standing over him, big as he is, but Dante don't got no choice 'cept to go with him.

After they leave, my moms flash me a look like, what's up with them? I shake my head like I don't know, 'cause I don't want her to know I told Regg. I don't need her going off on me any more than she already do.

It don't take long for Regg and Dante to get back. Dante still walking and ain't got no broken bones or blood coming outta his body, so it don't look like Regg laid a finger on him or nothing. Regg go back to eating, and so do Dante, but he eating mad fast now. Like three minutes later, he done. He throw some money on the table and say he gotta go. Nobody hardly pay him no mind though, 'cept my moms, and soon as he leave, she look 'bout ten times happier and more relaxed.

I don't know what it is, but something 'bout the way Dante was looking at my moms and pops, and something 'bout how my moms is acting, make me think shit is even worse than I thought. I been thinking they only hooked up for them couple days, 'til I got my moms her own place, but now I can tell that ain't what happened. They probably ain't stop this whole time, knowing my moms. She don't know how to be by herself.

When we through eating, my pops and Regg go over to another table in the corner and count the money. Regg get a piece of what everybody pay at the door, so they always count together. After they through, my pops come over and pay the other guys. When he come over to me, he hand me some cash and before I can even count it, he go, "Tomorrow, I'ma gonna need you. We gotta get all the furniture and shit out the storage place, into the new apartment. I got some guys helping out, but I'm still gonna need you."

"What time?" I ask.

"Early. I'ma call you when I'm on the way." He don't wait for me to say alright or nothing. He just go back over by my moms.

I ain't gonna lie. I'm confused. My pops say he want me to help him move into the new apartment, but what that mean for me? I'm s'posed to move in there or not? Or I'm s'posed to help him move and then keep staying with Cal?

I'm still sitting there when Regg come over to me and say my pops asked him to drive me home. He laugh and say, "Your pops don't wanna take no time away from your moms."

I get up from the table. "They too old for all that."

"Never too old," he say, still laughing. "Your pops is what? Forty-one? How old is your moms?"

"Thirty-five. Gonna be thirty-six next month."

"They young, Ty. They still wanna —"

"A'ight. I get it."

Regg still laughing when we walk outta the restaurant and 'cross the parking lot to his truck. "I can drive," I tell him. "If you too tired, I mean."

"I got this," he say. "I already risked my life one time this week."

I get in the passenger seat and right away start counting my money. Eight hundred dollars, all in twenties. It's more than I thought he was gonna pay me, but I still need a lot more.

The second we get out the parking lot I ask Regg what he said to Dante, how he got him to break outta there so fast.

"I told him that from now on, he need to know that your moms got a order of protection out on her. From me. If he see her, he need to back away. And if he don't, he gonna hafta deal with me."

I smile. "Good." I shoulda did that myself.

Then Regg tell me again 'bout not saying nothing to my pops 'bout what went down with my moms and Dante.

"I ain't," I say a couple times before he actually believe me. "I'ma let them handle they business. I got my own problems anyway. I don't need no more."

"How you and your pops doing? Y'all looked like y'all was okay playing together tonight."

I shrug. "I was just looking to get paid, that's it."

"But y'all talking, right?"

"Nah. I ain't got nothing to say to him." Then I tell Regg 'bout what my pops did to me at the storage place yesterday. "The way he did that shit, it came outta nowhere. He, like, crazy or something, I swear."

"Try and make it work with him, Ty. Y'all used to be real tight. A lot of kids your age ain't got that with they old man."

The way Regg talking, I know he thinking 'bout his own life. When we was driving down south he told me he ain't never knew his father. When he was my age he had to leave his moms house 'cause he ain't get along with her boyfriend and he ain't had nowhere to go for a long time. Regg was living out on the streets, not like what I'm doing, staying with Cal and them. Regg had it real bad.

As we get close to Bronxwood, I'm still thinking 'bout everything Regg told me. "Regg," I say, "was the whole reason you brung me down south with you 'cause you wanted to talk to me 'bout my pops?"

"Not the whole reason," he go. "I wanted to get you outta the Bronx for a while. And yeah, I wanted to talk to you too. Make sure you was ready for your pops to get out. I knew you since you was a little kid, Ty, and I don't want you going through the kinda shit I had to go through."

"You think I need my pops or something?"

"It ain't about what you need. I'm just looking out for you."

For some reason what Regg saying kinda get me a little mad, at him and my pops. Like the two of them is on the same side or something, trying to get me to do something I don't wanna do.

"You can let me out here," I tell him before he can turn into Bronxwood. "I need to get something from the store." And I need to stop talking to him.

He pull over, and as I'm opening the door to get out, he say, "Just so you know, I'm going outta town for a while."

"A'ight." I get out the truck and close the door.

"Don't get in no trouble," he say out the window.

"You too."

He laugh. "They ain't caught up to me yet, right?"

Even though I don't wanna talk to him no more right now, I can't help but ask him again, "What you do, anyway?"

"Mind my business," he say.

"When you gonna trust me?"

"I trust you, Ty. But I ain't trying to get you involved in my shit."

Now that just make me madder at him. I'm sixteen and he treating me like a fuckin' child that can't handle nothing. "Thanks for dropping me off," I say. "Holla at me when you back."

"Count on it," he say, and drive off. Another dude that can't stay in one place too long.

I go in the bodega and buy a Pepsi and some chips and cookies. Then, on my way to my building, the second I turn the corner, I almost run right into Novisha and her moms. They look like they on they way to church, and I'm like, damn, it's Sunday morning. People been to sleep and woke up and got dressed, and me, I'm now getting home.

I don't wanna stare at Novisha, but she look real fuckin' pretty, wearing a light blue dress and heels. She don't never dress sexy. That's not the kinda girl she is. But no matter what she wear, she look good. She real short and little, and her body kick ass. And she got a cute face too. Back when we was together, I could never get tired of looking at that face. No lie, it used to make me feel real good that she was mines.

But I ain't with her no more, so I stop looking and instead just turn to Ms. Jenkins and tell her good morning.

"Good morning to you too, Tyrell." She used to always look happy when she seen me, but now that me and her daughter is broke up, she only half smile and it's real fake. I don't know if it's 'cause me and Novisha ain't together no more or if it's 'cause I'm living with Cal and them and maybe she think I'm in they business now. She probably glad I ain't Novisha boyfriend no more. "You're up early on a Sunday morning."

The way she say it, I can't tell if she actually believe that shit or if she really know I been out all night. So I just nod and go, "Yeah." Then, so Ms. Jenkins don't think I'm disrespecting her daughter, I say, "Hi, Novisha."

"Hi, Ty." She open her mouth to say something else, then close it again.

And for, like, five seconds, we don't say nothing. We just standing there on the sidewalk, not moving and not talking 'til finally, Ms. Jenkins say, "Well, we better get going."

"Yeah," I say. "Okay."

They walk to the corner and stop, waiting for the light to change. Crazy thing is, I'm watching them. I don't know why. Then, while I'm still standing there, Novisha turn her head back and look right at me, like she wanna say something. Her eyes is right on mines, and damn, that face. I'm waiting for her to say something, but she don't. She just turn back 'round.

ELEVEN

By the time I get upstairs, I'm all 'bout sleep. Between being up all night and the big fuckin' Beast, damn, I can't hardly stand up. But, course, shit don't work out the way I want it to. Even before the elevator open on my floor, I can hear the baby crying. Damn. I forgot. Cal told me he was gonna have his son today.

When I walk in the apartment, Cal standing in the living room holding CJ, who crying the brains outta his head. He only, like, seven months, but still, why he gotta scream like that? "What you doing, killing the boy?" I ask Cal, locking the door behind me, which take a minute 'cause they got three fuckin' locks on they door.

Cal look like he through. Already. He still in the raggedy sweatpants he sleep in and he look half awake, holding his son like he a football. "I don't know what he want," Cal say. "He wildin' out for nothing."

Cal don't get to watch CJ all that much, not by hisself. Tina don't hardly be letting Cal take the kid outta her sight, and definitely not bring him over here 'less she here too. Most of the time he only get to see him when they at her moms house. Tina say it's 'cause she don't want CJ in Bronxwood, 'round where he do business. "Why she let you have him today anyway?"

"Told you. Her cousin getting married."

"Funny that it ain't all that dangerous over here now, when she need something from you."

He shake his head. "You should know by now, females is like that."

"You mean, full of shit, right?"

Me and him both laugh 'cause it's true. If I ever started understanding girls, I would write a book or something. Make some real money.

"You shoulda been here," Cal say. "The second Tina set foot in this apartment, she was arguing with me and complaining. Telling me this place is too nasty for her kid, like he ain't my kid too, and telling me I don't know how to take care of him right. She was all in my face. I swear that girl gonna turn out just like her mother and I ain't gonna be around when she turn." He shake his head, looking mad frustrated. "I'm so fuckin' tired of arguing with that girl." He don't say nothing for a while, just look down at the floor, and I don't know what to say neither 'cause he right 'bout Tina. She is kinda off the hook most of the time. After a couple seconds he look at me and go, "Where was you anyway?"

I tell Cal all 'bout the party and how Dante showed up and wouldn't leave for shit. And how he was at the diner and kept looking at my moms. All that. Cal shake his head 'cause he know all 'bout what happened and how fucked up it was. He know there really ain't nothing I can do 'bout it, that I did what I could already.

"Damn, I'm tired," I say, but the second it come out my mouth, it sound stupid 'cause when I work all I gotta do is spin some records for five, six hours. But for Cal, when he work he gotta bust his ass all fuckin' night and put his freedom on the line at the same time.

"Your pops want you to move back in with them?" Cal change CJ from one arm to the other, but it don't work to shut the baby up none.

"Nah, not yet. They moving to they new apartment tomorrow, and it look like him and my moms is working on something. I don't know."

"He ain't tell you what they up to?"

"Nah. Probably some kinda new business, something to make fast money. Something illegal, knowing him."

"That's who he is," Cal say.

"Yeah, I know." Which is why I ain't gonna move back in with them even when my pops try and make me come back. Why I'ma go through all that trouble, moving my shit over there when he only gonna get locked up again a couple months later, if that? When we only gonna end up losing that apartment too?

I go into the kitchen and put my Pepsi in the refrigerator. The sink is full of dishes, and all I know is somebody need to start bustin' some suds up in here. And it ain't gonna be me.

The baby keep crying and Cal try walking 'round with him. He come in the kitchen, then go back in the living room and walk 'round in a circle, but nothing work. I remember when Troy was that little. I was eight when he was born, and sometimes my moms couldn't get him to shut up, no matter what she did, and she couldn't handle that shit for nothing. My pops used to tell her to just put him down and let him cry hisself to sleep, but when she did that, I used to sneak over to his crib and pick him up 'cause I couldn't take him crying neither. It ain't seem right to just leave him alone like that.

I go into the living room. CJ look real tired, but he crying and fighting hisself to stay awake. "Look at him," I say. "He must not wanna miss nothing. He wanna be in it."

"I don't know why babies do that."

"Give me him," I tell Cal even though I'm tired and not in the mood for none of this. "Go take a shower or something. I mean, I ain't sayin' you kickin' or nothin', but damn, you definitely got a hum jumpin' off you."

Cal laugh. "Oh, it's like that?" But it don't take him a second to hand off the baby to me, like he been ready to make that pass for a while. "I ain't gonna take that long," he say, and he gone down the hall, and I'm standing there with a screaming baby and no idea what the fuck to do with him.

I know babies be liking music, so I walk 'round the living room with CJ and start rapping to him, anything I could think of that got the word "baby" in it. I'm rapping shit from back in the day like,

"Baby, don't cry, I hope you got your head up
Even when the road is hard, never give up."

I just do that part over and over 'cause the rest of that rap is 'bout some fucked-up shit, and no baby need to hear that, no matter how young he is. Tupac lyrics is deep.

I ain't lying when I say rapping to a baby work. I mean, he ain't relaxing really. He still moving all 'round and looking like something bothering him, but he ain't crying no more. Maybe he gonna grow up and be a rapper or something, make back some of the money Cal spending on him. Keep his father in style with cars and clothes and shit.

And his father friend Ty too.

Yeah.

'Bout half hour later, Cal still getting dressed. He got music playing in his room and he must be taking his time or something 'cause how long it take him to put some clothes on? And right then, outta nowhere, Andre show up. He don't ring no bell or nothing. He just unlock all the locks on the door and walk in like he still live here. True, his name is still on the lease, but he act like he got the right to just roll up in here anytime he want, just 'cause he the boss of the business and the man of the family.

The thing 'bout Andre is he don't never show up nowhere by hisself no more. After he got shot he bought this stupid pit bull he call Bin Laden. Crazy dog, you ask me, that never stop barking and act like he don't know nobody, no matter how many times he seen you.

Andre close the door fast and lock all three of the locks like somebody chasing him. Dude mad paranoid and shit, thinking the drug dealers that shot him are still out to get him. Like anybody even care 'bout his ass or where he at. All he do is run a small-time weed business. It ain't no Scarface up in here.

"Cal, where you at?" Andre go, talking all loud over the barking, and acting like he don't even see me standing there. I don't get no "Hey, how you doin', Ty?" or nothing.

Cal come down the hall. He wearing jeans and nothing else, and now his face look all confused and his mouth is open all wide.

Before he can say anything, Andre say, "Me and you gotta talk." He grab hold of Bin Laden collar and walk past Cal down the hallway, fast, even with that fucked-up limp he got going on now. Cal give me a look like, what the fuck? Then he turn 'round and follow his brother. A second later, his bedroom door close and I'm still out there in the living room with the baby. Stuck.

Cal and Andre don't come out the room for 'bout a half hour, and the whole time I can't hear a thing they saying in there 'cause that dumb dog is losing what's left of his stupid mind. Even through all that noise, I do get the baby to go to sleep in his stroller and I lay on the couch trying to relax my own self, but I sit up when I hear Andre coming down the hall. I ain't sure why, but I don't want him seeing me sleep.

Bin Laden still barking and shit when Andre get to the living room. "How long he gonna be here?" he ask Cal, and for a second I think he talking 'bout me. 'Til he go, "'Cause you gotta work tonight."

"I know," Cal say, breathing kinda funny. "Tina coming to get him by four thirty."

Andre nod. Then he look at me. "What's going on, Ty?"

"Chillin'," I say.

"Your pops out, right?"

"Yeah. Friday."

"You still gonna stay here?"

"Yeah," I say. I ain't think he was just gonna come out and ask me like that. I ain't mind when Cal asked me, but this is different. To be honest, I don't even know why I said yeah when I don't really know what I'm doing. But something 'bout the way he asked made me wanna have a answer.

"Look, Ty," he say. "We need more guys out there working for us, you know, guys we can trust. I don't mind you

96

living here, but you not really helping us out like this. We gotta work, all of us. This is business."

"I know, Andre, but I been paying a third of the rent and buying food and shit. I know that ain't a lot, but —"

"That ain't shit," he say. "We need you bringing in money."

"Yeah, I know, but —"

"You need to make some decisions."

"I know," I say again.

Andre never used to be like this, all hard. He used to be cool, back when he lived here and they was just selling weed here in Bronxwood. Now he all serious and got his brothers scared of him. I don't get it. Just 'cause he running two projects, he think he gotta be a asshole now.

Andre just stand there looking at me for a couple more seconds, hard. Even Bin Laden staring at me now. Then Andre unlock the door, stick his head out, and check the hall real crazy and suspicious, then leave. Damn. That dude losing it.

I wait 'til I hear the elevator doors open and close before I ask Cal what up.

"He say I ain't making enough. Shit is hard now. The economy is fucked up."

"What else he want you to do?"

Cal shake his head. "Work harder. That's all he said."

Cal already working hard, and Andre act like he don't see that. Nothing good enough for him. And he think I'ma wanna work for somebody like that? Yeah, right. "Don't worry 'bout it," I tell Cal. "You know how Andre act when he on his period."

Cal smile. "It's that time of the month again?"

Me and him laugh loud, and I gotta point to the baby so we don't wake him up. Last thing we need.

After a while Cal go get his shirt and finish getting dressed in the living room, and I finally get to my room. I put on some music in case the baby start crying again, so he don't wake me up, and change into some sweatpants to sleep in. Not that it's gonna be easy sleeping after dealing with Andre. I would be lying if I said he ain't got me thinking. I do got some decisions to make. Not only 'bout where I'ma live, but 'bout a lot of things.

I mean, it was alright being here when my pops was locked up, but now I don't know. If Andre think he gonna get me to start selling for him just 'cause I'm here, that ain't gonna happen. I don't need to. All this time I been taking care of myself by just throwing parties and charging kids to get in. I wasn't living large or nothing, but I paid my bills and my moms bills and still kept myself looking good.

And I see what selling is doing to Cal. Yeah, he walking 'round with a lot more money than me, but it ain't worth it, putting up with Andre and looking out for the police and all the other shit that go with it.

Me, I ain't looking for no more stress in my life. I already got enough to deal with.

TWELVE

It's after five o'clock when I wake up and I only got one thing on my mind — the rest of them Cocoa Puffs. I get up out the bed, cut the music off, and go out into the hallway. When I pass by Cal room, the door is closed and I can hear the bed squeaking and all kinda moaning and shit. Tina musta came to get CJ early, and from what they doing in there, it sound like they not still fighting. Even the baby ain't crying no more.

I go to the kitchen, and all I see is Cocoa Puffs all over the table and floor. And damn, the box is still on the table and there ain't even hardly none left in there. The whole kitchen is jacked. A glass is broke on the floor and soda is spilled all over the place. My Pepsi.

Everything 'bout living here is starting to piss me off. But then I think 'bout my pops and I don't know where it's worse, here or with him.

I'm 'bout to knock on Cal door to find out what happened to the kitchen, not even caring that I'ma be breaking up whatever him and Tina is doing in there, but before I even get down the hall all the way, Greg come home. I hardly seen him the whole time I been back from down south.

"What up, Ty?" he go.

"Chillin'," I say. "What up with you?"

"Working hard. Trying to stay ahead." He go in the kitchen and say, "What the fuck?"

I shake my head. "Cal and Tina musta been fighting in here or something."

"Where he at?"

"His room. With Tina and the baby."

"He did this?"

"I don't know. Pro'ly. Or the baby."

"Your friend losing his mind," Greg say. "And he losing money for us. You need to tell him to start working harder, you know what I mean?"

"I ain't got nothing to do with y'all business, Greg. You know that."

"That's fucked up, Ty. Least you could do is help when we need you. We ain't saying you gotta do this shit forever."

He leave the kitchen and go to the living room, right for the PlayStation. He turn it on and say to me, "Don't touch that game. Me and my boys gotta get our guys outta this battle and kill them Vietcong assholes. Shit taking too fuckin' long." He go down the hall, looking pissed, like any of that shit is real. I hear him pull out this big set of keys he walk 'round with so he can get in his room 'cause he always keep it locked.

Even though Greg in charge of handling the weed, Cal always tell me that Greg don't keep no big stash of drugs here in this apartment 'cause he ain't stupid like that. From the little I know from hearing them talk, Greg s'posed to be keeping the drugs in different spots, and making sure the guys they got out there selling always got what they need. And he also s'posed to be driving 'round, making sure them guys is alright out there all night. That's all I know.

My whole thing is this, I don't wanna be the one to go down for some shit they doing. All three of them brothers know how I feel 'bout that. I'm not 'bout to live in no apartment that got drugs stashed in it, 'cause it ain't gonna matter to the police that I'm not part of they business. They gonna arrest my black ass just for living here.

Greg go in his room and close the door. I ain't never stepped foot in his room, but the way he lock it all the time make me wonder what he got up in there. I know he got a lot of clothes and sneakers and shit, 'cause ever since he started working harder for Andre, he definitely making more money. But that ain't no reason to lock his door like we even care what he got in there.

I go to the bathroom, take a shower, and get dressed. I missed most of the day working for my pops, helping Cal with CJ, and sleeping. Now I wanna have some fun.

While I'm passing the living room, Greg on the couch with his headset on, screaming battle commands into the microphone real loud. Dude think he really in the war or something. On the TV screen, shit is blowing up and heads is flying off and blood is shooting out all over the place. Greg don't even see me. He too busy shouting crazy dumb shit like, "I wanna see dead bodies on that bridge, men! Make them motherfuckers taste they own blood!"

I gotta get up outta here.

It's nice outside. Hot. Too hot to be sitting inside, which is probably why everyone hanging out. Not Novisha, not that I'm looking for her or anything. I know she been back from church for a while, but she don't be hanging out no matter how nice the day is. She always upstairs in her apartment.

Or, for all I know, she could be out with that dude.

I walk over by her building, the same building where Adonna live at. Man, I used to come over here so much when me and Novisha was together that now, for a couple seconds, it's like I'm walking over here to see her.

I pass by Kenny truck and ask him if Adonna 'round.

"She's somewhere around here," he say.

"Yeah? She with somebody?"

"She ain't with no boy," Kenny say, staring me down like he wanna know what up. "She's with Asia, probably watching them knuckleheads play basketball behind Building C."

I nod, trying to play it off like it don't really matter to me who she with or what she doing. "A'ight," I tell him. "I'ma go over there and see if I can get in the game."

I walk a couple steps away and hear Kenny go, "What, you like my sister or something?"

I turn 'round and Kenny leaning out the window to his truck and shit. "We talkin'," I tell him, 'cause it ain't none of his business. "I gotta go, Kenny. Check you later, a'ight?"

I'm walking 'cross the street when Keith come up behind me. He trying to ride his scooter and carry a cherry icee at the same time and it ain't working.

"You gonna bust your head," I tell him.

"Not me." He smile big. "I'm gonna be a stuntman in Hollywood. A famous one. Watch."

I wanna tell him he gonna hafta stop working with Cal and them first, but I don't wanna bust on the kid for trying to make money, 'specially when I don't know what his family situation is like. I mean, this kid is thirteen and he out to, like, midnight almost every night. No way his moms don't know what he doing and ain't using the money he bringing in. So I tell Keith I'ma look for him in the movies and he keep on scooting down the street.

Adonna right where Kenny said she was gonna be. Sometimes I think he be sitting in that damn truck keeping track of everybody and what they up to. Adonna and Asia is running they mouths and watching the guys play ball. I gotta figure out a way to get Adonna away from her friend this time, 'cause ain't nothing gonna happen with them two girls together.

Adonna smile when she see me coming 'cross the playground. That's a good sign, I'm thinking. She do like me. As usual, Adonna looking hot today. She got on another pair of shorts and one of them tops that leave the whole back out, and she still rockin' my pops chain. Make me walk faster past the basketball court over to where they sitting.

I say hi to the girls and sit down next to Adonna. Her legs is looking nice and smooth. Girls don't know what they be doing to guys when they show this much skin to us. We weak. We lose our minds when girls is this sexy.

"Why you hiding out back here?" I ask her. And I ain't gonna lie. I make my voice a little deeper, kinda like one of them baritone brothas girls be getting excited over. "You ain't want me to find you?"

She look me in the eye and smile so damn cute. "Can't you tell? I like to be chased."

I smile my own self. "I like chasing." And just like that, I lean over and give her a kiss on the lips. Nothing like we was doing the other night in the elevator, just something to keep her wanting more. And it look like she do too, 'cause when I stop kissing, she still leaning into me like she thought it was gonna go on for a while longer. "I wanna talk to you," I tell her real quiet so Asia don't hear me. "Alone."

It ain't easy, but after 'bout twenty minutes of me sitting there, talking and joking with both them girls, trying not to show how bad I wanna spend time with Adonna, Asia finally take the hint and say she gotta go home and help her moms cook. I think that's what she say, but to be honest, I ain't really paid her no mind. This time 'round, my mind is focused on what I want.

As soon as Asia gone, I grab Adonna hand and get her to walk with me away from the basketball court. I'm trying to find someplace where me and her can go where there ain't a whole bunch of other people 'round, but that's hard to find in the projects. They got us packed in here like fuckin' rats. I mean, I don't know why we don't all go crazy at the same time.

I take Adonna back 'cross the street over to the side of the community center that's closed now. They only open in the morning on Sunday to give the old people 'round here breakfast and a sandwich or something to take home with them. I lean up against the building and bring Adonna close to me, and before she can start talking, I go in for the kill. My mouth is on hers and we doing some long, hard kisses. I know it ain't easy to turn me down, but at the same time I'm kinda surprised that Adonna kissing me outside like this, even if there ain't a lot of people that can see us. I mean, she don't never mess 'round with guys from Bronxwood, and now it's like she letting everybody know she like me or something, and that's cool. Funny thing is, if Novisha in her apartment right now, she could see us if she was looking out her kitchen window.

My hand is on Adonna back, right on her nice smooth skin, and I start sliding it down to her ass real slow so she won't even hardly notice. It don't work though. She pull her lips away from mines and is like, "*Where* is your hand going?"

"I don't know," I say, and try to go back to kissing, but she keep her lips away. I smile. "Both my hands got a mind of they own. But this one, the right one, it's a bad hand."

"Bad hand?" She raise her eyebrows, but she still got that little smile on her lips.

"Yeah, it always been like that. When I was in fourth grade, you ain't gonna believe this, but this hand actually threw a Pokémon eraser 'cross the classroom and almost hit Mrs. Milner in the back of her head while she was writing on the board."

Adonna laugh.

"And when she turned 'round and was like, 'Who threw that?' I ain't say nothing, 'cause I ain't do it. My hand did it by its own self."

Adonna shake her head. "You are so full of it."

"I'm serious."

"All I know is, you better find a way to keep that bad hand off my ass."

"I don't got no control over it." I try and make myself look innocent, but I can't help smiling myself.

Next thing I know, I'm putting my arms 'round her and we hugging, and I'm kissing her ear and neck, and she trying to act like she ain't a hundred percent into me, but she still letting me do what I want. Damn, I'm starting to like this girl. And the way her body feel against mines, it's all good. I could get used to this. "When you gonna let me take you out?" I whisper in her ear. "Show you a good time."

She smiling. "How good?"

"Real good." In my head, I can't believe she actually gonna go out with me. Cal ain't gonna believe this when I tell him. I give Adonna another kiss.

"My mother's not gonna let me go out with you 'til summer school is over on Friday."

"No problem. Let's go out on Friday, then. I'ma come over and say hi to your moms, and take you to see whatever movie you wanna see and then we gonna go for something to eat. How that sound?"

"Good," she say. Then she kinda wiggle herself outta my arms, just trying to be extra sexy. "I have to go now, Ty."

"You sure you can't come back to my place for a little while? I got some new music we can listen —"

"Remember what I said before," she say. "I like to be chased."

Damn. "A'ight. I get it. I'ma let you go home and sit in that apartment all bored outta your mind. That's cool. But let me get your digits so I can call you."

Adonna pull her cell outta her pocket and I tell her my number and she call it. After I save her number I walk her to her building but don't go upstairs with her this time. I'ma be patient. Ain't no rush. Friday gonna be here in five days and I know I'ma get her. I can tell. That girl is so into me it ain't even funny no more.

On the way back to my building, I'm thinking that I just told Adonna, of all the females I know, that I was gonna show her a good time. A *real* good time. Why I say that shit to her? She probably thinking I'ma spend crazy money on her when I ain't even got it like that. It's true what they say, girls can really get a brotha in some deep trouble.

It ain't 'til I'm upstairs that I'm like, shit, I forgot to get my pops chain back from her.

THIRTEEN

My pops get me up mad early again and make me meet him downstairs. It's crazy the time he be waking me up since he been back. He probably still on prison time or something.

Me and him still don't say a word to each other in the van. Nothin'. This time, though, I'm the one that put the radio on.

Two of my pops friends is waiting for us at the storage place. I don't know where my moms is at, if she gonna do anything to help out with the move, but she don't never do nothing, so why she gonna start now?

The four of us get to work, loading as much of our furniture and shit in the van that can fit at one time. There ain't no room for all four of us in there too, so I'm the one my pops make stay behind and wait, like them other guys is stronger than me or something. I'm bored out my mind standing there, but least I don't gotta spend more time with my pops.

Since I gotta be here anyway, I start looking through a lot of the stuff we got in here. It take me a while, but finally I find the stuff that used to be in my room. Not only my clothes but my TV, laundry basket, alarm clock, DVDs, and fan. And I find a box of stuff I used to have on top of my dresser, shit I forgot 'bout. A bullet I found behind my building when I was, like, ten. My ashtray, a folded-up two-dollar bill, my incense. Then I see this strip of photos me and Novisha took last summer at Rye Playland. After we got on practically all the rides a couple times, we was walking 'round for a while and found one of them old-skool photo booths. We went in there and kissed and acted stupid and had fun wasting money. The pictures came out real funny. She took some and I took some. That was a year ago, back when my family still had a apartment and we was all still together. But everything is different now.

The day we was evicted from that apartment, man, I ain't never gonna forget that feeling I got when I came home from school and seen my moms and Troy standing in the hall outside our apartment. Troy was crying and my moms was cursing and going off on how they threw us out our place. That's when I seen it, that big, giant padlock on our front door, and the sign that was stuck on the door by the marshals, telling us we was evicted and all our property was in storage.

First person I called was Novisha. And even though she never been through nothing like that herself, she was always by my side through the whole thing, making sure I was okay and not getting too depressed while we was going through the shelter system. What me and her had back then was good. I ain't gonna say it's messed up we not together no more 'cause things happen for a reason. I just ain't think it was gonna end.

I take out my cell and text Adonna. All I say is: hi.

She text me back a minute later: getting in the shower. dont peek!!!

That girl is trying to kill me, I swear. I don't need to be thinking 'bout her all naked and soaped up right now.

While I'm waiting, my pops and his friends come back, get more stuff, and leave again. Only thing left now is the living room furniture and four boxes of pots and pans and dishes and shit.

It take a long time for Adonna to text me back: did u keep ur eyes closed or were u a bad boy?

i seen everything. i need a spanking.

omg!!!

Even when she text, I can see her pretty face smiling and laughing.

Me and her text back and forth 'til she say: gotta go 2 school. last week!!!!!!!

I text her back telling her I'ma call her later, then my pops come through the door by hisself this time. Me and him carry the rest of the stuff outta there. Only thing we leave is the DJ equipment 'cause them speakers is too big for the apartment and 'cause my pops got a regular system to listen to his music at home.

Me and my pops drive to the new apartment, which is on the other side of the Bronx from where Bronxwood is at. Jasmine don't live all that far from here. I mean, she ain't 'round the corner or nothing, but I could walk to her place from here if I felt like it. I need to talk to her anyway, find out how she doing, if she got to talk to Reyna and if everything alright. It don't matter that I'm trying to get with Adonna. I'ma always gonna look out for Jasmine.

I gotta admit, this part of the Bronx is kinda okay. I mean, for the Bronx. The place where the new apartment at got, like, four buildings that all look the same, with grass and shit. Regg don't live too far from here neither. He over in Riverdale. This place ain't as cool as Regg place, but it's way better than where we was living before. When we get Troy back, he ain't gonna believe this is where he gonna be living now.

The apartment is on the eleventh floor and, even though it's a mess right now with boxes and furniture and stuff all over the place, I can tell it's gonna look nice when it's hooked up. My family ain't never lived like this before. It got a big kitchen and living room, two bathrooms, and three bedrooms. Me, I don't know why they need all them rooms if I ain't gonna be living here. I don't even know what I'm doing here now, helping them move in this place.

But I am here, and so is my stuff from the storage room. My moms is in the kitchen, leaning up against the counter, looking bored.

"Lisa," my pops say to her. "Put away the kitchen stuff."

"I don't have no way to open them boxes."

He grab a box cutter from the kitchen table, like a foot away from where she standing, and open up two boxes for her. "Go on. Start."

For the next couple hours I don't think 'bout the fact that I ain't gonna be living here. In my mind, only thing I'm thinking is that I want this apartment to look good for Troy. Just in case. So I just work hard, carrying furniture and putting it in right rooms, hooking up TVs to the cable boxes, and fixing bed frames and dresser drawers and everything else that need fixing.

Only furniture I don't fix or set up is my shit, which we put in a room right next to Troy room. It's bigger than my room at Cal apartment, and even bigger than my old room at our place on Pelham Parkway, the apartment we got threw outta. Every time my pops come outta jail, it seem like he always try and do better, try and get a bigger apartment and more stuff to put in it. Only thing, it never last. Then it just be harder for us to hold on to all that shit, keep paying for all of it, when he go and get hisself locked up again.

And that's another reason why I ain't even thinking

'bout getting my room together and moving back in here with them. 'Cause I know it ain't gonna last. And when shit fall apart, it's gonna be worse then, 'cause we gonna be losing a apartment that's real nice this time, and that shit's gonna hurt. Not me. It's my moms and Troy that ain't gonna get over it easy.

I put the last box in Troy room, a whole box of cars and fire trucks and Pokémon cards. I ain't even sure if he still into that shit or not, but I know I want all his toys here when he get back. Troy got the smallest room, but it's cool 'cause when he look out this window he gonna see the playground they got down there, and he gonna know if his friends is out there playing before he go out.

A few minutes later, I'm back in the living room fixing this little drawer on the coffee table when my moms come in. I don't know what up with her today, but I can tell she ain't really feeling this new apartment, not as much as my pops think she is. 'Cause when he 'round, she smiling and shit, but now that he working in they bedroom, she stand here, looking 'round and shaking her head. "I don't know, Ty. This place. Why we gotta be in the apartment where the terrace don't even face the street? Who gonna wanna look at a parking lot all day?"

I put down the screwdriver. "What, you don't like the whole apartment 'cause of where the terrace is at?"

"Not only that," she go. "I just don't understand why your pops is putting me in a place that's only just a little better than the last apartment me and him lived in, you know, before. He put me through a lot of shit this year, had me worrying 'bout him being in that prison. When he got out, he should of at least found us a bigger —"

"Just be happy your man is back."

"I am," she say. "I'm not saying I don't like this apartment. It's better than where *you* had me living all this time, damn straight. That's one thing about your father, Tyrell. He just got out, and look how fast he got us a new apartment. Just like that." She snap her fingers. "That's how he do. He ain't perfect, but he know how to take care of his family."

I know what she trying to do, but I ain't gonna let it work on me. "Regg the one that got this apartment for y'all," I tell her. "So he the one that took care of your family, and not just now neither. He the one that helped me get some of them parties to DJ at, he the one that brung me down to Atlanta to make money. How you think I was paying your bills all this time? Answer is Regg."

"And Regg work for your father."

"No, he don't. He just help him out 'cause they friends. You think Regg need that little chump change he get from them parties?" I laugh. "You should see the house he getting built for him down in Atlanta. We could put ten of these apartments in that joint and still have room left over. He got a pool and a basketball court and inside he got a jacuzzi and shit. It ain't no joke."

Now my moms look real interested. "What Regg do to make that kinda money?"

I shrug, not only 'cause I don't know but 'cause the look on her face tell me if she knew what Regg was up to, she would probably figure out a way to get my pops into it too. She look like she could already see herself swimming 'round in a pool like Regg got, spending his kinda money.

She go into the kitchen and I hear her complaining half under her breath 'bout the stove and how it ain't electric like we had before, and how the refrigerator ain't got no automatic ice maker. "I don't know how long I gotta wait, what I gotta do to get me a dishwasher," she say. "I don't know why your father left it up to Regg to pick out a apartment for us when he coulda asked me to find the kinda place I'm gonna wanna live in. Don't make no kinda sense to me."

A few minutes later, my pops come down the hall and my moms cut that noise fast. He sit down at the kitchen table and, without him even saying a word, she get him a beer outta a bag of food she musta got somewhere. Then she take out the bread and cold cuts and make him a sandwich. She give it to him and give him a kiss, then ask him if he need anything else.

"I'm good," he say, and start eating. My moms take some dishes outta one of them boxes and start washing them, smiling like she happy all of a sudden.

I go back to the coffee table, but it ain't easy watching the two of them sometimes. I mean, yeah, I know they love each other, but I don't get how my moms can just take him back like he wasn't gone for a year. And not only that, how she just act like what her and Dante did never happened? What, she forget?

Even though I don't wanna think 'bout Novisha, my mind go there. The whole time we was together it was like she forgot 'bout all the shit she did in the past, and when everything came out, it was like she expected me to forget too and get back with her, just like everything was okay. I ain't never gonna be that kinda guy.

At the same time, I would be lying if I ain't say watching my moms take care of my pops, the whole thing remind me of the way it used to be between me and Novisha. She was always feeding me when I was at her apartment, she used to braid my hair, and when her moms wasn't 'round, she always knew how to get me off. I don't miss Novisha, but I gotta say, I miss the way she treated me 'cause she did know how to take care of her man. I don't know if I'm ever gonna find somebody that's gonna make me feel as good as she did.

I mean, Adonna is a cool girl, but I don't know. I ain't sure she the kinda girl that's gonna wanna take care of no man. From what I know 'bout her, she more 'bout what a man can do for her. But I don't know her that good yet. What I do know is she fine enough to keep me interested for a while. Just to find out for myself.

FOURTEEN

When the table is fixed, I come into the kitchen to get myself something to eat and drink. My moms don't make nothing for me. She too busy talking to my pops, or actually listening to him. He through eating now, and he sitting there drinking another beer and going on and on 'bout his problems, number one being money.

Then, like, outta nowhere, he tell my moms, "Right now, while I'm thinking about it, call that fuckin' caseworker and tell her you ready for them parenting classes, and you wanna start soon as you can."

My moms look surprised. "What? Why I gotta call today when — look at all the work we gotta do around here. Why you want me to —?"

"Where your cell at?" he ask her.

She pick it up off the counter and hand it to him like a little kid who in trouble with her pops.

"What that bitch caseworker name?"

My moms fold her arms in front of her. "Ms. Thomas," she say, and suck her teeth.

He click 'round on her phone for a couple seconds and hand it back to her. "It's ringing."

Damn, he really know how to handle her.

While she stand there talking to the caseworker, I just sit at the table with a double ham and cheese sandwich and a Pepsi. It's the first thing I'm eating all day, and it's good.

Crazy thing is, sitting right 'cross from my pops, it's weird that we not talking. I mean, the whole day. Nothing.

"Tonight?" my moms say to Ms. Thomas. "I told you, I'm moving today and . . . hold on." She cover the phone with her hand and say to my pops, "They starting a class tonight, but I ain't ready. And it's for three times a week. I don't know. That's a lot of time and — what I'm supposed to tell her? I don't think —"

"I'm back home now," my pops say, not even looking up from his beer. "You don't gotta think no more."

Damn.

"Now get back on that phone," he say, and don't even raise his voice none, "and tell that bitch you gonna be there tonight."

My moms sigh real loud, but then she do what she was told to do. She tell the caseworker to sign her up for them classes. When she hang up, she say to my pops, "Why you make me do that, sign up for them classes now when you see how much work we gotta do around here? I need to go the store and buy some food for this apartment, and —"

"We can buy food tomorrow."

"What if I'm not ready to start them classes?"

"You ready," my pops say. "What I tell you when you came to see me at Rikers? I told you I wanna get things back to the way they was before I got locked up, right? That mean Troy need to be back home. And that mean you gotta take them classes, and you ain't missing none of them."

My moms don't say nothing back. She mad, but she know better than to talk back too much and get him mad. She turn her back to us and keep washing the dishes.

It's good my pops doing what he gotta do to get Troy back, but half of me, nah, not even half, is waiting to see what he gonna say 'bout me. I mean, Troy wasn't the only one that was living with them before my pops got locked up. My pops don't say shit and I try to keep my mind on the fact that Troy the one we need to think 'bout. Not me. All of us want the same thing.

Only thing, if Troy living here with them and I'm still over at Cal place, me and Troy still ain't gonna be together. Nothing really gonna change, not for me.

I finish my sandwich and make another one. That's when my pops try to explain to my moms how she gotta dress and talk and act at them parenting classes. "You gotta take this shit serious now," he tell her. "They looking for a reason to keep Troy 'cause that's how them foster care agencies make money. They charge the state a whole lot of fuckin' money for every kid they snatch. If you give them any reason to keep him there making money for them, they gonna use it against us."

Then he turn to me and tell me that he want all us to go to the agency on Wednesday 'cause that's when we s'posed to have our time to visit with Troy.

"I don't need to go to the agency." First thing I said to him all day. "I see Troy all the time, and he call me on my cell when he wanna talk to me."

"That don't matter," he say. "The agency make a report to the judge when it come time for us to try and get him back. We need to start doing everything right."

I can't stand going to that agency and having to deal with Ms. Thomas. Back when ACS took Troy, that caseworker found me and tried to get me to go live in some kinda group home or something. She was like, "Your mother can't take care of you. You're not safe with her." Meanwhile, the only shit my moms did was leave Troy alone at the shelter. But he was only seven. She could leave me alone all she want and nothing gonna happen to me. I don't need her looking after me.

So I told the caseworker that if she tried to put me in a group home, I was gonna go AWOL like two minutes after she left me there. So she checked with the judge, then told me it was alright if I stood with my moms, but only if I went to school and all that. And she had to come and check up on me every couple weeks.

Both us know I wasn't never really living with my moms 'cause first of all, the place my moms was living at was too small for me and her. I mean, she only had one fold-out couch/bed. But for the past seven months me and Ms. Thomas and my moms been going through the motions just so Ms. Thomas could leave me alone and cover her ass at work. She would tell me when she was coming by my moms place so I could be there. Then she come over and make sure the place wasn't too dirty and that my moms had food for me, and she would ask me a couple questions 'bout how me and my moms getting along and if she treating me good. All that kinda shit. Like she care 'bout me.

I would lie, she write it down, and then she tell me the next time she coming by. Then Ms. Thomas was gone, and I was gone outta my moms place right behind her. Whole thing was a waste of everybody time, 'specially mines, but least it got the agency off my back all this time.

But I tell my pops I'ma be there at the agency visit just so he can stop talking 'bout what we gotta do and how we all gotta work together to get Troy back and all that shit. My mind ain't on that right now. I'm trying to solve my other problem.

So while they still talking, I get up from the table and go into the living room and pocket the key for the storage room.

I don't got no other choice. I'm broke as a joke. I'ma hafta use my pops equipment next Saturday for Jasmine party.

Anyway, it ain't like the man gonna miss that key. He too busy thinking 'bout Troy to worry 'bout the storage room or the equipment. Or me for that matter.

Since I ain't too far from Jasmine apartment, I walk over there when I leave my moms and pops new place, just to see what Emiliano want from me and get this shit over with already. Jasmine live on Grand Concourse and it don't take me more than fifteen minutes to get to her building. I stand in between the two front doors and press the intercom, then some female voice come through, but it ain't Jasmine. Emil girlfriend probably. I ain't never met her before, but I'm glad Emil getting it from somebody and don't gotta try nothing with Jasmine.

I take the elevator upstairs and the second Jasmine open the door, she smile big and throw her arms 'round me. "Tyrell!"

I put my arms 'round her waist but only for, like, a second 'cause I can see into the apartment, and Emiliano is sitting on the couch, and I don't want him thinking I'm into Jasmine or something. I don't need no crazy Dominican bodybuilder after me.

I'm not even in the apartment yet and the smell of whatever cooking hit me. "It smell good in here," I say to Jasmine. "I know you not cooking nothing that good."

She slap me on the shoulder. "Yes, I am. Ana's teaching me. Come in."

I step inside. In the living room, Emiliano sitting there drinking a beer, watching the Yankee game on the big-screen TV on the wall. He don't look up and say nothing to me, he too into the game, so I follow Jasmine into the kitchen. Ana standing at the stove, stirring something that look like tomato sauce. She alright-looking for somebody that's probably in her thirties or something. Least Emiliano ain't only into teenage girls.

Jasmine introduce me and Ana and we say hi. She seem okay. Nice.

"Sit down," Jasmine tell me. "You want anything to drink?" She open the refrigerator. "We got Pepsi, but it's flat, Sunny D, Malta, water, and that's it."

"I'll take the flat Pepsi," I say. Them choices is bad.

I sit there looking 'round, waiting. The thing 'bout Emiliano apartment is, dude got it hooked up. Not only do he got the big-screen TV, he got all the new sound equipment and a weight-lifting bench in the corner. I could see myself living like this one day.

Jasmine don't only bring me the soda, she bring me a whole plate of chocolate chip cookies. Emiliano drive a truck that deliver some Spanish bread and all kinds of donuts and cookies to stores, and he always bring home extra shit. "Tell me, what did you do today?" Jasmine ask me, all up in my business as usual.

The first thing I think is, what, do I stink or something? I mean I was doing a lot of heavy lifting and shit today. Probably shoulda went home and took a shower before coming over here.

But she sit down next to me so I must not be too funky. I tell her 'bout the move and the new place and all that. But it's like she only paying half attention to me 'cause every couple minutes Ana call her back to the stove so she can show her something. Ana got Jasmine putting more spices and shit in the sauce and tasting everything. Then she got her cutting up some Italian bread and putting it in the oven.

Watching this whole scene make me mad, like, what Emiliano got going on in this apartment? Dude got two women cooking for him, making sure everything taste good, and all he doing is sitting on his ass.

But that ain't the real problem, the way I see it. The thing that really piss me off is that it look like Ana teaching Jasmine how to be a wife or something. Why Jasmine gotta know how to cook like this at her age?

Jasmine come back over to the table and sit down next to me again. "I'm so excited about this party," she say, giggling like a little girl. "I'm thinking about it, like, nonstop. I found a dress already and, *ay dios mio*, I can't wait for you to see it. They're altering it so it fits perfect and *tight!*" She laugh. "But let me tell you about it. It's kinda purple but, like, between purple and lavender with little white lacy edges. I mean, off-white. Whatever. It looks so good next to my skin, Tyrell. It costs a ton of money, but it's the only time I'm gonna turn sixteen so it's worth it, right? And —"

"God," I say. "Take a breath."

She laugh. "I can't!"

"You making me tired."

"You don't understand, Tyrell. This is a big deal for a girl. You boys don't understand nothing."

Yeah, she talking my head off, but it's good to see her happy like this, 'specially after what happened to Joanny. I thought she wasn't never gonna get over that shit.

Finally, at a commercial, Emiliano get up off the couch and come over to the table to sit down 'cross from me. Without him even saying nothing, Jasmine take the empty beer bottle from his hand, and get up to get him a new one. Ana don't do that. Jasmine do. Why she the one taking care of his old ass?

"Tyrell," Emil go. He don't hardly speak no English, but he try. "I want Jasmine to tell you to visit here because the party, it is —" He stop talking 'cause he trying to find the right word or something. Face look like he all confused and shit.

"He's trying to say," Jasmine tell me, sitting back down next to me, "that he wanted you to come over because the party is coming up real fast and he wants to make sure you know what to do and what to play." Then she translate what she just said to Emil and he say something back. "He says he wants this party to be special because I'm special."

I nod and look over at Ana real fast out the corner of my eye, just to see if she got a reaction to that, but she don't. She just busy wiping off the counter. Probably, only reason Emiliano with Ana is 'cause Jasmine too young and he don't wanna end up in jail. The same reason he got with Jasmine sister, Reyna. He was just using her while he waited for Jasmine to grow up.

Ana probably don't even see it yet. She don't know she training Jasmine to take over as Emiliano girlfriend.

Damn.

The rest of the time I'm there, me, Emiliano, and Jasmine go over all the details of the party. Everything. They tell me shit I don't even need to know as the DJ. But I get it. They wanna make sure I know how the whole thing gonna run. Then, before I'm 'bout to get up outta there, Emil give me a list of songs he say I'ma need to play at the party, and he even tell me when to play them. They got a song to play when Jasmine come into the party and a song to play when she opening her presents. Dude thought of everything. Course I ain't never heard of none of this music. I got a lot to learn 'bout Spanish music. Fast.

Soon as I leave outta there, I head straight back to Bronxwood, not to go home but to go see my friend Patrick who be bootlegging CDs and DVDs and selling them on the street and shit. He come with me to most of my parties and help me out, and I let him sell his stuff there too.

I'm just hoping he got some of that Spanish music on Emiliano list.

Patrick moms let me in, and for the first time in a long time, music don't be blasting from Patrick room. They apartment ain't never been this quiet. Never. "He here?" I ask.

"He sure do be." Patrick moms always look tired.

"He dead or something?"

"Maybe." She shake her head. "Go on back and see."

I knock on Patrick room door, but he don't answer so I go in anyway and hope he ain't jacking off or something. He ain't. He 'sleep. The room smell like weed and he got a empty box of Devil Dogs on the bed next to him. And all he got on is Batman boxers.

This a sad scene.

I can't figure Patrick out. He ain't ugly and, yeah, he kinda outta shape, but he ain't really fat or nothing. Still, he the most non-life-havin' dude I know. When he ain't out on the street selling his CDs and DVDs, he in this room burning them. I don't never see him going out with no females or nothing.

Only time Patrick ever really go out is when he come to one of my parties. He do help me set up and keep the records straight, but the real reason I bring him is 'cause he need to have some fun. In my mind, I'm helping him more than he helping me.

It take me a while to wake his ass up, and when he see me I know he kinda embarrassed. Which he should be.

"Dude," I tell him while he get up outta bed. "You can't keep living like this."

He start putting on his sweatpants. "What you mean?"

"Getting high by yourself, eating like this. C'mon. You need to hit the gym or something, tighten all that shit up. Then you need to start getting something going with girls. What's wrong with you, man?"

"You go to the gym?"

"Nah. But I play ball and my body just stay this way. My pops is like this too. We don't gotta work too hard."

Patrick grab a T-shirt from off the floor, smell the pits, make a face, then put it on anyway. I'ma hafta work with this brotha.

After he go to the bathroom and come back in his room, I show him the list and he say he got most of them songs and a lot more new shit they gonna like too. Patrick my boy.

While I'm there, he start playing some Spanish music from his deck and saving it on my flash drive. "When the party?" he ask me.

"Next week. On Saturday."

"You need me, man? 'Cause I ain't doing nothing that day."

Like I ain't know that.

"Nah, I don't think so. It ain't the kinda party you can sell shit at. This Jasmine Sweet Sixteen."

"I know, but I like them Puerto Rican girls."

"You ain't gonna talk to none of them," I say.

"So what."

"You can come," I say. "Could always use help." And Patrick got a uncle with a truck that he don't mind lending Patrick to carry the equipment. Another problem solved.

Patrick on his computer looking for more music. "Listen to this. It's reggaeton. Just came out, straight from San Juan."

He crank that shit and next thing I know he lighting up a blunt and we getting high. Good shit. He musta got it from Cal.

Meanwhile the music seem like it's getting louder. I don't know if I'ma be able to get into this. Even when he change to salsa and merengue, it all sound the same to me, like a bunch of trumpets and bongos and words I don't understand. And everything so fast, I'ma need to listen to a lot between now and Jasmine party and practice mixing this shit. Jasmine all excited 'bout this party. I don't wanna mess nothing up for her.

While I'm waiting for him to finish putting the music on my flash drive, I ask Patrick when the last time was that he got a girl.

"I don't know," he say. "A while."

"I ain't never seen you with nobody. Why you don't ask out none of the girls 'round here?"

"Bronxwood girls?" He shake his head. Something 'bout the way he look make me think he scared.

"You ever had a girl?" I ain't trying to embarrass him or

nothing, but it's like I'm now seeing what I gotta work with here.

He laugh, but it come out real fake.

"Seriously," I say. "If you ain't never had a girl, that's a'ight. You still only, what, sixteen, seventeen?"

"Seventeen."

Damn. "You still got time, you know. But you ain't gonna change nothing in here eating Devil Dogs."

He sigh. "C'mon, Ty. I ain't —"

"You gotta get some confidence, you know."

"It ain't gonna matter. Females don't like me."

"A'ight, look, I'ma help you out, man. But you gotta work on yourself. Tonight, you can do what you want, but tomorrow, no more of this shit." I throw the Devil Dogs box over by him. "And starting tomorrow, me and you gonna start hitting the courts, a'ight?"

"Seriously, it's not gonna matter," he go.

"You gonna be looking good soon," I say. "Trust me."

I don't know why I'm doing this. I mean, what, I need somebody else to take care of?

FIFTEEN

I'm kinda pissed at myself for showing up at the foster care agency on Wednesday afternoon. Not 'cause I don't wanna see Troy but 'cause I don't want my pops thinking he can tell me what to do and I'ma just do it like a child s'posed to. I don't even know what I'm here for.

I can't stand anything 'bout this agency. The people that work here, them social workers and shit, all of them don't care nothing 'bout the kids. Like my pops said, the agency is all 'bout getting paid. Them caseworkers act like they care and write down that they checked up on the kids and everything okay. But course everything okay when you don't ask nobody enough questions to find out that nothing, not one thing, actually okay.

My moms and pops is already at the agency when I get there. They sitting real close, holding hands. Our visit s'posed to start at 5:30 and I get there, like, a minute early so I don't hafta spend more time with my pops than I need to. They in the waiting room with a whole bunch of other people, and before I can even sit down, my pops say to me real quiet but real threatening, "Don't forget what we trying to do here, Ty. We trying to show these people that we back to being a family. A strong family."

Why he think I'm here for?

"What, you don't know how to say hi to your moms?" he ask.

"Hi," I say to her. She look nice, all fixed up and shit. Before my pops got out, she wasn't walking 'round looking like this.

My moms kinda smile at me and say, "Hi, Ty. How you doing?"

"A'ight." I wanna ask her how long it's been since she came to one of these visits. The courts said she could have a supervised visit every Wednesday, but it was up to her to call Ms. Thomas and set it up. She did it for a while after Troy was took from her, but then she would set up the visit and not show up. She did that a lot and Troy would be so mad. And Troy old foster mother too. She used to hafta leave work early to pick up Troy at his after-school to get here on time, only to find that my moms couldn't bother to show up. Shit got old real fast.

But I don't bring up nothing 'cause my pops right 'bout something. This ain't the time or place to start no fight. And knowing him, he just gonna take her side and tell me I'm wrong for saying anything even if it is the truth and we all know it.

When Troy and his foster mother, Ms. Woods, get there, man, the look on Troy face when he see my pops, that shit is for real. It's like he can't believe what he seeing. He see my pops and then look to me like he want me to tell him what he seeing ain't something he dreaming. I just nod and then he run over to my pops like he still a two-year-old or something. My pops snatch him up in the biggest hug and I'm like, good to know my pops got it in him to be happy to see one of his kids. My pops is laughing and shit, and Troy is just going, over and over, "Daddy, you back. You back!"

I ain't gonna front. I got a smile on my face too, 'cause, damn, I ain't seen Troy this happy for a while. And I ain't think I was ever gonna see him like this after all the shit he been through since my pops was sent up. Little dude is smiling so big his face 'bout to crack in half.

Ms. Thomas finally come out and tell us a room ready for us. She not a bad-looking woman, kinda thick, but it's her attitude that make her look so rough. She always look like she mad 'bout something, and that she don't have no time for us. Like she just doing what she gotta do to get paid.

But anyway, all of us 'cept for Ms. Woods go down the hall with her. And that's when Troy really start to lose his mind. He running 'round and shit, acting like he 'bout to be free from foster care jail. It ain't easy to watch, 'cause I know that by the end of this visit he gonna be going back home with Ms. Woods and ain't nothing really gonna change for him right now.

This how the whole visit go. The caseworker bring us to the broke-down room where they must put the oldest tables and chairs that nobody want no more or shit they find on the street. They got some old toys in the room too, a lot of dolls with dirty hair and plastic cars and a racetrack thing with three levels and a ramp, but shit so nasty looking even Troy don't wanna touch it. But he don't hafta 'cause my moms brung him a Hulk action figure, like he all that into the Hulk. He give her a big hug anyway and sit on the floor and try to get it outta the hard plastic shit they got it in. I don't know who think to put toys in them things, 'less they just wanna make kids lose they minds or something.

"Let me help you," I say, getting up from where I'm sitting and going over to where he at.

I'm 'bout to sit on the floor with him when he jump up. "Daddy can do it." And he run over to my pops.

I go back over to where I was sitting before, like it ain't nothing.

The visits only last thirty minutes, which ain't shit when you got a eight-year-old that ain't seen his pops in a year. Troy bouncing 'round for, like, fifteen minutes, and all my pops can do is try and calm him down even though it ain't working.

I try to talk to Troy too, ask him 'bout camp. But Troy ain't hardly paying me no mind. He all 'bout my pops. And I get that. Still, though, I'm sitting thinking, knowing, that Troy gonna do it again, get all attached to our pops and all that. And then, a couple months or a year from now when my pops get locked up again, Troy gonna get let down.

But what can I do to stop it? He still young, and when you that age, all you want is your pops.

So what I do is act happy, like everything with our family gonna be okay. My moms is smiling while Troy show everybody what he can do with the Hulk. And we all talking and having fun with him, and basically we don't say nothing 'bout nothing. That way, nothing could get used against my moms and pops in court when they go to try and get Troy back.

'Cause the other thing 'bout this visit is this. Ms. Thomas right there the whole time 'cause the judge said my moms gotta be supervised while she visit with her own kid. Ms. Thomas sit at this little table in the corner doing paperwork, trying to act like she ain't listening to everything we saying, but meanwhile if anybody say anything wrong, she gonna write that shit down fast.

Just like I knew was gonna happen, when Ms. Thomas tell us the visit is over, Troy lose his fucking mind. He start crying. "I wanna go with you," he say, holding on to my pops arm. "I hate Ms. Woods. I wanna go home with you!"

My pops take him to the corner of the room and tell him, "I need you to be a little man. And men, we don't cry like little girls, you know'm saying?"

Troy nod, tears still sliding down his face and shit.

"I'm back now," my pops say, "and I'ma do everything I

can to get you back home. But you gotta try hard to be good to Ms. Woods, okay? Don't worry 'bout nothing. You gonna be back with us soon as we can."

Troy hug my pops again real hard. I hate this. I hate the way Troy hanging on to him like that's gonna stop my pops from fucking up again and having to go away. Troy can't see it though. And he the one that's gonna get hurt the most.

Cal outside working, but what else is new? The whole situation at the agency pissed me off so much I don't think I wanna chill with him tonight. I just wanna get upstairs and be by myself.

But he get me to start talking anyway. "Problem with pops?" he go.

Man. How he know? I tell him 'bout the visit and how my pops told Troy he s'posed to man up when the kid only eight and don't need to hide his feelings for nobody. "He used to pull the same shit with me," I say. "When my moms used to take me to visit him in jail, when I was a little kid. All I wanted was for him to come home, and I would cry and shit, be like, why they ain't letting you outta here? And he would tell me the same shit. 'Be a little man, don't cry.' I wish I coulda told him back then to go fuck hisself. How he gonna tell me not to cry when he was the whole reason I was crying in the first place? If he woulda kept his ass outta jail . . ." I shake my head. "Cal, that visit was fucked up."

"I feel bad for the kid," Cal say.

For a while me and him don't say nothing. 'Cause both of us been there where Troy at now. Cal pops been locked up forever. Dude a straight-up criminal. Probably never gonna walk free again for all the shit he did.

When Cal go over to the curb to handle his business, I take out my cell and call Adonna to see if she could come out for a little while. Seeing her could change this whole fucked-up mood I'm in.

She answer the phone. "Ty?"

I'm already smiling. "Just wanted to hear your voice."

"What you doing?" she ask me.

"Nothing. Bored. You could come outside?"

"No, I'm actually studying. My final is tomorrow and we get the results on Friday. And if I don't pass, my mother is gonna go off on me."

Damn. I wanted to see her. "Okay, I'ma let you go, then. We still going out on Friday though, right?"

"If I pass."

"A'ight. Go back to studying, then. I don't want nothing to get in the way of our date."

She giggle. "Okay."

"Bye."

Two days. I can wait.

I go upstairs, grab a beer, and sit on the couch. And 'cause I can't get the agency visit out my mind, I call Jasmine. "What you doing?" I ask her when she answer her cell.

"I'm in bed, reading one of those books from the list. It's called *The Stranger*, but it's kinda slow and depressing so far. You okay?"

"Yeah. It's just that, I'm thinking, you know, 'bout Troy and —"

"He okay?"

"Yeah. I mean, I think so." I tell her 'bout the visit, everything that happened, and how bad it got at the end.

And just like I knew she would, she listen to me and try and say the right thing. "Troy knows you the one that's always been there for him, Ty. You two are real close now and nothing's gonna change that."

"I know, but . . ."

"Listen to me, Ty," she say, real serious. "He's gonna be alright. Remember, he got you as a big brother."

Jasmine always know the right thing to say to make me feel better. And she mean what she say too. Me and her talk for a little while, 'til she tell me she getting tired and gotta get up early for work. "I thought you was gonna try and read some more of that book," I say.

"I am. If I read a few more pages, I'll be asleep in five minutes!" She laugh.

"A'ight. I'ma let you go, then."

We say bye and hang up, and I sit there finishing my beer. Jasmine right. I don't got nothing to worry 'bout, not when it come to Troy. He gonna be okay. I'ma make sure of that.

SIXTEEN

Even though I seen Troy at the agency yesterday, I go by his camp on Thursday anyway so me and him can talk. That was the first time he seen our pops in a year and I wanna make sure he doing okay, that he understand what's going on, how we all trying to get him back. Not only that, but I want some one-on-one time with the kid 'cause of the way he said he hate Ms. Woods. I wanna know if there was something more he wanted to say to us but couldn't 'cause Ms. Thomas was right there in the room the whole time we was together.

I mean, it mighta been nothing. Maybe he was just wilding out 'cause his whole family was there and all of us was acting weird and shit, putting on a show, and maybe Troy ain't know what the fuck was going on.

As usual, me and Troy play 'round for a while like we always do, but then I calm him down and ask him how he feel that our pops is out.

He shrug. "I don't know."

"'Cause it's okay whatever you feel."

He quiet for a while, then he go, "How you feel?"

Why he gotta ask me that? "I probably feel the same way you do," I say. "But me and you is gonna be a'ight no matter if he stay out or if he get locked up again. Don't worry 'bout nothing."

Troy don't say nothing. Sometimes I think he getting more and more like me, thinking too much and not saying what he feeling. Keeping a lot of shit inside.

"Everything okay at Ms. Woods house?" I ask him. "'Cause it looked like something was bothering you yesterday. That right?"

Under his breath, Troy mumble, "I hate her."

Man, hearing him say that get to me. Make me feel that there has to be more I can do to get him outta this situation. But course only my moms and pops can do that. "Why you hate her? She do something to you?"

"She don't like me. She always yelling at me and I know she don't like me."

"Come over here." I walk Troy over to the fence and me and him lean against it for a while. He look mad. He squinting his eyes and breathing hard. Finally, I go, "Talk to me. Tell me what's going on over there."

And he do. He tell me a lot of things, like how she always tell him he eat like a animal 'cause Troy don't like to use forks or nothing. He be pretending he a dog and picking up the food with his mouth. And she always making him mop the bathroom 'cause she say some of his pee got on the floor. "I can't help it, Ty," he say. "I'm trying."

I shake my head. "It ain't your fault. You a boy."

"And she say I gotta watch what she wanna watch on TV and all she wanna watch is the news and other stupid things. And then the babies is always crying and they too little and I can't play with them. I'm boring there."

"Bored," I say. And I would be too. "I'ma handle it, Troy. Okay?"

He nod.

"Don't say nothing to Ms. Woods. Just try and do what she want and don't backtalk her."

He look down at the ground. "Okay."

"I'ma work to get you out of there."

Even as I'm saying this, I'm thinking, why don't I just shut the fuck up? How I'm s'posed to get him outta there? My moms and pops is doing what they gotta do, but my moms gotta take them parenting classes for, like, a month before they can go to the judge and try to get him back, and I know for a fact that the city don't never do nothing fast. It could be months before he home.

I know my pops is out now, but I can't help but feel responsible for Troy. I was like a father to him while my pops was away, and it ain't easy to turn off that button and go back to being a brother again. Anyway, in a way I'm the one who got him into this situation in the first place. I should be the one to get him out.

On the way to the train, I call Troy old foster mother, Ms. Reed, the one that treated him okay. While it ring, I don't really know what I'ma say to her when she pick up, but the main thing I wanna know is why she let Troy go like that and what Troy can do to get her to want him again.

But nobody answer. It go to voicemail. I don't know what to say, so I just tell her it's Tyrell, Troy brother, and ask her if she can call me when she get the chance, that it's important.

I hope she call me back. Soon.

SEVENTEEN

By Friday afternoon, I still ain't heard back from Ms. Reed, and waiting for her to call is making me mad. So when Cal tell me he going to shoot some hoops, I go with him, and me and him spend the whole afternoon playing ball behind Building C with some of them same dudes that was playing out there on Sunday. I know it's summer, but damn, that don't mean they can't have something else to do with theyself too.

It feel good working up a sweat in the heat though. Me and Cal used to play all the time when I first moved in with him. We used to hang out and have fun. Back then, he used to get a day or two off every week so it wasn't like he was working every day the way he hafta now. Shit changed fast.

Another reason I wanna play hard today is 'cause me and Adonna going out tonight and I wanna be chill, so it's good to burn off as much energy as I can now. I don't want Adonna knowing how bad I wanna get with her. Girl like that, it's best to wait 'til she begging me for some.

Like that gonna happen.

When we done, me and Cal go 'round the corner and get a couple meat patties from the Jamaican place and eat them on the way back to his apartment. I ain't gonna lie, I'm dragging my ass. Been a while since I worked out like that. And I can tell from the slow way Cal walking, he feeling it too.

In the elevator, Cal go, "You know, you one funky nigga. Need a oxygen tank to be in a elevator with your ass." He laugh like he smell any better than me.

"Dude, I can smell your sweaty balls all the way over here."

"That's nasty, man," he say. "Why you gotta go there?"

Me and him laugh. A minute later we in the kitchen finishing our patties, still snapping on each other. Then his cell ring, and from what he saying I can tell he talking to Tina 'cause he telling her he can't give her no more money 'til next week. "And even then it ain't gonna be all that much," he tell her. "Only enough for what CJ really need."

It's good he finally telling her what he shoulda told her a long time ago. That girl don't get it sometimes. She don't know the kinda pressure he got on him.

Even though Cal my boy and he doing the right thing setting Tina straight, still, that don't stop me from laughing at him while he start arguing with her. Fucking guy used to just chill. Now he got a kid and a girl that think she his wife. And he gonna have eighteen years of this shit too.

When he hang up, he reach 'cross the table and try to punch me. "Fuck you, Ty."

"Don't blame me. You got yourself into that shit."

"Damn, man, why you gotta keep remindin' me?" He lean back in his chair and he quiet for a couple seconds. Then he smile and go, "Least my kid is cute."

I laugh. "You stupid. You know that, right?"

"Stupid? You talking? Who got third place in the science fair? Me or you?"

"That was fourth grade. And I wasn't even in that jacked-up ghetto fair."

Cal laugh. "'Member Rodney Webber and that broke-down volcano he made. Dumb-ass dude."

"Rodney got second place, stupid. Beat your ass."

"Damn, you right." He reach 'cross the table again and this time he do punch me, right in the chest. Hard too.

Course, I gotta retaliate. I get up out my chair and before he know what's going on, I got him in a headlock and pull his chair back 'til he 'bout to fall. "You want me to let you go?" I ask him.

"You do and I'm gonna kill you in your sleep."

"Don't be a pussy." I let the chair back down. "Man, if you gonna kill somebody, you gotta do it to they face. When they awake."

He slap me and I slap him back, and this go on for, like, a minute, us acting like kids. Two funky kids. Sometimes me and him act real dumb.

When we through, I go in the refrigerator for a can of Pepsi while Cal tell me all the shit Tina wanna get for CJ and how much everything gonna cost him. He like, this ain't never gonna stop with her 'cause she want everything she see. "She like a baby herself that can't understand that money is tight."

Then he start talking 'bout Andre again, and how he told Cal that he want him working extra hard this week-end, making as much as he can. "He was like, weekends is when we make most of our money, like I don't know that." He shake his head. "So now I'ma hafta start earlier and stay out 'til I'm half 'sleep, and make enough to get him off my back for a while."

"Don't make no sense," I say. Then, just so he know he ain't the only one that got problems, I tell him 'bout snatching the storage room key from my pops and how fucked I'ma be if he find out. "You know how much that equipment gonna cost me if I hafta buy it? No way I can play Jasmine party."

"You can't just ask the man to borrow that shit? He ain't throwing no party next week, right?"

"Nah, not 'til the week after, but I don't wanna ask him for shit just to hear him say no. Then I'ma have him thinking I need him or something."

"You know I would help you out if I had it like that, right?"

"Yeah, I know."

Me and Cal sit there for a while, talking 'bout how fucked up everything is. Me and him used to have fun

24/7. Now we like two old dudes talking 'bout his kid and how broke we are. This time last year we ain't had nowhere near this kinda stress.

A couple minutes later, I get up from the table and say, "I got a date." I can't help smiling 'cause the word "date" sound like something you see on them TV shows or something. When me and Novisha was together I don't think we ever went out on a real date. Yeah, we used to hang and go out and eat and shit, but we never called it a date or nothing. I don't know. We was just together.

Course, Adonna ain't Novisha. Adonna gonna need to go out on a real date. And sometimes a brotha gotta step up.

Cal shake his head. "You sit here all this time talking 'bout how you broke, and now you getting ready to take Adonna out. That girl gonna take every last dollar you got."

"I know, I know," I say, but I ain't looking to hear that right 'bout now. What he saying is true though. He know it and so do I. Only thing, something tell me that a girl like Adonna is worth it. "I asked her out and I'ma take her out. And I ain't gonna be like them other dudes that pro'ly be trying to hit it right away. By the time I make my move, she gonna be begging me for it."

Cal laugh, but he don't know. My plan gonna work.

"That's the thing with girls like Adonna," I tell him. "Guys always be moving too fast with them."

"And you think you gonna get some by being a turtle?"

"Nah, not a turtle," I say. "A gentleman."

EIGHTEEN

And I am a gentleman. I dress up nice in jeans and another new shirt I got in Atlanta. It was expensive as hell, but I go over to Adonna building looking good. Clean.

The second I walk into the building, I'm like, shit. Novisha coming outta the elevator. It don't take her two seconds to see me, and when she do, she stop dead in her tracks a couple feet away from me. Me and her stand there looking at each other, the first time we together by ourself with nobody else 'round since we broke up in January.

"Tyrell," she say, and give me a almost-smile. "Um, how — how are you?"

I don't even know what to say to her. 'Cept for hi and bye, we ain't really conversated since January.

Seeing that I don't say nothing, she keep on talking. "How's Troy? Did your mother ever get him back?"

"Nah." I ain't even know she knew 'bout what happened to Troy. "He still in the system."

"That poor little boy."

That's the thing with Novisha. She do really care 'bout Troy. She mighta lied 'bout a lot of things when we was together, but by the look on her face, I can tell she really do feel bad for Troy. "He a'ight, Novisha. Don't worry 'bout him. I see him all the time."

She sigh. "Oh, good."

"Yeah."

I don't got nothing else to say so I start walking again. I get past her, almost at the elevator, when she go, "Why didn't you ever return any of my calls? I left you a ton of messages."

I press the button for the elevator and say, "I never listened to none of them."

"Why?"

I don't even turn 'round when I say, "'Cause I was through." I'm hoping the elevator will come fast 'cause I ain't in the mood for none of this right now.

"Oh," she say, sounding all surprised. "Well, since you never listened, I can tell you what I said. I said I was sorry, you know, for lying and, um, hurting you. And messing everything up. I wanted you to know that."

I don't know what to say to that.

Out the corner of my eye, I see her start walking closer to me, talking 'bout, "If you ever wanna talk, Ty, and clear everything up, we could — um, is that the cologne I got you for Christmas?"

Shit. I ain't even think 'bout that when I put it on, but she right. It is. 'Stead of answering her, I go, "Where your new man at?" and I turn 'round to see the look on her face. "You standing here talking to me. You think your man gonna like that, Novisha?"

"My *man*?" Only Novisha can make her face like this, like she looking surprised and at the same time, I can tell she know exactly who the fuck I'm talking 'bout. "I don't — oh, are you talking about Marcus? He's not . . . He's just a —"

"A what? A guy you brung 'round here to try and get me jealous? That what he is?"

"It's not like that, Ty," she say, and it look like she 'bout to start explaining, which for Novisha mean she 'bout to start lying.

So I cut her off. "Novisha, I ain't into none of your games today. I got plans."

The elevator come and I get in and press 19. Novisha stand there and ask, "Who are you going to see? Adonna?"

The doors close before I can answer her. Like who I'ma be with is any of her business. That girl got a lot of nerve, 'specially since she the one that fucked us up in the first place. We had a good thing, but every time I see her now, all I think 'bout is her with that other guy, Jamal. Regg was right what he said 'bout how guys can't ever get the visual out they head when they woman is with another guy. That shit is true. 'Cause just knowing that she was with him, I can see it in my mind. And being that me and Novisha never actually had sex, I don't got no other picture to cover that one up with. Jamal the only guy she ever got with. Not me. Him.

So by the time I get to Adonna floor, I'm through thinking 'bout Novisha. I'm back to being a gentleman, 'cause I'ma charm the shit outta Adonna moms. I'ma be the kinda guy she happy her daughter is going out with. Just like Novisha moms used to be.

I know how to work them moms.

By the time me and Adonna is leaving outta Bronxwood, I can tell her moms like me and we even stop and talk to Kenny at his truck before we go to the corner to catch a cab 'cause Adonna too good for me to take her on the bus or train. I'm gonna show her off in style.

We end up going to the movies at Bay Plaza and I let her pick the movie she wanna see, some stupid shit 'bout a female that can't get no man and all her friends gotta try and find her a dude. Meanwhile, the girl so hot, the whole movie don't make no kinda sense to me. They shoulda hired a ugly-ass actress if they wanted folks to believe that shit.

At the movies, I'm still trying to be a gentleman, playing it cool and not trying to be all over Adonna, even though it's dark in there and ain't nothing more I wanna do 'cept kiss them pretty lips. But all I do is hold her hand. That's it. I'm all 'bout making her feel comfortable with me. So when the time come, I'ma be in there.

After the movie, I take her to City Island, where they be nothing but seafood restaurants up and down the street. And most of them, you can look out the window and see the water and shit. This the kinda date a girl like Adonna deserve.

"This is nice," Adonna say, looking out the window. It's after nine o'clock, but it ain't so dark outside that we can't still see the water. Adonna lean 'cross the table and whisper, "Are you sure you can afford this restaurant?" Only thing, the way she say it ain't like she worried 'bout me spending too much. Girls like Adonna don't think a guy could ever spend too much on them. She just wanna know how much I got.

"Yeah, I'm sure," I tell her. "Order what you want."

She smile, but only a little bit. Then her eyes kinda light up and she open the menu and start talking 'bout how much she love lobster, but she can't never afford it. Me, I don't react. I'm cool. But damn. Cal wasn't lying when he said I ain't gonna have a dime when I leave outta here.

After we order, the waiter bring over this basket of bread, and I sit back and watch Adonna spread a ton of butter on a roll and eat it, talking nonstop in between bites. I just like watching her 'cause she happy eating and talking.

The last time I brung a female to City Island was back in April, right when the weather was starting to get nice. I was talking to this girl from school and we came to one of these restaurants after hanging out one night. But she was one of them salad-eating females that act like they don't never eat, even though she wasn't no skinny girl. She probably got home and ate everything in her moms house.

Adonna ain't nothing like that. She keepin' it real. Real expensive.

A hour and fifteen later, me and Adonna leave the restaurant and take a walk so all that food we ate could settle down in our stomachs. Adonna talking 'bout something, but all I'm thinking 'bout is the fact that I spent almost ninety dollars on food, plus, like, forty dollars at the movies. And this date ain't even over yet.

We walk for a while holding hands, past all the other restaurants, then down to the pier. I lean up against the railing and put my arm 'round her waist and bring her close to me. I wanna get some good kissing in and this spot is mad romantic. Females like this shit, with the water in the background and all that.

And it's good. We standing there tonguing and shit for, like, ten, fifteen minutes. Something 'bout being with a girl like her. Seriously, I don't need to think 'bout nothing else. Nothing 'cept her. Standing out here, kissing her, it's worth it, spending money like that on her.

After a while we stop long enough to look down at the water and talk 'bout what a nice night it is and all that. Looking down at the beach with all them rocks make me think 'bout what Adonna said last week 'bout not going to the beach this summer, and before I know it, I'm like, "We should go to the beach tomorrow, let me get a chance to see you in that bikini."

"I told you, you couldn't handle it."

I smile. "My heart's beating harder already. Damn, girl, you gonna give me a heart attack."

She laugh. "Don't say I didn't warn you."

"So let's go tomorrow, get you in that water and have fun." I put my arm 'round her waist again. "Get you on that blanket."

"I can't, not tomorrow. My father's coming by and hopefully I'll get him to take me shopping for school clothes."

"Then how 'bout Sunday? Me and you, and I can ask Cal and Tina too. And why don't you bring Asia, and I'll get my boy Patrick to come and we could try and set them two up."

Adonna shake her head. "Asia?"

"Yeah. What?"

"I don't know about that," Adonna go. "I mean, about bringing Asia."

"Y'all not still friends or something?" I know girls go in and outta being friends with other girls real fast, but damn, last week they was tight.

"We're still friends. It's just, I don't like bringing other girls around guys I like. I been through some stuff, you know, trusting girls around guys and —" She just shake her head. "I don't know."

What I'm really getting from her is that she like me. And that's all I need to get. "I hear you," I say. "You wanna get me alone. Am I right?"

Adonna look down for a minute. "That's not what I'm saying."

"I know what you saying. And you don't gotta even think 'bout me looking at no Asia. I'm only looking at you and thinking 'bout you. Asia a'ight, but she ain't you, know what I'm saying?"

Adonna look up at me, in my eyes, like she trying to read me or something. But I'm for real. I'm putting a lot of time and money into getting with Adonna. Nothing gonna keep me from closing this deal. Definitely not Asia. Shit, when I got my mind on something, I don't let nothing get in the way.

"Okay," she say. "Sunday."

We kiss some more and hang out and I'm really having a good time with this girl. I mean, I ain't gonna say that in the back of my mind I ain't still thinking 'bout how broke I am and how fucked up Novisha was acting. Adonna almost take my mind off all that. And she probably the only girl that can.

NINETEEN

Sunday morning, me and Patrick meet up with Adonna and Asia in front of the girls building. Cal went to get Tina and they gonna meet us at the beach. It's something after eight o'clock, but it's gonna be a nice day and we ain't the only ones in the Bronx planning to go to Orchard Beach today, that's for damn sure. We gotta get there early.

Adonna looking good in a white sundress and sandals. And she wearing sunglasses even though the sun ain't hardly out yet, so I can't see her eyes, but I can tell she ain't acting like herself for some reason.

The whole time we outside waiting for the cab, Adonna and Asia is off to theyself, talking 'bout something. I can tell Asia trying to get Adonna to let something go and have fun, but it ain't working. Not yet. I hope Adonna ain't gonna be like this the whole time we at the beach, 'cause the whole reason for me bringing her there is to get close to her and have fun. Let her know I'm a good guy that she could trust.

The beach ain't all that crowded when we get there, so we get to choose where we wanna be. I'm looking for a spot on the sand that's kinda outta the way so me and Adonna could spend some time getting to know each other better, but the girls wanna be close to the food stands. So we find a spot somewhere in the middle and I text Cal to let him know where we at.

It's nice being out here this early. Even the water don't look too nasty today. A couple hours from now, there ain't gonna be no space left, not only on the beach side, but over by the grass too. Folks is gonna be setting up they grills and shit, and whole families is gonna be out here playing loud merengue and reggae and hip-hop music, all at the same fucking time. A day like this, it's gonna feel like the whole Bronx is here.

Since we ain't gonna have it like this forever, after we put down our blankets and shit, I grab hold of Adonna hand and we take a walk together down near the water, like the way they do in them movies females be watching over and over. I'm hoping the water remind Adonna of the other night and how long we stood there kissing on the pier.

Only thing messing it up now is the fact that Patrick brung this big-ass old-skool boom box with him, and we can hear his music blasting all the way 'cross the beach. Dude getting to spend time with Asia by hisself and he busy playing music so loud he can't even talk to the girl.

For a while, me and Adonna walk and don't say nothing. I just wait for her to feel comfortable with me and tell me what's on her mind. 'Cause I need her to get past it and have some fun, or this gonna be one long-ass boring day.

After 'bout five minutes I ask her if she okay.

She shrug.

"'Cause you could tell me anything," I say. "I don't know if you know this, but I'm one of them sensitive brothas."

Adonna give me a half smile.

We still holding hands, and I'm taking that as a good sign that she okay being with me and maybe she starting to feel close to me now.

"I'm not like most of the guys out here," I tell her, all serious. "Them dudes only talk to females 'cause they trying to get with them, but me, I'm different. I like talking to girls. Y'all deep."

What I'm saying must be working, 'cause her smile get bigger and she finally start talking to me. "This doesn't really have anything to do with you," she say. "I like being with you, Tyrell. I'm just upset, from yesterday."

I wait for her to keep talking.

"I told you my father was gonna pick me up and take me shopping, but . . ."

"He ain't show up, right?"

She sigh real heavy. "He said he didn't know the date was 'official.'"

"Damn. That's messed up."

She stop walking. "That's the thing. Yeah, it's messed up, but that's the way he always is. I haven't seen him in, like, a year. No, more than a year. He keeps promising this and that —" She shakes her head. "I don't know why I keep letting him get to me."

"He your pops. Course you gonna get mad when he don't do what he s'posed to do." I wanna say he ain't the only pops that be like that, but I don't wanna make this 'bout me. I wanna let Adonna know she the only one on my mind right 'bout now.

Me and her stand there for a while talking. I let her get it all out her system and then I tell her her pops is stupid 'cause he missing out on having a real nice daughter. She tell me she know and then we end up hugging and shit. It's all good.

We walk down the beach a little more, real slow, talking some more. Then Adonna say she wanna go back to our blankets and relax. "A'ight," I say. Then ask her, "When you gonna put on your bathing suit?"

"I have it on under this." She smile all sexy and whatnot. She know what she doing to me. "Wait 'til you see it."

Then she start walking away, shaking her ass more than she do already, and I'm chasing after her, going, "It ain't too early to show it to me now. The sun out. It's hot." But she just laughing at me.

Seriously, females got all the power, and they know it too.

When we get back, Patrick and Asia is on they blankets, not even talking or nothing. Matter of fact, Asia 'sleep, all covered up and shit. Patrick turned the boom box down low, but all he doing is sitting there eating some leftover cold fried chicken his moms packed in foil for him before he left. Like her baby was gonna starve out here. The girl he was s'posed to be trying to make a play for is 'sleep and he eating chicken. Dude gonna be more work than I thought he was.

Cal and Tina is there. They blanket is right next to where me and Adonna set our blankets up, and they just starting to get comfortable, with Tina laying in his arms, when Cal ask her what time her moms is gonna watch CJ 'til. And that's all it take to set her off.

"Don't ask me," she say. "Why you always asking questions that don't have nothing to do with you?"

Cal look over to me, like he wanna know if he crazy or if it's Tina. I just shake my head 'cause I wanna stay outta it.

"CJ my kid," Cal tell her. "Why I can't ask you 'bout him?"

"You wanna know? Okay. I didn't tell my mother I was coming out here with you today. Why? Because I didn't wanna hear her mouth. I knew she was gonna be all like, take the baby with you, and I didn't feel like it. I'm tired. So I told her I was going to the nail place. And when I ain't back in a couple hours, she gonna call me and I ain't gonna answer."

"Why you do that?" Cal raise his voice high, but I can't tell if he mad or just don't get her. "We shoulda just brung CJ with us, then."

"You gonna take care of him?"

"I could help."

"Not the same thing, Cal. Who wants to come to the beach with a baby?"

"I woulda played with him in the water and on the sand. He pro'ly woulda liked that shit."

"Fuck you, Cal," Tina say, and she turn on her side, away from him.

Cal look like he don't know what to do, so I say, "Let's go get something to eat." Give him time to cool down.

I give Patrick the sign, and all three of us head over to the food stands. Cal is mumbling some shit under his breath the whole way, like he fighting with hisself. Dude 'bout to blow. For real.

It's too early for burgers and pizza, so we buy biscuits with sausage and egg, and some donuts and juice, enough for everybody, and on the way back to our blankets, I try and help Patrick 'cause he need it. "You gonna sit there the whole time we here and not say shit to Asia? You had her all to yourself and you musta bored the shit outta her for her to crash like that."

"I don't know," he say. "A girl like that, man. Why you couldn't pick a regular girl for me?"

"You dumb, you know that, right? She a regular girl. She

just a *fine* regular girl. And you ain't no ugly dude. You could get her."

I can't believe the shit that's coming out my mouth, but as long as Patrick can't tell I'm lying, that's alright by me. Yeah, Asia probably ain't gonna get down with nobody like Patrick, but he could man up and get some confidence. He need to start walking 'round like he be collecting females and she lucky to be one of them. I mean, he don't gotta be no pimp or nothing, but nobody gotta know all he do is sit in his moms apartment all day.

Females can smell a virgin.

"What I'm supposed to say to her?" Patrick ask me.

"Ask her what kinda music she like, something you can talk to her 'bout. And when she tell you, tell her you gonna mix some cds, just for her."

"And I could get her back to my place to pick them up, right?" He all proud of hisself for figuring it out.

"Yeah? But go slow with her. You gonna hafta work her. And you gonna hafta spend some money on her too. She a nice girl, but she could get anyone."

"That's what I'm saying. Why she gonna wanna be with me, then?"

I don't answer. I can't do everything for Patrick. He gonna hafta learn something for hisself.

Cal walking behind us. He ain't mumbling no more, but he look like he don't wanna get back to Tina too fast. I still gotta blame Cal for his own situation. He knew Tina only got interested in him when he started making money. I ain't saying she a gold digger, but if Cal was still a broke nigga, he wouldn't have no kid by her.

We get back to the girls, and Asia awake now. Adonna on her knees behind Asia, putting her hair in one big braid, and she whispering something in Asia ear. I thought Adonna woulda took off her sundress by now so I could see her bathing suit, but that ain't happen.

"Food!" Asia say, smiling, when she see us. "I'm so hungry."

I elbow Patrick in the ribs. "Me too," he go. I give him a look like I could punch him. Dude just ate half a chicken. How the fuck he hungry? He must catch my drift, 'cause he go, "Asia, I got you breakfast and some chocolate milk."

"Wow, thanks, Patrick."

I give him a nod and he go give her the food and sit down next to her. Okay, he doing his thing.

I sit on my blanket close to where mines and Adonna blankets is touching and put our food down. Adonna smiling now. "Oh, you got me a Sprite."

"I know what you like."

Right away, she start greasing. Call me crazy, but watching her eat is hot as hell. Like she hungry for more than just food.

'Bout eleven o'clock the sun really start to get hot, and Adonna and Asia finally get outta them dresses, and I'ma tell you, it was worth waiting for. They both got on bikinis, but I'm only checking out Adonna 'cause, man, she fill hers out real good. She don't got real big titties or nothing, but she got more than I need. Anyway, to be honest, I'ma ass man. The bikini bottom she wearing is one of them little shorts with the ass cheeks hanging out the sides. And damn, looking at that ass, I know where all them buttered rolls and sausage biscuits be going.

Adonna take out a bottle of Hawaiian Tropic oil from her bag and start putting it on, nice and slow. Her and Asia is taking turns with the bottle, acting like they don't know me and Patrick is watching them. But they gotta see how we drooling and shit.

When Adonna finish oiling all the parts of her she can reach, I'm quick. "Let me put it on your back for you."

She eye me, suspicious. "You sure?"

"I got this," I tell her. "Watch. I'ma put it on nice and even, and your tan gonna be beautiful. Trust me."

I don't know why, but she lay down on her stomach and let me rub oil all over her back. It feel good too. Her skin is smooth like butter. I put the oil all 'round her bikini top and even slip my hands under the bows. Them girls in the movies be taking off they bikini tops when they lay on they stomachs, but Adonna ain't like that. After I get her all relaxed and shit, I start getting lower and lower, and finally I'm putting that oil on the sides of them ass cheeks and acting like it ain't no thing.

She chillin' so hard, it take her a minute to catch on to what I'm doing. When she do, she turn over on her side and face me. "Don't tell me. You were using your bad hand again, weren't you?"

I smile. "How you know?"

She snatch the bottle from me. "I'm gonna keep my eyes on that hand."

"And I'ma keep my eyes on that ass. *Damn*, girl!"

She slap my shoulder, and I gotta say, I like when she do that. 'Cause I know she don't mean it. She like me.

A couple minutes later, Adonna is laying on her stomach reading a book, and Asia laying next to her listening to her iPod. Both they asses is up in the air with the sun shining on them and it's a beautiful thing. I look over at Patrick and he grinning like a damn fool. But probably so am I.

The whole day is getting good. Even Cal and Tina ain't fighting no more. They musta made up 'cause they laying on they blanket all close, kissing every couple minutes. I don't know how long this gonna last though.

I lay down next to Adonna on my back and look at the cover of the book she reading, something called *Thugs and Lovers, Book 3*. "Book three?" I ask her.

"It's a series," she say.

"I can't stand when girls read them books 'cause y'all start thinking all guys is like the dudes in the book, treating they girlfriends bad and cheating on them."

"You don't cheat?" she ask.

"Nah, I ain't like that."

She turn over to look at me. "You never cheated on Novisha?"

"I told you. I ain't like that." My mind go to Jasmine for, like, half a second, and I think 'bout all the shit me and her did while I was with Novisha. But still, we never hooked up. Came damn close, but not all the way.

Adonna looking at me like she don't really believe me. "Then why did you and her break up?"

"Me and her, I don't know, it just —" I shrug. "It just stopped working, you know what I mean?" I don't like talking 'bout what happened between me and Novisha, not to no one, 'specially another female that live in the same building as Novisha do. I mean, I could tell Adonna that Novisha was the one that was with another guy, but I don't. It ain't like I wanna protect Novisha or anything. Not anymore. But still, why I need to blow up all Novisha business for?

It look like Adonna waiting for me to say more, but what can I say? That's it. She open her book again, but I don't wanna stop talking to her. "What's the book 'bout?"

"Some girl with a lot of guy problems and family drama."

"Which one you got?"

"Well, I already told you about my jacked-up family. And I don't have a man."

I look her in the eyes. "You *want* a man?"

She smile and look me up and down. "Maybe."

I lean in close to her. "You beautiful," I whisper, just focusing in on her. "Everything 'bout you is so beautiful." We kiss.

I put my hand on her oily back and pull her closer to me. It's nice, but I wish me and her was alone now. I know I'm trying to take it slow with her so she know I'm for real, but it's hard. Real hard.

The beach day turn out real good, 'specially for me and Adonna. I can't say the same thing for Patrick and Asia. They talking, but she stay, like, two feet away from him the whole time. It look to me like she ain't really feeling him, but she just trying to be nice. After a while, he take her over to the other side of the beach where they got rides and games and shit. I'm hoping Adonna don't want me to win her one of them stuffed animals 'cause the way they make them games, no matter how good you are, you gotta keep playing over and over to get the big animals. Shit cost you, like, eighty dollars by the time you finished. And you gotta go for it 'cause your girl ain't gonna walk 'round with no little shit neither.

So me and Adonna stay on the blanket and kiss and talk. After a while, I end up telling her 'bout my pops being back and how I hope he ain't gonna try and make me leave Bronxwood 'cause I'm having a good time being my own man. Even while I'm talking, I'm thinking 'bout what I'm not telling her, like how my pops ain't even ask me to move back home. And how I don't know if he want me back there. I don't even know why I brung him up, but Adonna talk to me some more 'bout her father and I'm glad I did talk 'bout my pops 'cause it's something me and her have in common. The way we connecting, I know it ain't gonna be long before she let me in them pants.

Cal and Tina leave the beach 'bout three o'clock 'cause Tina phone start ringing nonstop. The rest of us chill. Then 'round five, I start to get hungry again, so I tell Adonna we should get outta there and go find somewhere to eat. Patrick look like he wanna come with us, but we just leave them there 'cause he need to either get somewhere with Asia or bring the girl home and forget it. Whatever he do, he need to do it on his own.

I wanna take Adonna somewhere nice, but not someplace expensive like City Island, even though we real close to there. So we end up at T.G.I. Friday's, and I gotta say, we have us a good time. We sitting on the same side of the booth, scarfing down chili nachos, then ribs and French fries, talking and laughing and kissing.

All I know is, right now, I'm happy. I need a girl like this in my life. For real. This the only thing that's working for me right 'bout now.

TWENTY

It's mad early in the morning when I hear him, and the only reason I do is 'cause I hafta get up and pee. I'm halfway down the hall when I hear the sound coming from the living room. It's Cal, and he moaning and crying, sounding like a dog that got hit by a car or something.

I fly out to the living room and Cal is on the couch, laying there, and all I see is blood — on him, on his clothes, on the couch, on the floor coming from the door. It's crazy. For, like, ten seconds I just stand there with my mouth open. What the fuck happened? Who did this to him?

"Cal." I run over to him and bend down over him. "Cal, what happened?"

But all he do is keep on moaning.

"Shit. Shit." I'm just standing there cursing to myself, but that ain't helping Cal none. I get down on my knees next to couch so he can see me. "Cal, you gonna be a'ight, okay?"

Shit, Cal face is jacked up. He got blood running down from his forehead and landing in his eye that's all busted up and bloodshot. And his lip and nose is bleeding too. And with all that, the thing he holding is his ribs. Shit, probably they broke too. Whoever did this fucked him up bad.

"I'ma call 9-1-1," I tell him and get up, but he grab my arm.

"Nah. You can't," he say. "Andre gonna find out."

"Fuck Andre," I tell him.

"No, Ty. Hold on, hold on. I'm a'ight. Hold on."

He actually try and sit up, but just by moving a inch, he practically scream in pain, and his face get all tight. That's when I see the tears. Damn, I ain't seen him cry since we was little kids.

"Cal, don't move. How the fuck you even get up here?"

"I don't know," he say, then it look like more pain shoot through his whole body and he close his eyes for a second. Then he go, "Get Greg," and it's like he can't hardly talk no more than them two words.

I go down the hall and knock on Greg door hard, but he ain't there. I call his cell and I know from the way he sound that I just woke his ass up. Asshole was s'posed to be driving 'round all night keeping Cal and the other guys that sell for them safe out there, and he 'sleep. "Where you at?" I yell into the phone. "Why you ain't doing your fuckin' job?"

"Ty? What the fuck you calling me —?"

"Cal hurt. Somebody beat the shit outta him. He need a ambulance."

Greg start cursing. "Where his weed at? Don't call nobody 'til you make sure he don't got nothing on him.

Nah, Ty, matter of fact, don't do nothing 'til I get there. I'ma be right there."

I don't never know Greg to do nothing fast, so after we hang up, standing there watching Cal in that much pain ain't easy. 'Specially when it look like he can't breathe all that good. I don't know what to do. I don't wanna call the ambulance up in here 'cause they be showing up with the police most of the time and I ain't looking to get nobody locked up, including me. But I can't just watch Cal die.

So I go to the kitchen and get a bunch of paper towels and sit by the couch with him, holding him 'round the shoulders, and telling him to try and calm down so he can breathe slower and it won't hurt so much. Like I know what I'm talking 'bout. Then I wipe some of the blood off his face. Shit is thick and nasty. "It ain't that bad," I tell him. "You gonna be a'ight." But I'm straight up lying to the dude. His face look like someone went twelve rounds with him.

Every time he try to talk, I tell him to relax, that he can tell me what he wanna say later, but he wanna talk now. But all he doing is mumbling and moaning.

Greg show up 'bout forty minutes later and I'm like, "What the fuck?"

"Shut up, Ty." He go over to the couch where Cal at and try talking to him and shit. Cal can't hardly breathe now, so he kinda panting.

"What we gonna do?" I ask Greg. "He been like this for a while."

"Ty, shut up and let me think."

Shit. If I let him think, Cal fucked. "I'ma call a ambulance if you don't do something, Greg. He your brother, man."

"I know. Shut up."

I sit on the chair 'cross from Cal and watch Greg and Cal talk. Greg ask him what happened, and it take a while, but Cal finally tell him two dudes came up on him and tried to take all the money he had on him. Cal say he tried to fight but they was both bigger than him and he ain't know if they was strapped. They ended up taking all the cash and the weed and said something 'bout how they was doing this to teach his brother not to go where he ain't s'posed to be. Then they kicked him 'til he couldn't hardly move.

When Greg get the whole story outta Cal, I can tell he don't know what to do. "Andre gonna go off," he tell Cal, like Cal need to hear that shit right 'bout now.

"Don't tell him," Cal say.

Greg shake his head. "He gonna find out."

Cal let out this long moan, and I don't know if it's 'cause he don't want Andre to know or if the pain getting worse. Or both. He look bad. How long Greg gonna have him dealing with it?

Finally, Greg decide to take Cal to the hospital, but he don't want no ambulance people in they apartment, so me and him hafta get Cal out to Greg car by ourself. Crazy thing is, on the way downstairs we see all the blood Cal left in the hall and elevator and lobby when he came upstairs. Damn.

By the time we get Cal outside, me and Greg can't hardly hold him no more and keep him walking. His ribs must be broke for real 'cause he damn near doubled over in pain. And his face is so fucked up. We barely get him to the curb when Ms. Lucas from Building D come down the street and I'm like, shit. That woman known for running her mouth. Now the whole Bronxwood gonna know what happened to Cal in 'bout a half hour. Shit can't get no worse for Cal.

At the hospital, they don't make us wait, but the nurse yell at us for not calling a ambulance. Even though we don't tell her what happened to Cal, she know. She like, "It doesn't matter what he was doing when this happened. You all should have called an ambulance. He could have a punctured lung."

While they checking Cal out, me and Greg sit there in the waiting room not even hardly talking. What I wanna know is this, where was he at while Cal was out there? Wasn't he s'posed to be driving 'round? This whole thing just prove my point that Andre and Greg just using Cal to do all they work for them.

But I ain't looking to fight with Greg now. He worried 'bout Cal just as much as me. And he worried 'bout what to tell Andre who probably gonna wanna know where Greg was at too. I mean, that's the fucking question.

It take almost two hours before the doctor come out to tell us how Cal doing. I was thinking she forgot 'bout us out there, but she ain't. She say two of Cal ribs is fractured and he got a sprained wrist and all kinds of cuts and shit. He even had to get five stitches over his right eye.

"We're going to admit him for a couple of days to monitor his breathing and his pain," she say. "Then he can go home and finish healing there. He'll be alright. We need to talk to his mother."

"I called her," Greg say. "She coming now."

"Can we see him?" I ask her.

"Are you family?"

"We his brothers," Greg go.

The doctor don't look like she believe us, but she let us go in. Cal still in the ER 'til a room could get ready, so we gotta walk past all these other people that be bleeding and shit. Cal in a small room with the curtain closed. The doctor open it for us and say, "Your brothers are here, Calvin."

Real fast, Cal open his eyes wide, scared. Then when he see it's only us, he close them again. I go over to him, looking at his face all swole up with this big bandage over his eye. The rest of his body is under the sheet, but man them dudes broke his ribs. That shit gotta hurt like hell.

But the real thing I'm thinking is what Cal must be going through, and I ain't only thinking 'bout the pain neither. Cal ain't no punk, but two guys beat him anyway. If it was me, I would be feeling like a big pussy.

So when Cal say, "Y'all shoulda went home already. You don't gotta watch me." I get it and I don't blame him.

I don't know what to say to him neither.

So for a while I don't say nothing. I just stand there watching him breathe. Every time he take a breath, I can see how much that shit hurt.

Me and Greg don't stay there too long. We just sit on these chairs next to his bed, not really talking or nothing. Just being there with him.

When Cal and Greg moms get there, the second she walk in the room and see Cal, she start crying. Then she look at Greg and start yelling at him. "What happened to your brother? What you let them do to him?"

Before Greg can answer, I get up to leave. "Cal, I'ma see you tomorrow, a'ight?" I don't wanna stay and listen to Cal moms act like she care 'bout him 'cause she ain't all that good a moms, you ask me.

First of all, she don't live with him. Andre got her a apartment in Co-op City and he pay her rent and buy her whatever she need. She living okay and don't even see Cal 'cept for when he decide to stop by her place, which is only 'bout every two, three weeks. Not only that, she just let Cal live with Andre and Greg and get caught up in they business. She know what he doing and don't never tell him to move in with her.

Now she gonna come to the hospital and put on this big show, but she not doing what she s'posed to be doing for Cal neither. Nobody is.

They got a McDonald's inside the hospital, which kinda seem weird for a place that's s'posed to be all 'bout making people healthy, but still that's straight where I go after I leave the ER. I'm sitting there eating two Egg McMuffins when my cell ring.

My pops.

I click my phone and say hello.

"Ty, I need the storage room key. You got it? 'Cause I been looking all over this apartment and it ain't here."

For a second I think 'bout lying to the man and saying I don't got it, but then he probably just gonna go to the storage place and get them to open the room for him anyhow. So I say, "Yeah, I think I got it."

"I'm coming by for it," he say.

"Nah, I ain't home. I'm at the hospital. With Cal." Then I tell him all 'bout what happened to Cal and how messed up he is, and how we don't know when he gonna get out or how long it's gonna take for him to get better. All that.

When I'm through talking, he go, "His brothers better find out who did that to him and take care of it."

"Nobody know who did it, not even Cal."

"Let me tell you something, Ty. When somebody do something wrong, there gotta be a consequence. Every time. Somebody gotta pay for what they did to Cal, or folks 'round there is gonna know they can get away with shit like that and it's gonna keep happening."

"I know," I say 'cause I don't want him to go into that thing he do where he think he always gotta teach me stuff 'bout life. Piss me off.

"I'm gonna be coming by the hospital for the key," he say, like nothing I just told him 'bout Cal matter to him. Or even that I'm living in the middle of all this violent shit. "You sitting in the waiting room?"

"Nah, don't come. I don't got the key on me. Why you need it?"

"Don't worry 'bout that. When can I get it from you?"

Damn, now I'ma hafta try and dodge this man 'til after Jasmine party or I'm screwed. "I could bring it on Wednesday, to the agency visit," I say.

"Okay, that's good."

We hang up and right away I know I ain't showing up at the agency on Wednesday. I'ma hafta go see Troy at camp today 'cause I need this key. I don't wanna be the one to fuck up Jasmine party.

TWENTY-ONE

I go to the hospital to see Cal the next day, 'round two o'clock, but when I get there, a nurse on the floor tell me he don't wanna see nobody. I'm like, "Tell him it's me, Ty." She go in his room and come out shaking her head. "He's very tired," she say. "He hasn't wanted to see anyone today."

I tell her thanks, but part of me just wanna bum rush the door to Cal room and tell him he don't gotta do this. Nobody blaming him for what happened and he ain't do nothing wrong. His brothers was the ones that was s'posed to have his back.

I leave the hospital feeling bad for Cal. He probably laying in that bed feeling like shit. And there ain't no need for that.

All last night I was thinking 'bout what happened, just sitting in that hot-ass apartment making myself madder and madder. The situation just feel heavy on me, like something that's so messed up, but something I can't do shit 'bout. That's a feeling I don't like.

I don't know what Adonna is doing today, but she could probably cheer me up. She answer the phone on the second ring. "What you doing?" I say to her.

"I'm on Fordham Road shopping with Asia. She's taking *forever* picking out a pair of jeans. It's crazy!" She giggle. "What about you?"

I tell her 'bout what happened to Cal and how he don't even wanna see nobody. "Don't tell nobody 'bout this at Bronxwood," I say. "Even Asia. He don't need this getting out."

"Don't worry. I won't say anything." I can tell she feeling real sad for Cal, just like me.

"Good," I say, hoping she keep her mouth closed. Then I ask her, "What you doing later? Wanna come over for a little while?"

"Okay, but something tells me I won't be done shopping anytime soon. I'll try to come over around five."

"Cool. See you in a while."

Talking to Adonna definitely help. I can't say Cal out my mind all the way, but least when I'm with Adonna I can think 'bout somebody else for a while.

I stop by Troy camp again, but he ain't there. They on a trip to the science museum and ain't getting back 'til after six, so I stop off at the bodega to get a two-liter Sprite and some barbecue chips for Adonna, then go back home to wait for her to get there. Second day of being in this apartment without Cal and it ain't the same. Nobody home to complain to 'bout shit, which is what it seem like me and him do all the time now.

Guess we gonna have more to bitch 'bout now.

I paid Keisha to come clean up this morning before I left for the hospital, so least the place ain't nasty. I'ma try and keep things slow with Adonna 'cause I can tell this plan is working on her. After Sunday, me and her is close. Course if she wanna go in my room and let me give it to her, I ain't gonna be the one to say no.

A brotha can dream, right?

Something after five, the doorbell ring and I'm like, good, she right on time. But when I open the door it ain't Adonna standing out there. It's Novisha.

Before I say anything to her, before I can even think of something to say, Novisha go, "I heard about what happened to Cal."

She still standing in the hall, and I ain't gonna let her come in neither, not with Adonna on her way over. "What you want, Novisha?"

She look kinda surprised by how I'm acting, but that don't make no sense to me. She know why I'm this way. She the one that made me like this. "I want to know if Cal is okay, and if you're safe, living here with those guys. I'm —"

"Oh, I get it. You worried 'bout me." I gotta laugh at that one. The girl that hurt me worse than anybody else is worried 'bout me. Shit is funny.

"What?" Novisha ask. "Why are you acting like this?"

"Novisha, you gotta go. I don't have time —"

"Talk to me."

Why she sound like she begging me? Why can't she take a hint already? "Look, Novisha. I'm okay. Cal okay. Just stay outta this, a'ight?"

"But —"

"Your moms know you here? 'Cause you know how she feel 'bout Cal and them."

"Of course she doesn't know I'm here, but when I heard about what happened to Cal, I couldn't stop thinking about him. It sounds horrible. How's he doing? Is he in the hospital?"

"Novisha, you gotta go." I step out into the hall and push the button for the elevator.

"I wanted to talk to you about something else," she say. "I want to tell you something."

I shake my head 'cause I shoulda knew she wasn't coming over here for what happened to Cal. All this 'bout how she worried 'bout Cal ain't nothing but bullshit. Yeah, her and Cal know each other, always did, but they ain't friends or nothing. She don't care 'bout him. I press the button again, but don't say nothing.

"I don't know why you're acting like this, Ty. I just want to tell you something."

"Keep it to yourself," I tell her, and finally I hear the elevator coming. "Go home, Novisha. Just go."

The elevator doors open and before Novisha can even move, Adonna come out. She look at Novisha and then at me and the look on her face say it all. She fucking pissed.

And me, I can't believe this shit. Adonna looking at me like I'm the lying asshole she thought I was, and with me standing out here in the hall with Novisha, I can't say nothing 'cause nothing I say gonna change what she thinking.

Adonna don't never step foot off the elevator. All she do is press the button for the first floor and stare at me 'til the doors close again. And when she gone I'm standing there with Novisha and I swear I could kill that girl. She standing there looking like she in shock, but I know she happy for what she did.

"Ty, I'm —"

"Save it, Novisha. Just go."

I go back in the apartment and leave her standing out there alone.

TWENTY-TWO

Cal get released from the hospital the next afternoon, and me and Greg go to pick him up. They moms is there too, but the second we get Cal into Greg car, Cal say he don't wanna go to her apartment. He wanna go home.

For a second I think Cal moms is gonna be like, no, you gotta come home with me. Then I remember who she is. Woman don't say a word to try and change his mind.

The whole way to Co-op City to drop off they moms and even on the way to Bronxwood when it's just us, Cal don't say nothing. He sitting in the backseat looking kinda depressed, and nothing me and Greg say to him bring him outta it.

Cal need help getting out the car, but since folks is outside, as soon as he out, he push Greg away from him and say, "I'm a'ight. Damn."

Then he walk real slow up the path to the building. It's obvious he in pain and trying to play it off. Me and Greg look at each other, but what we s'posed to do?

It take a while for us to get upstairs to the apartment, Cal walking so slow and stiff. Cal say he can't lay in no bed no more, so we set him up on the couch. His ribs is still hurting real bad and his breathing ain't back to normal. The nurse gave him this little machine thing with a hose that he gotta blow into so his lungs can get stronger, but Cal get lazy sometimes and I know he ain't gonna hardly use that thing.

I give Cal a bag of Doritos, a Pepsi, and the remote control. Greg must be happy he home 'cause he don't even try to play one of his PlayStation games. He just chill and let Cal control the TV.

We all sitting in the living room watching TV for a while when the doorbell ring.

Cal go, "Oh, shit."

For a second, Greg even look scared. That's 'cause nobody still told Andre what happened to Cal and they don't know if he found out yet.

But Andre don't gotta ring no bell to get in. So I go to the door and ask who it is.

"Me. Tina." Damn, I swear, that girl musta shoved some kinda tracking device up Cal ass or something. "Let me in."

Cal let out a moan.

"A'ight, hold on," I say through the door. I give Cal the signal like, what you want me to do?

He just shake his head, not really saying no, don't let her in, but more like, why she gotta come here?

So I open the door and Tina come flying in with CJ in his stroller. She take one look at Cal and suck in her breath. Then she just go crazy. For real crazy.

First she start crying and saying over and over, "I can't believe this. I can't believe they did this to you."

She sit down on the arm of the couch by Cal and lean over and start stroking his head and shit.

Then she flip. She curse him out for not letting her come and see him at the hospital. "How could you do that to me?" she ask. "Me!"

Least I ain't the only one he flat-out disrespected.

Cal hardly get a word out when she flip again. "We got a kid, Cal. Your son needs you alive and well, not laying in the street somewhere dead. You gotta think about what you're doing, protect yourself. This shit is crazy." She turn to me and Greg. "Don't you think this is crazy? Why can't y'all talk to Andre?"

Greg shrug and just look dumb.

I go, "I ain't in they business, Tina."

"So you don't care what happens to him? Is that what you're saying, Tyrell? Your best friend."

I stare at her for a couple seconds and then tell Cal I'ma be back. I ain't gonna start arguing with Cal girl.

I leave the living room and go to my room. I sit on the bed and try and cool myself down, but it ain't working too good. I wish Adonna wasn't pissed at me 'cause she could take my mind off all this shit.

I tried calling her, like, three times last night and she ain't answer her phone for none of them. I left a message, trying to tell her that Novisha came over here by herself, not 'cause I asked her to come over, but I guess Adonna ain't trying to hear it.

While I'm waiting for Tina to stop acting like a crazy fool in the living room, I try calling Adonna again. This time she answer. "I don't want to talk to you, Tyrell." Damn, her voice all hard and tight.

"C'mon, Adonna. You gotta let me . . . how you not gonna let me explain?"

"Explain what?"

I take a deep breath and try to relax myself. "I wanna see you, talk to you. See you."

"I'm on my way back from Bay Plaza. I'll call you when I'm close, but I'm only giving you five minutes. That's it." She don't sound like she even wanna give me that. "I gotta go."

We hang up and I don't know. I ain't feeling all that good 'bout none of this. She sound like she already made up her mind. But all the time I put into that girl. It's worth trying to make up to her.

I lay on the bed and try to relax. Right 'bout now, my moms and pops is at the agency visit and I ain't there. I know Troy probably wanna know where I'm at, but I hope he understand. I can't let go of that key yet.

Finally, Adonna text me. 1 block away. u got 5 mins.

I check myself in the mirror to make sure I'm looking cute. I hope Adonna gonna let me explain. I mean, I ain't even do nothing wrong, but still, I know females don't always make sense. And no matter what I say, I know for a fact Adonna definitely not gonna make this easy on me.

Adonna coming down the street by the time I get downstairs, and I can tell she in a pissed-off mood by the way she walking. She carrying all kinds of shopping bags and shit, and she walking and swinging them like she don't care that I'm walking up to her. It's like she trying to prove she through with me.

And damn, that bad attitude is fuckin' hot.

Me and her finally get close enough for me to talk to her. "You doing all this shopping for school already?"

"Kinda," she go, and keep walking down the block.

I hafta follow next to her 'cause she ain't slowing down. "Y'all girls kill me with the way y'all be shopping all the time."

She don't say nothing. She just keep walking. This ain't going too good. If I don't stop this now, she gonna be walking into her building and this whole thing gonna be for nothing. "Adonna, c'mon. Slow down."

She take another couple steps, but I stop walking. She ain't gonna play me like this. It take her a couple seconds, then she actually turn 'round. She sigh. "Where are you —?"

"Adonna, you gonna talk to me or not? You said you was giving me five minutes. You ain't even gave me five seconds."

She sigh.

"Come here," I tell her, and I feel that I'm kinda taking control, kinda the way my pops do with my moms. Just tell her what she need to do. "Come over here, and me and you gonna talk. That's it. Talk."

It work too. I mean, she still got that attitude and everything, but she follow me to the side of her building, over by the parking lot. A couple people going to they cars and coming into the building, but it's still the best place me and her could talk.

I take her bags from her, and put them on the ground, then take both of her hands in mines, real romantic. "I like you," I say. "A lot."

She shake her head and pull her hands outta mines.

"Listen to me," I say. "I like you and I wanna spend time with you, just me and you. And what happened yesterday, that was straight-up —" I try to find the right word, but I don't even know what the fuck happened. "That was just bad timing or something, 'cause like I told you before, me and Novisha is nothing no more. Yeah, she my ex, but I'm not thinking 'bout that girl."

"You keep saying that, but —"

"Let me finish," I say. "Let me tell you what happened." And I tell her the whole story, how Novisha just came by outta the blue to see how Cal was doing and how I was trying to get rid of her when Adonna came by.

"That's not what it looked like," she say.

"I ain't lying. Why I'ma bring her over there when me and you had plans to watch a movie together?"

"I don't know why guys do anything they do." She look down at the ground.

"Why you being like this, Adonna, huh?" I know she wasn't gonna be easy to get, but this don't make no sense already. "I told you. The way that girl treated me, ain't no way I'ma get back with her. You see me spending time with her? No. You see me spending time with you. That's it. That's 'cause you the one I want."

I'm hating the way I'm sounding right now, like I'm begging this female for something, and yeah, I wanna get with her, but I'm not liking the way I'm going 'bout this.

Adonna pick her head up and she got tears just rolling down her face. Shit. I don't even know what I said to make her start crying. "This is what I wanna know, Tyrell. What's wrong with me?"

"What? You?"

"Why am I always the one nobody wants?"

"You crazy or something? Every dude up here in Bronxwood want you. We be drooling when you walk by."

"Then what am I doing wrong? I thought I was making you happy. Yesterday, I wanted to, you know, really let you know how much I liked you, but then —" She shake her head. "Forget it."

"You was making me happy, and you coulda made me real happy for a long time, Adonna. No doubt. Me and you together could be alright if you just would let it."

"I can't," she say. "I can't be with somebody if I'm gonna have to worry about who they're with when they're not with me. I'm tired of chasing guys."

"C'mon, Adonna. I been chasing you for —"

"I gotta go, Ty. If you want, me and you can be friends, but that's it. Sorry."

Damn. That "friends" bullshit hurt. No way me and Adonna gonna be friends. What, me and her gonna go play ball or something? I already got one female friend and Jasmine enough for one guy. Besides, how I'ma have two girls in my life and I ain't getting with none of them? That don't make no kinda sense.

"Bye," she say, and she just 'bout to go when I see that she still got on my pops chain. If I don't get it back from her now, I ain't never gonna see it again.

Yeah, I feel like shit, but I hafta do it. "Adonna, I need my pops chain back. He been asking me for it."

She just stare at me for a couple seconds. Feel more like a couple hours though. "I thought you gave it to me."

"I ain't give it to you. I told you —"

"Whatever," she say with all the attitude she got, turn

'round, and move her hair out the way. I undo the chain and take it off her neck fast before I do something stupid and say she should keep it.

I slip the chain in my pocket while she pick her bags up off the ground.

"I'ma see you 'round, then?" I ask her.

"Yeah. I'm not going anywhere."

And that's it. I stand there watching her carry her bags 'round the building to the front door. She don't look back neither. She gone.

The whole thing is fucked up. All this 'cause of Novisha. On my way back to my building, I can't help but think maybe me and Adonna wasn't s'posed to get together. I mean, going after a girl like that was fun, but I don't know if that was enough.

When me and Novisha was together it was different. We had something deep. I need a girl like that again. Somebody. I'm tired of being like this.

I can't help but be pissed at myself that I never got none from Adonna though. Trying to be a gentleman and go slow was a bad idea.

The day only get worse from there. Second I'm close enough to my building, I see that black van double-parked out front and know I'm fucked. My pops is here at Bronxwood. I'ma lose the storage room key. And the equipment.

"Where was you?" my pops ask me when I get close to the van. He sitting inside, smoking a cigarette.

"Cal got out the hospital. I had to help bring him home. He jacked up, in a lot of pain and shit." He don't say nothing, so I keep talking. "I know I was s'posed to come to the agency, but —"

"I told you we trying to show that agency that we a family, right? I ain't gonna make it a habit to tell you the same thing more than once. You understand me?"

"I know."

The way he looking at me, staring me down, I don't get him. "We had to tell that caseworker that you had a cold. And don't you think your brother wanna see you?"

"I know, but I don't need to go there to see him."

"Where the key?"

"Upstairs. I gotta go get it."

"Go on, then. I don't have all day."

I can't believe the way he think he can have me running and getting things for him like I'm a slave or something. But I go upstairs anyway, just to get the stupid key and get him to leave me the fuck alone. But I'm pissed. I know he ain't having another party 'til next week when he throwing that big party he gonna make lots of money from. He don't need that equipment now.

Only reason he taking the key is 'cause he don't want me to make no money from it. He trying to keep me in line and make me need to go back home or something. But he don't know, I'm my own man now. Ain't no going back.

Still, I can't act like what he doing ain't getting to me. I gotta DJ Jasmine party on Saturday and I don't know how I'ma do it. This day is fucked up. I feel like I don't have nothing right now. No equipment, no money. No girl.

TWENTY-THREE

By night, I'm fucking miserable. I'm sitting in the living room watching TV with Cal, who kinda in and outta it. The pills they got him on must be good 'cause 'bout five minutes after he take one of them things his eyes is rolling back in his head and he passing out with a smile on his face. It ain't a deep sleep 'cause he wake up and say something 'bout every ten, fifteen minutes, but none of it make sense. Dude is fucked up and feeling no pain.

But I'm feeling my own kinda pain. Not only 'cause of the cold way Adonna broke up with me but 'cause of Jasmine and what I'ma do 'bout her party. I can't think of no way to get the kinda money I'ma need for new equipment, not in two days. I gotta figure something out.

"You okay, Cal?" I ask him. "You hafta go to the bathroom or something?"

He mumble something I don't understand.

"A'ight," I say. "Just don't piss on the couch." I'ma hafta get him into his bed somehow. Wish Greg was here to help, but he downstairs doing Cal job like he been doing for the past two days.

It ain't a minute later that I hear all them locks on the door open fast and the door fly open. And that damn dog barking.

Shit. I shoulda knew Andre was gonna find out.

Andre stomp into the apartment, and when he see Cal laying there on the couch, the muscles and veins and shit in his face start twitching and popping. This ain't gonna be good. Greg running into the apartment right behind him, trying to catch his breath 'cause Greg ain't known to do nothing athletic. He look at me like this ain't his fault.

But it is. Nothing woulda happened to Cal if he was watching him.

Andre point to Cal, who kinda awake now, and say, "When you was gonna tell me about this?"

Greg go, "I know I should of told you, Andre. It's my fault. Don't blame Cal."

Least he stepping up now like a man.

"Why I gotta find out about this on the street?" Andre screaming now. "How that make me look out there? That my own workers is keeping shit from me."

I'm sitting there in the living room and I wish I could get up and leave outta there 'cause I ain't in this, but if I get up now, Andre probably gonna turn on me again. So I don't say nothing.

For a while it work too. Andre going off on Greg for not telling him nothing. Then he get mad at Cal for getting beat up and robbed in the first place. "What kinda pussy get beat up right in fronta his own building?"

Cal just close his eyes and moan.

Damn. I can't stand by and watch this happen. It ain't right. "C'mon, Andre, man. Leave the guy alone. He hurt."

"Ty, you the one always talking about how you don't wanna be in this business, so why you putting your ass in it, then."

"He my friend, Andre. Why don't you let him get better first, then go off on him?"

Cal mumble something that sound like, "I can work. I can go back to work."

"No you can't," I tell him, even though I don't think he half awake. "Andre, back up off him. He drugged up on pills he got at the hospital, and he got broke ribs and a busted eye. Leave him alone."

"How long you want me to leave him alone for?"

Greg jump in here. "Doctor said he need to rest for a couple weeks. The ribs take a while to heal."

"Weeks?" Andre look like he can't believe what he hearing. "We losing money out there! What I'm supposed to do?"

"I'm working his job," Greg say.

"And who gonna collect for you?"

Both Andre and Greg turn to look at me. "Ty?" Greg say. "We need you, man."

Andre nod like everything settled now. "All you gotta do is go around and collect the money from some guys we got working for us. You ain't gonna have to take no weed with you 'cause I know you too fucking scared to do that. Help out, Ty."

I shake my head. All this time, me living there and I ain't get involved in what they doing yet. Why I'ma start now?

"You collect from four guys, and I'll pay you two hundred dollars."

I don't gotta think too long. I don't wanna do it. It's stupid. But I'm not gonna have no drugs on me. And I need the cash. If I get through this, I'm two hundred dollars closer to getting what I need for Jasmine party. I can't say no.

The four guys I gotta collect from live in the Bronx, Washington Heights, and Harlem, so I don't gotta go too far. I take the train to Harlem first, then work my way back uptown. Tell the truth, the whole thing is mad easy. Andre told the dudes I was coming and told them what I was wearing and shit. It wasn't nothing. Most of the guys was, like, my age, living with they moms and sisters and brothers. Small-time guys trying to make a little money.

The last guy I collect from look like he thirteen or something. He live in the basement of this broke-down, need-to-be-tore-down building on 178th Street near Webster

Avenue. Kid look mad starving too, all skinny, hair messed up, rotten teeth and shit. Sad.

Everybody give me they money in a plastic bag, all wrapped up in tape and rubber bands. I don't even open nothing, just take it and leave. I mean, even though I'm doing this, I'm still trying not to be 'bout this. I'm only doing this so Andre will get off Cal back.

And for the money.

I'm back home 'round midnight. Cal still 'sleep on the couch. Damn, them pills is no joke. I should take one of them myself to get to sleep 'cause my mind can't stop running, thinking 'bout everything, all at the same time. I'm thinking 'bout Adonna and how fucked up it got between us and it wasn't even my fault. And thinking 'bout my pops and how he the reason I'm even in this situation in the first place.

But most of what I'm thinking 'bout is how Andre did it, got me into they business when I said I wasn't gonna never do that. I don't even know what I'm doing no more. I mean, even though everything worked out okay and I made some fast cash, still, I put my freedom on the line for two hundred dollars. And that shit is stupid.

TWENTY-FOUR

I don't know why, but the next day I go out to Astoria, to this DJ store my pops used to take me to all the time back in the day. They got everything, equipment and all the vinyl albums a DJ could want. All the expensive equipment is in the front of the store, and they got the best shit. Denon, Bose, Yamaha, Pioneer. Man, I wish I could afford any of it.

But I can't. So I stop looking at that stuff and go to the back of the store where they got all the crap, shit no real DJ with any kinda respect for hisself would buy, only some dude trying to look like he something he ain't. And that's the kinda DJ I'ma look like at Jasmine party. Fake.

My pops fault, all of this.

I know I can use Patrick turntables and deck, but his bullshit amp ain't gonna work with the big speakers I'ma need to get to make the music fill the room Emiliano rented for Jasmine party. And there's a lot of other stuff I need for the DJ table, like some records I could mix with and a microphone and lights and shit. Adding up it all, I'ma need, least, a thou, and that's for the cheapest gonna-break-in-two-days garbage.

Jasmine call me while I'm walking back to the train, and she ain't just crying, she doing that nasty, snot kinda crying, and for three whole minutes, she don't say nothing and I'm like, "Jasmine? Jasmine, what up? Jasmine, you a'ight?"

Nothing.

Part of me know this just her being emotional, and that's just who she is, but I been looking out for her for a while now, and the other part of me need to make sure nobody hurting her or nothing.

"I'm sorry, Ty," she say finally, in this little-girl voice. "I, I don't know why I called you. I —" She back to crying again.

I'm just 'bout to walk up the steps to the train, but she sound like she need to talk, so I light up a loose and lean up against the wall on the side of a cell phone store.

"Jasmine, c'mon, talk to me. What's going on? You thinking 'bout Joanny?" Some days the whole thing just hit Jasmine again and she can't get outta it.

"No, it's not that."

"Emiliano, then? He did something to you?"

"No," she say. "No, it's Reyna. I still can't find her and I want —" More crying.

"C'mon, Jasmine. You know Reyna okay. She know how to handle herself."

She sniff in all them boogers. "I know that, but I need to see her."

"The party still gonna be hot, Jasmine, even if Reyna don't come. Don't worry 'bout that." I'm saying all this but meanwhile I ain't got no equipment or money, and if I don't do something fast, this gonna be the kinda party where kids gonna hafta stand 'round talking and shit 'cause there ain't gonna be no music.

"You don't understand, Ty. I really need her."

I don't get it. Jasmine sound desperate all of a sudden. I ain't think it was all that important to get Reyna to come to her party, but look like females take this Sweet Sixteen shit real serious.

"I wanna go look for her," Jasmine say. "I'm gonna call in sick tomorrow and go to New Jersey, to the last place she lived to see if she's still there." I know the next thing she gonna say before she say it. "Come with me, Ty. Help me find her."

Oh, damn. The day before her party when I need to be thinking of a way to get the speakers and shit, she gonna have me running 'round Jersey trying to find a woman like Reyna, who move from one guy to the next like it ain't nothing. Like Jasmine ain't her responsibility no more.

"A'ight," I tell her. "I'll go with you."

Can't say no to her.

■　■　■

When I get back to Bronxwood I spend a couple hours at Patrick apartment, practicing DJing with the Spanish music, and finding the right old-skool music that I can mix with it. Can't just give up my style 'cause the music kinda different. Gotta turn this party out no matter what.

Then Andre text me and say he got another job for me. I don't tell none of this to Patrick. Not like I need to keep shit from him, but the fact that I'm even doing this is embarrassing as hell. To be broke enough to hafta work for Andre mean I'm as hard up as I could get.

When I get downstairs, Tina there taking care of Cal. She got him to sit up a little on the couch and she trying to get him to use that machine thing he s'posed to use so his lungs could get stronger. Andre there sitting in the chair in the living room talking to Cal real serious, like what he saying is so important, shit like, "You need to get better so you can help out the family. Remember, it's all us in this together. I take care of you and Greg, and Greg take care of me and you, and —"

"He get it, Andre!" Tina scream. "He ain't stupid. Leave him alone already! How many times he gotta hear the same thing? God!"

Tina a pain in the ass sometimes, but she do speak her mind, which is a good thing when it come to Andre.

I go over to Cal and watch him use the machine. He gotta try and breathe in air for as long as he could so that this yellow thing on the side move up. But he can't hardly get it halfway up, and he can't hold it for more than half a second. "You doing good," I tell him.

Tina roll her eyes. "You gotta keep working on this, Cal, even when I'm not here. Your child needs you to get better."

Cal try the breathing thing again, but I can tell he exhausted from it. It's hard seeing my boy like this, all helpless and shit.

Andre get up and come over to me. He hand me a list that got names and addresses on it. Some of the same dudes I went to yesterday, a couple new places, but they all still not that far. "A'ight," I say. Then I tell Cal, "I'ma be over by that spot we got them ribs from, remember? I'ma bring you back some of them, long as you don't get off that couch and you just chill 'til I get back."

"He's not going anywhere," Tina say.

Andre shake his head. "Y'all need to stop treating him like a baby."

"C'mon, man," I say. "He just got out the hospital. Give him a little time. He can't even hardly breathe good."

"I see that, Ty."

"He need least a couple weeks to get back out there, Andre. I'm picking up his slack, right? The whole reason I'm doing this is so you could back up off him."

Andre nod a couple times. "Okay, you right, Ty. Long as the work getting done. That's what matter, right?"

"Yeah."

"You know what, Tyrell. I got a better job for you." Andre lower his voice. "I'ma give you the job I give my best guys. It's gonna take you more time, but it's only one stop and I'ma give you five hundred. You down?"

All I hear really is the amount of money I'ma get and I'm in. With five hundred dollars I could probably put together what I need for the party. I'ma be straight. "Yeah," I tell him. "Where I hafta go?"

"Brooklyn," he say. "Bed-Stuy."

It take me more than a hour to get to Bed-Stuy. I get off at the Kingston-Throop stop, deep in hard-core Brooklyn, and soon as I come up the steps to the street, I see all these dudes hanging 'round the subway station like they waiting for somebody. It's after ten, but there's still people out. They got a lot of stores on this block, all kinds of Jamaican patty and soul food restaurants, hair braiding and nail places. All the gates is down though. Only store still open is a bodega on the corner with bright lights, so the block ain't all that dark. Still, the way them guys stare me down as I cross Fulton Street, I know something up. I can feel it.

Them dudes don't follow me 'round the corner to Kingston Avenue or nothing, and I find the building real easy. It's one of them low buildings, only four floors, with fire escapes and piles of garbage bags right in front. But getting there only half the problem. The front door locked and there used to be a buzzer, but the shit is busted with wires hanging outta it. I don't got the guy phone number that I'm collecting from, so all I can do is stand there and wait. Meanwhile, I'm watching my back too.

It take ten minutes, then this female come up to the building and she must not live there neither 'cause she just start screaming up at one of the windows, "Tony! Throw down the key!" She wait half a second and scream again, "Tony! I need the key! Throw down the key!"

A window on the second floor open and a key on a thick string come flying down. She snatch it off the ground and open the door and don't say nothing to me when I go in right behind her.

The guy I'm collecting from live on the top floor. Me and the girl take the elevator up together, but I don't say nothing to her. When I get to the guy door I'm s'posed to collect from, there's a big sticker on it that say JESUS LIVES HERE and I ain't sure I'm at the right place 'cause that's wild. But I knock anyway and this short dude in his twenties answer the door.

"Jimmy?" I ask.

"Come in," he say, looking down the hall like he making sure I'm there by myself. "I got it in my room." He close the door behind him, then go down the hall, and I'm standing there looking at a old lady in a sweatsuit watching TV. She gotta be his grandmother or great-grandmother or something. The apartment nice and clean and smell good too, like she just finished cooking something.

"Hi," I say to her, but she don't hear me. I ain't even sure she know I'm standing here.

When the guy come back, he hand me the plastic bag and go, "You the new guy Andre got working for him?"

"Kinda."

"How long you been with him?"

"Not that long."

"Watch your back," he say. "You know how he could get."

"Yeah, I know." I stick the bag in my pocket. "I'ma go now." I get out in the hall, still thinking 'bout what Jimmy said 'bout watching my back. This whole pickup giving me a bad feeling. Something ain't right.

I take the stairs down 'cause I need time to think. When I get to the third floor, I stop and pull all the tape and shit off the bag and, damn, there gotta be, like, three thousand dollars in there. I take my five hundred out and stick it inside my sock and push it all the way down 'til it can't go no more. Then I wrap the rest of the money up and put the tape back 'round it and stick it in a pocket in my backpack.

When I get to the first floor, I don't see them dudes down there or out in front of the building, so I go outside and walk the other way this time. I don't really know where I'm going, just not to the same train stop I got off at in case they waiting for me. I'm just trying to get back to Bronxwood with no kinda problems.

But that don't work. I ain't even halfway down the block when a dude come flying out one of them alleys and bum rush me. He a big dude, and the way he hit me feel like I been hit by a bull, but he don't knock me down or nothing, he just knock me off balance. And that's all it take for three other dudes to come outta nowhere and attack me.

Everything happening so fast. I'm getting punched in the head and pushed, but I don't really feel none of it. And they all talking and saying shit that don't make no sense. I can't tell what the fuck is going on. I feel them going through my pockets and trying to grab my backpack, but I ain't giving it up that easy. Yeah, there's, like, four of them on me, but shit, I ain't 'bout to pussy out now. Not 'cause of no Brooklyn dudes, that's a fact.

So I fight back. I punch one guy dead in the mouth and another guy in the eye. But that's it. There's too many of them. So I try and get away, but they pulling me, trying to get me in the alley with them, but I ain't going there.

I'm, like, a foot away from the alley when it happen. One of the guys, the one that look the oldest, grab me by the head and press a nine millimeter to the side of my face. "The money," he say real slow.

One of the guys try again to get my backpack, but I ain't 'bout to give up all my shit just to try and hold on to Andre money. I don't even know what I'm fighting for. Fuck Andre. I take the backpack off my shoulder, reach into the pocket, and take out the bag. Then I throw it into the alley and take off running down the street. My heart is beating fast and hard and I'm feeling like a chump. I just ain't trying to get shot.

I get to the corner and turn back to see if they following me, but they ain't. So I start walking, trying to cool myself down. It ain't easy. I had a gun to my fucking head. I could be dead right now. And for what? For some drug money? For Andre?

I walk for a while, thinking and thinking. By the time I find another train station, I know what happened. And I shoulda knew what was up from jump. Andre set my ass up. I shoulda knew something was gonna go down from how he started whispering when he told me where he wanted me to go and how he threw the five hundred in my face.

Andre ain't sent me here to Brooklyn for nothing. He trying to get back at me for something. Trying to get me scared.

Them guys wasn't trying to kill me. They was sending me a message. That Andre could do whatever he want to me. That he got guys all over the place. Even Jimmy was trying to tell me 'bout Andre.

But I don't care. Yeah, Andre could hire some dudes to attack me, but I know he ain't no big-time gangsta. That shit is in his mind. He just don't want nobody telling Cal he don't hafta listen to him and do everything he say. He don't want Cal to be his own man. He like my pops that way.

■   ■   ■

Back at the apartment, Cal in his room. It's late, and I don't know if he 'sleep or not. Music is coming from the radio in there, but it's low. He could definitely sleep through it. Probably took some of them Vicodins and passed out again, knowing him. Shit. I could use a couple of them to stop the headache I got from getting hit in the head.

I sit in the living room for long time, having a beer and going over everything. The apartment is real quiet. I don't know where the fuck Greg at. I send Andre a text: got robbed.

I wait for him to text me back or call me, but he don't. I ain't telling him nothing he ain't already know.

I hold the phone thinking 'bout who I could call, but it's late. All this shit that happened tonight and I don't got nobody to talk to. I don't even got a girl.

I think 'bout calling Jasmine, but she probably 'sleep already. Besides, I don't want her knowing 'bout none of this. Girl would go crazy if she knew I was working for Andre. And if I tell her what happened tonight, she only gonna start worrying 'bout me too. That's the last thing she need.

It take two beers before I start to calm down. My head is still hurting, but weird thing is, what I'm really feeling is the pressure on the side of my face from the gun. Right there, at that spot, it's still cold.

TWENTY-FIVE

Going to Jersey City was a waste of time, straight up. We started off at the last apartment where Reyna was s'posed to be living at, and course she wasn't there no more. But some woman that lived on the first floor told us that Reyna was working at some club, and I don't know why we listened to a woman that was drunk at, like, eleven in the morning, but we did.

Turned out, yeah, Reyna worked there, but she quit, like, four months ago to work at some strip club. Course the strip club was all the way in Newark and they was just opening up 'cause I guess dudes like to go to strip clubs for lunch or something, but they wasn't letting two kids in. Some guy that work there told us Reyna don't work for them no more but he see her in the neighborhood, so Jasmine left a message with him to give to Reyna, telling her 'bout her party and where it's at. Doubt he gonna give Reyna the message though. Anyway, why he hafta? Reyna know when Jasmine birthday is. Why she need some strip club dude to tell her to come to her own sister party?

Meanwhile, Jasmine been crying off and on all day, every time we left another place where Reyna wasn't at. And no matter how many times I tried to tell her that Reyna probably okay wherever she at, Jasmine wasn't trying to hear me. Finally, we ain't had no other choice 'cept to come back to the Bronx.

"I don't wanna go home," Jasmine tell me on the train. "I wanna go to your place just until I can stop myself from crying."

"A'ight. I want you to hear some of the music Patrick got, stuff that wasn't even on your list."

By the time we get back to Bronxwood, it's after three. I'm trying to be cool, but inside I'm shitting bricks 'cause I need to start setting up for her party in exactly twenty-seven hours, and I don't know how I'ma make that happen. Only good thing is Jasmine ain't crying no more, but I can tell she still upset and still worried. And I get that. Reyna ain't no kid, but she still Jasmine sister.

Me and Jasmine go to my room 'cause Cal 'sleep on the couch. Probably took one of them pills 'cause he out cold with his mouth open and shit. "How's he feeling?" Jasmine ask, sitting on my bed.

"He in a lot of pain. Every time he breathe, you can see in his face how much it hurt."

She shake her head, and I don't want her getting even

more sad than she already is. So I put on some Spanish music to cheer her up and remind her 'bout her party.

Jasmine try to smile, but it look like her mind still ain't there.

"C'mon," I say. "Don't let nothing mess up your big day tomorrow. I mean, how many times you gonna turn sixteen?"

"That's the point. It's *my* day, right? I been talking about what kinda party I was gonna have since I was, like, twelve or thirteen. Reyna knows that. So why isn't she here? It doesn't make sense, Ty. Unless something's wrong. How can I not think about that?"

I sit down next to her and slip my arm 'round her waist. "You right," I tell her.

"And she's a stripper? How stupid is that? Stripping."

"I know you worried 'bout her and I don't blame you, but tomorrow I want you to have fun, you hear me? And I'ma do the best I can to make your party hot, okay?" Long as nobody wanna hear music.

"Alright." She rest her head on my shoulder. "I'm okay."

I kiss her forehead, then she turn toward me and we kiss on the lips fast, but good. Then, just as I'm 'bout to kiss her again, my cell ring. Shit.

Andre name come up on the screen. Fuck. I click the talk button and right away he go, "Ty, I need you to do the Bronx/Harlem pickup again."

"You ain't serious," I say.

"What you mean?"

"The shit you pulled yesterday. You remember that, right?"

"You said you got robbed. I still need you to —"

"Andre, I'm through." I make sure my voice real strong, so he know my mind's made up.

"Through with what?"

"Through with you."

I click the cell off and lean back into Jasmine and try to get back to what we was doing. But she pull away and say, "Who was that?"

"Look, Jasmine, I know you like to know everything 'bout what I do, but —"

"Just tell me."

It take me a couple seconds to think of a way outta this, but there ain't none. So I just tell her. "It was Andre. I did some work for him and now —"

"What?" Jasmine eyes bug out and she cover her mouth with her hand, all shocked and shit.

"I ain't sell no drugs, Jas —"

"You promised me you wasn't gonna do nothing with them. Didn't you promise me? I remember you promising me."

"Yeah, I did, but you don't understand everything that's been going on, like, since my pops got out and . . ." I stop talking 'cause if I tell her any more, I'ma hafta tell her that my pops took his equipment back and I ain't got nothing to use for her party. Then I'ma hafta deal with more tears than I already put up with all day.

"You're so stupid," Jasmine say. "God!"

"Look, Jasmine. I gotta take care of myself 'cause nobody else gonna do that for me. Why it matter to you so much what I do?"

She shake her head over and over and roll her eyes. "You're so stupid."

"You said that already. Yeah, a'ight. I'm stupid."

"You're stupid because you can't see that I got feelings for you, stupid."

Okay, now I don't even know what to say to that. Or what to do. But I don't gotta do nothing 'cause before I open my mouth to say anything, she back to kissing me. And this time our kissing is hard and nasty, like the kind that make me know she want it from me bad.

Me and her kiss for a long time, longer than I ever spent kissing a female. To be honest, I'm trying to slow myself down 'cause I been thinking about getting with Jasmine for so long, when we get going, I wanna make sure it last.

"Watch me," Jasmine say, standing up right in front of me. I wanna get up and keep kissing, but she put her arm on my shoulder. Then next thing I know she taking off her clothes, and I'm still sitting on the bed trying to be cool and keep my mouth closed. But damn. Damn. I can't believe this shit is 'bout to go down. "You looking sexy as hell," I tell her.

She smile and throw her top on the dresser. Then her bra come off and now I'm the one smiling. I swear, Jasmine titties is bigger than the last time I seen her naked, one time back at the shelter when she was changing and she thought I was 'sleep. Now they probably a D cup or something, and she only now turning sixteen. By the time she twenty, they gonna be least a double D.

I know she trying to strip for me, but I can't take it no more. I gotta get my hands on them things. On her. I get up from the bed, put my arms 'round her waist so she don't think I'm only going after her titties and we stand there kissing for a while. Finally, I move my hands up slow 'til they where they wanna be, and man, it was worth the wait, for real. I ain't gonna lie, just touching them make me ready to go. And I don't waste no time getting the rest of her clothes off while she taking off mines.

It don't matter that I don't know what Jasmine thinking and why she wanna do it with me all of a sudden. All I'm thinking is if she want it, I'ma let her get it.

And that's what I do. I grab a couple condoms from my top drawer and, in the same move, get her on the bed and kiss her some more. Then I lay it down hard. For real. I ain't gonna lie, girl got me breathing hard and sweating. Working hard. All the time I'm making sure she getting as much outta this as me. And I can tell she is, all the noise she making. She definitely know what a guy need to hear to know he doing the right thing.

When we through, we lay in bed with our arms and legs wrapped 'round each other and Jasmine talking and talking, but it's hard for me to stay awake. The girl wore me out.

"I wish I could stay here with you," Jasmine say.

"What time Emiliano getting home?"

"I don't wanna think about him now."

"I know," I say, 'cause I don't wanna think about him neither, not when I know he wanna do the same thing to Jasmine that I got finished doing. "I don't want you to get in trouble if you get home late."

She sigh. "I know. It's just —"

She stop talking and I wait for her to finish what she was gonna say, but my eyes is closing. Finally, I feel her pulling away from me. I open my eyes and try and keep her next to me. "Don't go nowhere," I say.

She sit on the bed with her back to me. "I have to go. I have to change trains and —"

I sit up and wrap my arms 'round her waist. "Stay here. Just for a while."

Next thing I know we back laying under the covers, kissing. Then ten minutes later I'm ready for Round Two. A girl like Jasmine ain't easy to let go of. Not 'til there ain't nothing left.

TWENTY-SIX

When we wake up, Jasmine start freakin' out 'cause it's after six. She sit up in bed fast and first thing she do is call Emiliano and tell him some bullshit 'bout how her and her friends went out after work and they was trying to get they nails done or something but the line was too long and now she on her way back home.

Soon as she hang up, and 'cause I'm thinking two steps ahead, I call Patrick to see if he borrowed his uncle truck for the party yet, and when he say he did, I tell him to meet us downstairs in five minutes. I can't hardly drive a regular car for shit. Ain't no way I'ma figure out how to drive a stick. Anyway, I ain't ready to let go of Jasmine yet, so why drive when I can let Patrick do it?

While Jasmine go to the bathroom, it's hard for me to move. Having sex with that girl came outta nowhere but that shit was crazy good. I knew if I ever got with her, it was gonna be something I wasn't never gonna forget, but I never knew she would be like that. She was like a different person or something, a female that did everything and let me do anything. It was like she couldn't get enough. Even trying to get outta bed, my legs is still weak. Good thing she ain't here to see it 'cause this shit is embarrassing.

I might hafta quit smoking for real and start going to the gym if I'ma get with Jasmine again.

Patrick uncle a plumber and he own the broke-down brown truck. He don't work on the weekend, so when I throw a party I pay him fifty dollars to rent it to bring my equipment to the party. While Patrick drive to Jasmine place, me and her squeezed in next to him, still kissing. Even with Patrick right there, I can't help myself. After what just went down between us, I'm feeling closer to her than I ever did before.

Then, when we get on Jerome Avenue, Jasmine stop kissing me and just put her arms 'round me and hug me for a long time. I hug her back, but I don't know. "You okay?" I ask her.

"Yeah," she say, and she don't let go of me for a while.

I'm like, what's she thinking? That she shoulda never got with me or something? But I don't wanna ask her nothing now, not with Patrick here, so I just keep my arms 'round her.

When we get in front of her building, Jasmine tell Patrick, "Don't stop here. Keep going and I'll tell you when to stop." Two blocks later, she tell Patrick he could pull over now. Before she get out, she give me a couple fast kisses on the lips. "See you tomorrow," she say, which just make me think 'bout how much I gotta do before the party.

"Don't worry 'bout nothing," I tell her. "All you gotta do is look good and have fun tomorrow, a'ight?"

She smile and nod. "Okay." But, damn, she don't look happy no more. And I don't know if it got anything to do with me or not.

I tell Patrick that we ain't going straight back to Bronxwood. We going to my moms and pops new apartment. I mean, I don't know how I'ma do it, but I hafta get my hands on that storage room key again. Ain't got no choice.

When my pops open the door, I can tell him and my moms ain't in the mood to have nobody visiting them. They in the living room watching some movie on TV and drinking, and my pops is only wearing boxers and my moms got on some long T-shirt thing, and I'm glad I told Patrick to stay downstairs in the truck 'cause nobody else need to see my moms and pops like this.

"You need something?" my pops ask me, standing in the door, blocking me from going in.

"What he want?" my moms call out from the couch.

I'm they son. They acting like I'm somebody trying to sell them *The Watchtower* or something. "I left something in my — I mean, I need to get something outta one my boxes."

"You couldn't call first?" my pops ask. And he serious too.

"I was over by here with my friend, and I ain't think it was gonna be a problem or anything."

My pops step aside and let me in, but I don't know why it even took this long. "Hurry up," he go. "We in the middle of something."

"I can see that," I say. "Y'all go back to what you was watching. I'ma be in and outta here." I go down the hall to the room where my stuff is at. I put the light on and start going through boxes looking for nothing. Only thing that get my attention, that I could say I came here for, is my old pocketknife. Shit kinda rusty, but my pops might believe this is what I came here for.

I hear the TV go back on in the living room and that's when I decide it's okay to sneak over to my pops room. I can't walk no slower or quieter, but I don't know what my pops would do if he catch me.

I don't wanna take a chance and put on the light in they room, so I'm looking 'round in the dark. My pops pants is hanging on a chair and I go through his pockets, but only thing he got in there is a lighter and a couple dollars.

"You find what you need?" my pops yell to me from the living room. Shit.

I fly out to the hall and go, "Yeah, I got it. I'ma just go to the bathroom, then bounce." I turn the light on in the bathroom and close the door, then run back to my moms and pops room.

I head straight for my pops dresser, which got all kinda shit on top. I'm feeling my way 'round in the dark and I don't know how, but I find his key chain. He got all kinda keys on there, but I recognize the storage room key just by how it feel 'cause it's bigger and thicker than the rest of them. Then I spend a while trying to get it off the key chain, 'cause my pops got all the rings hooked together like a crazy person. Shit take forever to take apart.

And I just get away with it too. The second I get the key and fly back to the bathroom, I hear my pops coming down the hall. I flush the toilet and wash my hands and come out the bathroom, cool, like I ain't got nothing to worry 'bout. My pops is practically right in front of the door, like he waiting for me or something. "Everything good?" he ask me.

"Yeah." I take the knife outta my pocket like I need to show him proof or something. "I needed this for —" Damn. Why the fuck I'ma need a knife tonight? "My friend wanna borrow it." Sound as stupid coming out my mouth as it did in my head.

I go back down the hall to the front door and say to both of them, "A'ight, I'ma see y'all next week at the agency, then." And I'm outta there fast as I can without looking like I'm up to something.

Me and Patrick go straight to the storage room 'cause I ain't gonna wait 'til tomorrow to get the equipment and give my pops time to figure out I stole that key. We grab the hand truck and the rope and shit, ready to load up that truck and get the fuck outta there, but the second I open that door, even before I turn on the lights, I can just hear the echo in the room and know the place is empty. Patrick flip the light switch and go, "Where —?"

"I can't believe this," I say, and it kinda feel like I got punched or something. "My pops, he musta rented it out or —"

"What you gonna do?"

I just stand there looking at nothing. "I don't know," I tell him. "I don't know." And I don't.

TWENTY-SEVEN

By six o'clock Saturday, me and Patrick is at the community center on Jerome near Bedford Park Avenue, where Jasmine party gonna be at. I'm tired as hell, trying to get myself awake by drinking Pepsi and Red Bulls, but they ain't working yet. I ain't gonna lie. I hardly got no sleep last night, not after seeing that empty storage room and knowin' I was gonna be the reason Jasmine gonna have a fucked-up, no-music party.

I been stressed out all night, counting and recounting my money, but all I had was the two hundred dollars Andre paid me, the five hundred dollars I never told him I kept, and some of the chump change I brung back with me from Atlanta. I had to get speakers and a amp, and all the other shit I needed before Jasmine party, and I ain't think I was gonna be able to do it.

But I did. Me and Patrick got all his equipment in the truck and drove to that DJ store in Astoria. I ain't even look at all the nice shit in the front. Nah, I went straight to the back. Still, after I picked out the amp and speakers I wanted to get, I still needed a hundred seventy dollars more, and I don't know why I still had that man chain in my backpack, but I went 'round the corner to this pawn-shop and sold that shit for two hundred twenty dollars. Got beat on the price 'cause that chain probably cost my pops three times that, but I ain't care. All I was thinking 'bout was buying what I needed to get through the party tonight.

Crazy thing is, my pops been calling my cell all morning and afternoon and I been ignoring every one of them calls. I know he figured out I took his key, but ain't no way he know where I'm at now. Shouldn't of never lent his shit out to whoever he gave it to. Now he gonna hafta wait to get his key back.

Fuck him anyway.

While me and Patrick set up the DJ table, three ladies is decorating the walls and the tables they got all 'round the dance floor. Everything, all the tablecloths and balloons and flowers is light purple and white, and all the chairs got big purple bows on the back. All the stuff they taping to the walls, the balloons, the streamers got SWEET SIXTEEN written on it.

On the other side of the room two ladies is setting up the food tables and even them tables got purple bows on them. The whole thing outta control, you ask me.

"Can't wait for the females to get here," Patrick say.

"I know they gonna be fine, 'cause remember them girls Jasmine came to your other party with, them dancers?" He laugh, all excited. "I hope she bring them again."

I'm plugging in cables in the back of the amp. "What you gonna do if she bring them? Ask one of them to dance?"

"Yeah," he go, but his voice don't sound like even he believe what he saying.

I'ma hafta see it for myself. I been so busy that I ain't had time to try and get him in no better shape. We only got the chance to play ball once. Dude was outta breath, running 'round the court without hardly picking his feet up off the ground. But I think it was a good thing for him, getting his heart beating fast and shit. And least he was outside for a change.

My cell ring. Again. This is getting annoying already.

"Your pops?" Patrick ask.

"He be a'ight," I say, turning off my cell and sticking it in my backpack. I got no time for him, not tonight. I need to focus on making this the best party Jasmine could think of.

It's, like, twenty minutes to eight when Emiliano get there. He walk in like he the man, in a black suit and a white shirt. Dude's shoulders is, like, three times the size of mines, but he short. Good. He come over to the table and give me this weird look like he sizing me up and say, "Everything ready?"

Why he looking at me like that for? The first thing I think of is, do he know what happened between me and Jasmine?

Even though I don't like the way he staring me down, I need the six hundred dollars he paying me, so I gotta put up with it. "Yeah, we ready," I tell him. "And I got all the music you want."

"*Bueno*, Tyrell."

That's all he say, then he walk away from my DJ table and go 'round the room talking in Spanish to everybody else that's fixing up the room.

I put on some music to test the sound out. My speakers sound like shit. Me and Patrick gotta adjust a lot of levels to try and make it sound halfway decent.

The party s'posed to start at 8:00, and I swear, them kids start coming in, like, 8:01. It's just like the parties my pops throw. Them people act like they never been out before. I know a lot of these kids from school but not everybody. And course I never seen none of them all dressed up like this. Patrick eyes almost fall outta his head checking out the girls. I don't blame him though. Jasmine got some bangin' friends.

I put my headphones on. Time to make this happen.

A half hour later and I can't believe I'm actually doing this, playing this kinda music. I'm getting into it too. Something 'bout the beat just keep my energy up. I'm talking on the mic and making people feel good. Having fun. Shit, I could probably get good at this and do more salsa parties.

Emiliano is walking 'round acting like he in charge, but the second he turn his back, I can see that some kids in the back of the room smuggled in bottles of vodka or something and they passing it 'round. They could pass a little this way too.

Everything working out alright, but I'm waiting for Jasmine to get there. I wanna see her. I gotta be honest, I can't stop thinking 'bout yesterday, everything 'bout it just been going 'round and 'round in my mind all night and day.

But I still need to look her in the eye and see if she really got feelings for me. 'Cause, yeah, I'm confused as hell 'bout what happened. What's that s'posed to mean for us? That we not just friends no more? That we together?

Finally, 'bout ten, fifteen minutes later, Emiliano come over to my table and tell me Jasmine ready to come in. He got a video camera in his hands and everything. I turn the music down to low and get on the mic. "Alright, everybody. I need y'all to turn and face the doors, and put your hands together for our very special, beautiful Sweet Sixteen girl."

Everybody do what I say and when the doors open up I put the song on that Emiliano told me to play, something called "Esta Es Mi Noche," and she come into the room looking so goddamn sexy in this long, light purple dress that fit her body tight in all the right places. My mouth probably hanging open, but I can't help it. I ain't never seen her looking like this, with all that makeup on and her hair curled. Man, my mind go right there, to trying to figure out a way to get that dress off her, to see what's under all that. She look hot, yeah, but I just wanna mess her up a little bit.

She walk into the room looking kinda nervous, which ain't like her. At school she love walking into a room with a whole bunch of people there. She do it like she the one everybody waiting for. But now, I don't know if it's just that there's, like, a hundred-something people here, or just that this place all big and Emil standing in the middle of the room videotaping everything, but she ain't acting like herself.

Some girl I never seen before come up to the table and practically snatch the mic outta my hand. She tall and pretty, but by the look in her eyes, I can tell she high on something. "Happy Birthday, Jasmine!" she yell so loud she don't even need to be holding the mic. "Now let's get wild, girl!"

I turn up the volume on the song and Jasmine and this girl and some other females all dance 'round in a circle, singing loud and laughing. Patrick lean over and say, "What you wanna play next?" but I'm not even listening to him. I'm watching Jasmine. She look like she having more fun, or least trying to have more fun. But I don't get why she ain't relaxing when she know everybody here and it's the party she been waiting for all summer.

Patrick cue up a song for me, something else Emil had on his list, and I mix into it hardly paying attention to what I'm doing. I'm still looking at her, but the thing is, I don't think she even look my way one time. It's weird but, okay, she just got here. We got time.

Three, four songs later, the party really taking off. Jasmine is still dancing and Emil still standing there video-taping her. Not nobody else at the party. Just her.

I swear, I ain't never gonna understand that dude. I know he spent a lot of money on this party and he wanna get it on video, but ain't Jasmine gonna wanna see the other people at her party except herself? Emiliano got real problems.

After a while, I can't take it no more. Jasmine been dancing and saying hi to people, hugging them and shit, but she still ain't come over to me yet. It's like she don't even know I'm there, even though I been talking on the mic and everything.

I gotta change shit up. Slow it down. Make a move.

I slap on some slow Marc Anthony song, something I know girls like, leave from behind the DJ table, and cut through everybody to get to Jasmine. I slip my arm 'round her waist real smooth and pull her real close to me. For a couple seconds I ain't sure if this is what she want, but then she wrap her arms 'round me and we start moving together to the beat. It don't take long for the whole floor to be filled up with couples.

For a while, me and her is dancing without even saying anything. For me, it just feel good to hold her again. Having her body next to mines like this make me remember everything that happened yesterday, and with the way she look and smell tonight, I'm just wanting more of what she gave me.

Out the corner of my eye, I look to see if Emiliano is still videotaping, but he ain't. He over by the food tables helping the caterers set up the hot food. Good. He busy.

"Jasmine," I say, trying to whisper but be louder than the music, "I wanna . . . You think we could go someplace, just me and you, and spend some time together?" The way she pressed up against me and moving her hips to the beat, all I'm thinking 'bout is putting it in her.

"Ty," she say, still not really looking me in the eye. She making it real hard to read her. "I can't."

I take her face in both my hands and make her look up at me. "Why not?"

"It's my party," she say, and look down again. "And Emil —" She look over at him real fast. "If I leave, he's gonna come looking for me."

This ain't what I wanna hear. "Where his girlfriend at anyway?"

"Him and Ana broke up last week."

"He look like he don't got nothing to do with hisself."

Jasmine shrug and rest her head on my shoulder and we finish the song. I wanted to be with her and talk, find out what's going on with her and with us. But dancing with her, with my arms 'round her, this alright too. If this is all I can get.

Patrick take over for me and play something else when Marc Anthony done. And since I don't want Emiliano thinking me and Jasmine is more than friends, I let her go. She give me a little smile, then turn and dance with some other guy I kinda know from school. And now I gotta walk by myself through all them couples slow dancing and kissing and shit.

I'm just 'bout back to the DJ table when I see her come into the room. Reyna. Jasmine sister. And straight up, girl looking busted.

TWENTY-EIGHT

Damn, I don't know where this girl been, but she look like
she been through a lot of shit since the last time I seen her.
Actually, I only seen her one day, when her and Jasmine
first came to the shelter in January. Back then, she looked
alright. Kinda hot.

Now she standing here looking damn-near crackhead
skinny, wearing a short, thin, almost see-through skirt, a
black T-shirt, and sandals with her toes hanging over the
front of them.

She tore up.

It take Jasmine only, like, a minute to notice her there,
and even then it's like Jasmine look like she ain't really sure
that's her. But then Jasmine fly 'cross the room all excited,
and her and Reyna hug for a real long time.

Jasmine so happy, even I start to feel better. Maybe
she ain't wanna be with me 'cause she was upset that
Reyna wasn't here. Maybe it ain't had nothing to do
with me.

Just to pick things up, I put on some fast salsa and put some hip-hop beats underneath it. More kids start dancing and the floor is full, everybody having fun, so I keep doing my thing, mixing they music with my old-skool shit, showing off my skills.

Meanwhile, Jasmine and Reyna is now in the corner of the room, standing up and talking. The music is loud and I know they having a hard time hearing each other so they talking real close. I gotta say, I'm glad Reyna showed up no matter how she look.

I play a couple songs, then Emiliano come over to my table again and say, "It's time for Jasmine, she needs to open her . . ."

"Presents?" I ask, 'cause I ain't got all day to wait for him to find the right word.

"Yes. Presents."

I know what he trying to do, but at the same time, he paying me to do what he want. Still, I wait a while, 'til the song through, so Jasmine and Reyna could get more time to talk.

Then I get on the mic and tell everyone to go over to the other side of the room where all the presents is set up, where they got a chair waiting for Jasmine to sit in. Then I put on the song they told me to play real low while she open her gifts. It take Jasmine a little while to leave Reyna side, but everybody waiting for her and she don't got no choice.

Next thing I know, the same girl that snatched the mic out my hand at the beginning of the party come back over and take the mic again. This time she pull it as far away from the table as it would go and as Jasmine open the boxes, this girl read the card and tell everybody who it's from. She taking over my job.

Jasmine get some nice shit too. Somebody give her one of them expensive leather bags girls be going crazy for, and she get silver bracelets, perfume, and a whole bunch of gift cards. She do alright.

So much is going on, it take me a while to see that Emiliano ain't over there no more. He in the corner now talking to Reyna, and by the way they look, it's hard to tell them two used to be together. Emiliano look pissed and Reyna look like she don't wanna hear whatever the fuck he saying. And both they faces is dead serious.

I don't know if he see me staring at them, but next thing I know Emiliano is taking Reyna into this little room that look like either a big closet or a little storage room, and he close the door behind him. What the fuck they doing?

Since Jasmine still opening her presents, I keep looping the song 'round and keep one eye on the door. They only in there, like, two minutes, then they come out. Reyna don't look all that mad, but she head straight for the door and she gone. Just like that. Without even saying bye to Jasmine or nothing.

I'm like, did Emiliano tell her she had to go, that he ain't want her here at the party? Or did he just tell her something that pissed her off enough that she wanted to get up outta here? And why she couldn't say something to Jasmine first? She know how hard Jasmine looked for her just to get her ass here.

When Jasmine through with the presents, and I get my mic back from that girl, I turn the music back up loud, and tell everyone to have fun and eat some more food. Before I get the word "food" out my mouth all the way, Patrick just stop what he doing and head straight for that table. And he cut right in front of a group of girls too.

I shake my head and go back to what I'm doing.

"Ty, did you see where Reyna went?" Jasmine ask, leaning over the table. "She was right over there."

Why I gotta be the one to tell her the bad news? "She left," I say. "I don't know —"

"She's gone?" Jasmine eyes open wide and they already full of tears. "Why would she do that? She should of told me if she —"

"C'mon, Jasmine," I say. She can't do this again. Not here. Not now. "This your party. You gotta hold it together and have fun for everybody here. All your friends is here and, look, they having a good time."

Jasmine nod a couple times.

"And least you know Reyna a'ight. You don't gotta worry 'bout her no more. She okay."

What I'm saying don't really work 'cause she crying. Just standing here by my table like a little kid. I'm 'bout to come 'round to her side and put her in my arms again, when the same girl that keep using my mic come up to her, give her a hug, then take her to a table in the back of the room.

Patrick come back with plates for both of us with all kinds of good Spanish food. He put everything on one plate, chicken and rice with beans, plantains, fried shrimp, some kind of roast beef with vegetables, a cake that look mad sweet with, like, five, six layers or something, and a little cup of something that look like rice pudding, but I ain't sure.

Don't matter neither. I start eating, and I'm so into the food that after a while the music actually stop. It's like dead quiet in there.

I drop the shrimp I'm eating and hurry up to find something to put on. Everybody is stopped dancing and they looking at me like, what up? I throw a song on and get on the mic and say, "Hey, y'all, don't blame me. Blame whoever made this food. *Damn.*"

All the kids laugh and then they start dancing again. And I start eating again.

"Look at that girl over there," Patrick go, all excited. "That's my type." He actually pointing his finger at some girl in a short, gray dress.

That girl is everybody type, for real. "Calm down," I tell him. "Wait a couple minutes, then go over there and ask her if she wanna dance."

Patrick kinda rock back and forth, like he trying to rev hisself up or something.

"I said calm down. I'ma put on some nice smooth shit for y'all to dance to."

Patrick start mumbling to hisself like he practicing what he gonna say. Finally, I tell him to go over there and make his move. And while he on his way, I put my headphones on and mix this Spanish song in with this vinyl record from back in the day called "Silent Morning," the instrumental version. When both them songs is playing at the same time, my opinion, it's gonna make that girl wanna dance with whoever ask her, 'cause she gonna feel like shaking her ass out there.

I watch Patrick do his thing and he definitely ain't no smooth brotha, but least he trying. Gotta say, he is stiff though, and his face look like he need to go take a dump. The girl must feel sorry for him or something 'cause next thing I know they on the floor dancing. I'm laughing when I get on the mic and say, "One point for Patrick." He look over and shake his head.

Jasmine still sitting at that table in the back and now I see what she been doing all this time. I see her pouring vodka in her plastic cup and drinking it down in one swallow. All the kids 'round her is doing the same thing, just drinking and laughing and acting stupid. The worst one is that girl that brung her over there to that table. It's like she pushing Jasmine to drink more. Least that's the way it look from here.

Then they get up and Jasmine is dancing and singing with that girl and spinning 'round in a circle like they trying to make theyself dizzy. I gotta say, Jasmine look like she finally having fun, but I don't think she gonna remember none of it tomorrow.

Emiliano is watching them, but he ain't videotaping and he don't look happy that Jasmine this outta control. But he don't do nothing. He just let her keep doing what she doing.

Patrick come walking back to the table. "What happened?" I ask him. "You got her digits?"

He shake his head. "Nah. She said she a lesbian, but I know what that mean."

"Maybe she is."

"I hear that shit all the time, Ty. C'mon, not every girl in the Bronx can be a lesbian."

I laugh. He do got a point.

A while later Jasmine and the girl is only getting more and more crazy. Now they ain't just dancing by theyself. Them two girls is dancing with guys and grinding on them and shit. I ain't never seen Jasmine like this before. Yeah, I know she upset that Reyna left, but I never even knew she liked to drink. When we was living in that shelter, she would always get mad when I got drunk or high. She would tell me I was stupid for doing that shit.

So it ain't easy watching her like this. I'm happy when it's time to end this party. We only got the community center 'til 3:00, so 'bout 2:20 I turn the music down a little bit and get on the mic to tell everybody we gonna hafta go soon. Jasmine come over to the table and say, "Ty! Did you have a good time because I did. Did you?" She smiling all stupid.

"Yeah, it was good."

"I know!" She come 'round on my side of the table and wrap her arms 'round my neck real hard and hug me. Girl is a hundred percent fucked up.

Then her friend come up behind Jasmine. She giggling for no reason. "This is Tyrell?" she ask, looking me up and down with them drunk, half-closed eyes. "He the one you were telling me about?"

Jasmine cover her mouth. "Yesenia!"

Yesenia smile at me and say to Jasmine, "He's cute."

Jasmine try to change the subject. She introduce me and Yesenia, who I find out is Emiliano niece. "She's from Connecticut. Remember I was telling you about her?"

"Yeah," I say, and nod even though I don't remember shit.

"We gotta go," Yesenia say. "Nice meeting you, Tyrell." She giggle again and pull Jasmine away. Jasmine wave to me as she go.

Even as Jasmine hugging everybody bye, I play one last song for the kids that ain't ready for the night to be over yet. Patrick start packing up the albums and everything.

Finally, Emil come over and hand me a envelope that's nice and fat. "You are very good, Tyrell."

"Thanks," I say.

When he gone, I turn away from the kids that's still dancing and count out the money. Seven hundred dollars.

He gave me a hundred-dollar tip.

TWENTY-NINE

I get up mad late, still tired from that crazy party. I swear, Sweet Sixteens is getting outta control. Them girls be acting like it's the last party they ever gonna get. But it's Jasmine that kinda surprised me. I definitely ain't expect her to be like that last night.

I text Jasmine. u happy wit the party?

While I'm waiting for her to text back, I drag my ass to the shower. After I'm dressed and looking good, I knock on Cal door to see if he alright. "You up?"

"I'm out here," Cal call to me from the living room and there he at, chilling on the couch. He still look like shit, face all cut up and stitches over his eye, but he outta bed. Got his leg up on some pillows and he drinking orange juice outta the container and watching Greg play some shit on the PlayStation. Least Greg ain't screaming at nobody on the fucking microphone. Probably too early for that shit.

"I thought you wasn't never gonna get out that bed," I say to Cal.

"Can't keep me down," he go. "You know that."

"You feeling a'ight?"

"Everything hurt like hell. Them pills ain't even working no more."

"Then give 'em to me." I laugh.

"Fuck you, Ty." He try to laugh too, but damn, I can tell laughing make everything hurt more.

"Watch this," Greg say, and me and Cal watch him steer his Humvee over these real steep mountains with all kinda folks shooting at him and shit. He just 'bout to make it 'cross this bridge when some kinda bomb or something go off and his truck fly off the edge, like two thousand feet down, and explode into fire when it hit the rocks at the bottom. "Shit. Fuck," Greg go. "Them dudes is vicious motherfuckers. Would blow they own mothers up, asshole bastards."

Me and Cal laugh. Personally, I can't believe how into video games Greg is. He take them serious. He sweating and shit.

"Help me up," Cal say. "I need to get in the shower. You know you funky when you smell your own ass."

"You sure you ready? I don't want you to fall in the tub and then I gotta drag your naked ass outta there."

"Nah, no way, man. Just let me drown if that happen."

Me and him still laughing. "You stupid," I tell him.

"Just help me up."

It take a while to get Cal down the hall to the bathroom, but when I get him in there, he say he got it, so I leave but tell him not to lock the door in case I gotta save his life or something. Dude do kinda stink, so I let him do his thing.

I go back to my room 'cause I forgot my cell there, and when I check it, there still ain't no answer from Jasmine. She probably too busy having fun with that wild girl to think 'bout me.

I'm still in my room when the doorbell ring. A second later, Greg yell out, "Ty." I actually know what he gonna say before he say it. "Your pops is here."

Shit.

I take a deep breath, a couple of them as a matter of fact, before walking back down the hall. I know. This is gonna be bad.

"Where the key?" my pops say before I even get down the hall good.

I look him dead in the eye. "What? You lost your key or something?"

He stare back at me. "Don't lie to me, Tyrell. Don't disrespect me like that."

"Like what? I don't know what you talking 'bout." I throw my arms open real wide and go, "What, you wanna search me or something?"

But nothing I'm doing faze him for a second. He get right in my face and say, "Ty, I don't want to embarrass you in front of your friend."

I look over at Greg, who got the game on pause for a change, watching us. Only thing, I can't tell if he look like he ready to jump in and help me fight if my pops attack me, or if he 'bout to cut and run.

My pops still in my face and I don't know what he 'bout to do. But he stay calm and say, "I rented the equipment to somebody for Friday night. Yesterday morning —"

"Who you rent it to?"

"Dante. You got a problem with that?"

I wanna say, "Yeah, I do." But I don't 'cause I don't want him asking me no questions 'bout Dante. I'ma listen to Regg on this one. So I just shrug and go, "Nah."

"So, yesterday, I get out my bed early in the morning to meet Dante at the storage place so we could lock all that shit back inside, and I pull out my keys and the only one not there is the one for the storage room. Now, how you think that key got off my ring?"

"I — I don't —"

"Get me my fucking key." He still not raising his voice, but I gotta be honest. The way he look make me think he 'bout to go off.

"I don't need your key. Or your equipment. Or nothing from you. I got my own equipment to throw my own parties, to make my own money. So why I'ma take your key for?" I turn 'round and start going back down the hall to my room. "I'ma show you."

He follow me. Right in the middle of the room I got the two new speakers. One of them got the amp on top of it, and all the records and lights and shit I bought is in a box on top of the other speaker. The DJ table folded up against the closet. "See. Told you. I don't need nothing from you no more."

My pops look 'round and outright laugh. I mean, I know he laughing at my cheap-ass equipment, but it feel like he laughing at me. 'Cause I'm the asshole that bought this shit. "You tried to steal my equipment," my pops go, talking like he got everything figured out or something. "You went to the storage place, the shit was gone, and you went out and bought a bunch of fucking garbage." He laugh again. "You pay more than fifty bucks for this shit?"

I don't say nothing.

"If you did, you was robbed."

"You finished here?" I ask him.

"I want my fucking key!"

He move over to the box that got the records and shit in it and, real fast, he just knock the whole box off the speaker. It hit the floor with a couple cracking sounds and I know something broke, but alright, ain't nothing in there that cost all that much. I don't care.

That's when I see Greg standing in the doorway to my room, and it's like, he got my back. I don't know how long he been there, but I'm probably looking like a pussy to Greg, lying to my pops like I'm scared to give him back a key I ain't even really use. So, before I think too much 'bout it, I go into my backpack and get the key and give it back to him. "Here."

He put the key in his pocket and then he just grab me by the throat again and this time I think he really gonna choke me. His hand is big and it just getting tighter and tighter. I know he gonna hit me or slam me into something and I'm, like, tightening my muscles, waiting for it, but it don't happen. Greg come in the room and say, "C'mon, now, Mr. Green. You don't gotta do this. C'mon."

My pops don't let up though. He laugh at me and say, "You keep telling me you your own man now, but you keep needing me and my shit." He let go of me. "You even need my friends."

Where the fuck that come from? "This don't got nothing to do with Regg," I say, still catching my breath. "Why you bring Regg into this?"

"If you don't need me, you don't need him. You ready to be a man, right? That's what you keep saying."

"That's what I mean."

"And where the fuck my chain at?"

Now Cal in the room. He still in his sweatpants and look like he ain't even got in the shower yet.

I ain't in the mood to lie no more. I stare my pops down and tell him, "You know, sometimes shit get lost when you leave it behind for a year. Sometimes shit get sold too."

He stare back at me for a long time, and nobody say nothing. Still, I'm getting myself ready for a fight. But he don't go after me. What he do is take both his hands and push the amp off from the top of the speaker, hard.

And when it hit the floor it crack and break like the cheap piece of shit it is. Just like that, it's through.

Before I get to say anything to him, before he say anything to me either, he just up and leave the room. He gone. Just like that.

A second later, I hear the front door close and all three of us look at each other like, what just happened?

Cal and Greg start talking on and on 'bout my pops being crazy and my amp, and all that, but maybe I'm crazy too 'cause I'm kinda feeling good.

Okay, yeah, I don't got no amp no more, but least I ain't back down. I stood up for myself no matter what he said or did to me. I mean, I ain't never disrespected the man to his face like that, and it feel good to do it now.

I don't care what he say. I don't need his ass no more. And now me and him both know it.

THIRTY

It's, like, a hour after my pops left, and all three of us been sitting 'round the kitchen, eating and snapping on my pops.

"And what the fuck kinda shoes was he wearing?" Greg say. "Damn, man. I ain't seen them shits since them old movies they used to put on late at night? What was that guy name? Shaft? Remember them movies, Ty? Your pops musta got them shoes from back in them days, man."

We all laugh. I know what they doing, trying to make me feel better, but truth is, I'm alright. The pressure off now. I did what I had to do, got through Jasmine party and ain't backed down in front of my pops. Sometimes you gotta show people that you different now, that shit change.

That's when Cal get up off from his chair real slow and put his bowl in the sink where there's already a whole pile of dirty dishes. Then he say outta nowhere, "I'm going back to work tonight."

I don't even believe what I'm hearing. "I thought you said you was still —"

"I know, I'm jacked up, but you know how Andre get." Cal start limping to the living room. "I'm tired of hearing his mouth. And all I gotta do is go outside and stand there."

What he saying is so crazy even Greg look surprised. Me and him look at each other like, what he talking 'bout? I don't know what to say, so I ask him if he sure. "I mean, what 'bout your ribs? They ain't even —"

"I'm good," Cal go.

I nod a couple times. "Okay, okay. You gonna be a'ight."

I can't say I'm feeling all that good 'bout this, but what I'ma do? He his own man too. He making his own decision.

Troy call me a while later from his foster mother phone. He whispering and talking fast. "Why you didn't come to see me for a long time?" he ask me. "I was looking for you and looking for you."

Damn. That make me feel bad. "I'm sorry, man. I been real busy." Busy getting with Jasmine. Busy working for Andre. "How you doing? Everything okay?"

"No." He sound kinda sad.

"Somebody do something to you or hurt you or something?" 'Cause I will roll up there if I hafta.

"No. I just wanna be at home and be with everybody else."

"I know, man. It's gonna happen. But —"

"I know, it's gonna take a long time, right?" He sigh all heavy. He sound too tired for a kid to be.

"Yeah, we working on it all the time, okay?" I hear Ms. Woods voice in the background like she talking to some people. "You ask Ms. Woods if you could use her phone?"

"Not really. She has company and I'm bored."

"Don't get in trouble, Troy. You know you s'posed to ask people to use they stuff."

"Sorry."

"It's okay. Just hang up and put her phone back before she catch you. And I'ma come see you tomorrow, okay?"

"You promise?"

"When I tell you I'ma be there, I'ma be there. I don't hafta promise. You got my word as a man, okay?"

"Okay."

Me and him hang up and I'm really feeling bad for that kid, stuck in the apartment with that woman all weekend with nothing to do and nobody to play with. I ain't gonna miss no more of them agency visits. I don't wanna do nothing to fuck us up from getting him back soon.

"The other day, me and Jasmine —" Even as I start to tell Cal 'bout what happened, I can't stop the big stupid smile that I get on my face. "She let me hit it."

Me and Cal is outside 'bout 7:30 and I'm hanging with him while he work. Dude look like he 'bout to fall over and I'm there to watch out for him, but I'm trying not to let him know that. I don't wanna make him feel like the pussy Andre told him he was the other day.

"You don't think I know that?" Cal say. "You know the walls in the projects made outta Legos and glue. All the noise y'all was making. Even them pills couldn't keep me 'sleep through all that moaning and shit. And that was coming from you!" He laugh.

I laugh with him, shaking my head. "I don't know what happened, man. I mean, me and Jasmine? That shit came outta nowhere. We was just hanging out, listening to music, and then she start talking 'bout she got feelings for me. And she taking off her clothes."

"Shit."

My mind go back to everything that went down in my room the other day. "That girl — she. She's —"

Cal laugh. "Look at you. You can't even talk no more."

"She wild, yo. That's all I'ma say." I know Cal want more details, but that's all I'ma tell him. I'ma keep everything to myself.

"She turned you out, man."

"Damn straight," I say, 'cause ain't no use trying to lie 'bout it. I been turned out. For real.

Which remind me. Why she ain't text me back? What I'm s'posed to do, wait all day and night to hear from her?

"You got too many girls, man," Cal say. "Never thought it could happen, but you got too many, son."

I kinda laugh, what he saying is so stupid. "I don't got none of them. Adonna kicked me to the curb, man."

I tell him everything that happened when he was in the hospital and how Adonna wasn't even trying to hear my side of the story.

"You gonna try and get her back?" he ask me, and I just shake my head 'cause I don't know if I wanna try again only to hafta see the back of her head as she walking away from me. Cal looking at me. "I mean, who you really want? Her or Jasmine?"

"I don't know anymore. Girls is making me crazy."

"You ain't still thinking about Novisha, right? I hope you ain't."

Cal never could understand why me and her was together. "Nah," I tell him. "Never." I don't know how many times I gotta tell him that.

A dude come out our building and hand Cal some money fast. Then he walk 'cross the street, over by where Keith standing. Cal give Keith whatever sign they worked out and Keith hand the guy the weed. Keith real smooth for a kid. The whole thing don't take more than a minute, and the dude on his way back to the building.

Then Cal ask me, "You love her?"

"Who we talking 'bout?" My head hurt from thinking 'bout females.

"Jasmine. You love her?"

"I don't know," I tell him, and it's the truth too. "I don't know."

Cal look me in the eye. "How many times you gonna say 'I don't know'?"

"I don't know, " I say again, and me and him both laugh. "I mean, I love her. Course. We friends. But I don't get what she mean by she got feelings for me. Girl got me mad confused and shit."

"My advice," Cal start, like I'm looking for advice 'bout females from him, a guy with the most fucked-up relationship I know. "Go for it with Jasmine," he say. "Y'all already tight. Y'all care 'bout each other. She hot as any female out here, and she giving it up to you. What more you want? You crazy to let that go."

I don't say nothing.

"Listen to me, Ty. You been walking around here for how many months now, no girl, all lonely and shit. Now you got one. Be happy."

He right. I do need a girl. My mind was set on Adonna. But maybe he right. Maybe it's s'posed to be Jasmine.

I don't know.

THIRTY-ONE

I go visit Troy at camp the next day like I said I would. It's raining and all the kids is playing inside. Just like before, Troy ain't playing with nobody. He in the back of the room sitting and watching a cartoon on the TV with a couple other kids, but none of them is talking to each other.

I don't know, but every time I see Troy he getting more and more quiet and to hisself. The agency sent him to this camp so he could make friends and have fun, but he just look bored and sad.

I sit with Troy for a little while, then when the commercial come on, I bring him over to the other side of the room so me and him can talk before Ms. Woods get there and bust me. The thing I wanna make sure he know is that, yeah, our pops is out and all that, but that don't mean things is gonna change for him right now. He gonna hafta be chill where he at for a while.

But I don't even get to say none of that 'cause when I ask Troy how he doing, he get real sad and say, "Ms. Woods.

255

She said, she told me that she gonna change my school. And I gotta go to another school where Ben and Dondre don't go, and I ain't gonna have no friends now."

Fuck.

I gotta take a breath and not say something that's only gonna make him more upset, if that's possible. "She say why she wanna do that?"

"She said my first school is too far, and she said they got a school that's really, really close, but I never seen it."

My mind running, trying to think 'bout what I can do, if I can even do anything. "I'ma talk to Ms. Thomas," I tell him. "You know, from the agency? I'ma try and fix this, a'ight?"

He nod, but I can tell he don't think I can do nothing. And I don't think so neither. But least I can try. I don't want Troy to hafta start going to a whole 'notha school now with no friends. How many things gotta change in this kid life?

I don't even get a chance to talk to him 'bout nothing else 'cause a couple seconds later I see Troy foster mother coming through the door on the other side of the gym. It's only like a couple minutes after five. She musta got off work early or something. And ain't nothing I can do now neither 'cause she looking right at me.

Ms. Woods come 'cross the gym, walking real fast. She fucking pissed, but damn, I'm like, I hope she don't start nothing in front of all these kids. And I hope she don't say nothing that's gonna make the counselors tell me I can't come and see Troy no more.

When she get to us, she say, "Tyrell, what are you doing here?" She ain't yelling or nothing. She look like she holding her anger inside.

"I came to see Troy," I say. I mean, why else she think I'm there?

"Well, isn't it enough to see him at the agency? Why do I bring him there if you're just going to sneak behind my back and see him here?"

Troy look from her to me and back to her again. "What's wrong?" he go.

"Nothing," I say, staring at Ms. Woods.

I tell Troy to put the cartoon back on and that I'ma be over there in a second. When he run back to the TV, I say to Ms. Woods, "He my brother. Just 'cause the state took him away, you know that don't mean I only wanna see my brother once a week."

"I understand that, but you have to see things from my point of view. Troy's been with me for a couple of months now and he's adapting to life in my house, a home with structure. Then every week, I have to take him to the agency, and most of the time, before your father was released from prison, your mother wouldn't even show up. And you weren't there either. So I had to bring him home and deal with his disappointment. That wasn't easy."

Damn. Why she gotta make me feel guilty?

She keep on talking. "Now your father is out and you all are filling Troy's head with promises, telling him he's going home and making him think he doesn't have to listen to me anymore. Now he's disobedient and mad all the time. You know, Tyrell, we all have to work together here. I'm not working against you. We're all doing this for Troy."

"You doing this for Troy? Then why you changing his school? That ain't gonna help him none. He 'bout to get put in the regular class, but if you move him, they pro'ly gonna keep him in special ed. That ain't good for him."

"Tyrell, I'm a working woman and I don't have time to take him halfway across the Bronx every morning to get him to school. There's a good school right near my apartment. And they have an after-school program with tutoring. It's a good thing for him. Don't worry."

"He got friends at his old school, you know."

"He'll make new friends."

I ain't in the mood to fight with Ms. Woods, not here in front of all these kids. So I drop it. I go over and tell Troy I hafta go, but I'ma be back soon. No matter what Ms. Woods say, no way I'ma let her keep me from my brother.

I try calling Jasmine again 'cause I still ain't heard from her, but her cell go to voicemail. She probably at work. Her boss don't let her use her cell and she usually too busy for that anyway. But I need to talk to her. This is stupid already. I need to know what's going on between us.

So I walk a couple blocks even though it's still raining and get on the bus and take it to the restaurant where she work at. The whole way there, I'm not sure why I'm even going there. Why she couldn't just call me back yesterday? Why she ain't acting like herself? Me and her used to be able to talk 'bout anything. Then we hooked up and now everything changed and I don't know why.

On the bus, I try calling the first foster mother again, but the call go to voicemail and I leave another message, asking if she could call me back real soon. Damn. I don't know why I can't get ahold of her. I wish I knew her cell number. Time running out. I gotta get Troy outta Ms. Woods house before she put that school transfer through. Then it's gonna be too late.

I get to Jasmine job at the Spanish restaurant and stand in the little waiting area for a couple minutes watching her work. She go by two tables smiling, checking to see if everybody okay, and then she go to another table and take the family orders. She look nice and she acting kinda friendly and everything, but something 'bout her is off. She acting kinda fake, you ask me. She just going through the motions.

Jasmine still don't see me standing there, and after she take the people order and start to walk over by the counter, I whisper to her, "Jasmine."

She turn 'round. "Ty? What? Why are you —?"

Weird thing is, she look kinda embarrassed or something. What, she don't want me coming to her job no more? She don't wanna be seen with me? "I ain't heard from you, so I —"

"I'm sorry," she go. "I know I didn't call you back, but I, I'm just tired, you know. We took Yesenia back to Connecticut right after the party and stood there all day yesterday. Then we had to drive back real early this morning so Emil could get to work on·time, and I had to come to work too." She look down.

"What time you getting off?" I ask her. "'Cause I wanna talk to you."

"I get off at seven, but Emil's gonna pick me up on his way home from the gym, you know, because it's raining. And he —"

"A'ight," I say, and stand there waiting for her to say something, tell me she wanna spend time with me too.

But all she say is, "I gotta get back to work, Ty. I'll call you when I get some free time."

She give me a real fast hug and turn back and go to the counter. It take me, like, two, three minutes standing there before I get it.

I been dismissed.

THIRTY-TWO

I wake up hearing banging. Banging. It's Tuesday night – nah, it's Wednesday 'cause it's something after three in the morning, and my first thought is that somebody musta broke into our place. Then I think somebody must be tryin' to attack Cal again. I remember that Cal crashed on the couch, and I jump outta bed and run down the hall, ready to kick ass if I need to protect my friend.

But the apartment dark and the banging still happening on the other side of the door. I can tell there's more than one person kicking 'cause no way one dude could kick that many times that fast. Even though it's dark, I can see that Cal awake now too. "You know who out there?" I whisper to him.

"Nah." He sit up straight. "What you think they want?"

"I don't know." But we both probably thinking the same thing — that they either the same dudes that attacked Cal last week or some other dudes that's trying to rob the apartment or something. They kicking so hard, for the first time I'm happy Andre put all them locks on the door.

When the kicking stop, I go closer to the door and look through the peephole to see who out there. I see two guys, both looking like they 'round twenty years old or something. I never seen them before so I know they ain't from Bronxwood, but least they don't got no weapons or nothing. Nothing I can see anyway. One of the guys see me and yell, "Where Greg? Get Greg."

Me and Cal look at each other. I'm thinking, Greg? What they want Greg for? I mean, yeah, he the one that handle the stash, but what they think he got here?

Cal get up off the couch. It take him a while but he come over to the door and look through the peephole. He shake his head. "I don't think they the dudes that, you know . . ." He stop talking.

I don't know what to say neither. Or what to do 'bout this situation. "Greg here?" I ask.

"I think. All I know is before I went to sleep he was coming in and out all night. I don't know what he was doing."

Greg don't never make no sense to me.

"I'ma wake him up," Cal say and go down the hall. He still walking real slow, so it's gonna take a while. I check the peephole again and the guys is still there. Matter of fact, one of them looking right at me. They know we in here and we just ignoring them.

I move away from the door just in case they do something stupid like shoot up the door or some shit. I don't know what they want or what they 'bout to do. Wouldn't be the first time somebody at Bronxwood got they door shot up.

Cal come back and say, "He coming." And me and him wait.

Finally, I hear Greg door open and slam behind him, and he come down the hall. He musta been dead 'sleep 'cause half his face is dented in and shit. He look mad too, but what he want us to do? Not wake his ass up and let some dudes keep kicking our door all night? I don't even get how he could sleep through all that noise. It probably woke up everybody on this floor. "What the fuck going on?" he ask. He mad but he whispering.

I shrug. "They want you."

"Me? What for?"

The kicking start up again and I don't know if it's 'cause they heard Greg voice and know he up now or what. If it's possible, the kicking even louder now. They wanna get in here. "Greg, you sure you don't keep no weed or nothing in the apartment?"

"How many times you gonna ask me that, Ty? I told you. Everything at the stash house. We don't even got no money."

"Then why they here for? They must know something?"

"I ain't lying to you," Greg say. But this time, even though it's half dark in here, I'm looking in his eyes, and I know for a fact that he lying his ass off. Probably been lying this whole time.

And while I'm thinking 'bout it, and while I got the chance 'cause for the first time I ain't hear him lock his door behind him, I take off running down the hall to his room so I could see for myself what he got in there.

When I push the door open all the way and flip the lights on, all I can say is, "Oh, shit," 'cause Greg whole room full of drugs. Not weed though. All I see is plastic bags of pills, all kinda pills with different colors and shit. Dude got enough pills in here to — "You running a side business," I say as Greg come up behind me. "You fucking —" Greg crash hisself into me and knock me down on the floor.

"Get outta here, Ty," he say.

I jump up, ready to fight if he wanna. "How you gonna do this?" I ask him.

Cal finally get to the room and his face go from surprised to pissed in, like, two seconds. The first thing out his mouth is, "This the reason them dudes is out there? This the reason why you wasn't where you was supposed to be when . . ." He shake his head. "You the brother they was talking about." His eyes is like stabbing Greg. I ain't never seen Cal this pissed. Never.

It all making sense now. Cal said they beat him up 'cause his brother was selling in somebody else hood. I thought they was talking 'bout Andre, but it wasn't him.

"You a asshole, Greg," I say. "'Cause of you, your brother almost was killed out there. How that make you feel?"

"I ain't do nothing," Greg say. "I'm just making my own money. You think I wanna work for Andre my whole life?"

"You were s'posed to be protecting Cal," I say. "But you too busy —"

"You don't know shit, Ty. Get the fuck out —"

That's when Cal run up on him. I ain't think he had the strength in him, but he must be working on crazy power or something 'cause he jump on Greg and knock him down and then Cal start swinging on his head. Hard. He ain't playing neither.

But as much as I wanna see Greg get his ass kicked, I don't wanna see Cal hurt hisself doing it. So I grab Cal under his arms and pull him up off Greg. "C'mon, man. C'mon." He stronger than I think. "Cal, c'mon. You don't wanna do this."

"Yeah, I do." He spittin' mad.

I finally pull Cal off him and make him leave outta Greg room. The second we out, Greg slam and lock his door like, what's the point now? We already know what he got going on in there. I take Cal back out to the living room real slow. I make him sit back down on the couch and go get him some Pepsi. He gotta calm down. Chill. Dude ribs ain't even through being healed.

"I wanna kill him," Cal say after a while.

"Me too."

Good thing Greg locked his ass in his room 'cause it take a lot for me to not go back down the hall and give him a little of what Cal got from them dudes. But Cal sitting on the couch breathing hard and back in pain again, so for now I gotta look out for him. 'Cause nobody else gonna do that. Andre all talk, saying how they running a family business and they doing everything for everybody else. But that's all bullshit.

They only looking out for theyself.

THIRTY-THREE

I couldn't hardly sleep, even after them dudes left and everything settled back down. Cal took one of his pain pills and passed out on the couch. And I went back to my room to try and sleep, but I was too pissed off for that. My brain couldn't stop thinking 'bout the fact that Greg been lying all this time, telling us what we wanted to hear. And all this time, living here, I been putting my own freedom on the line for some shit Greg doing just for hisself.

The thing that I couldn't stop thinking 'bout all night is, now that I know what's going on here, what I'ma do 'bout it? Can't stay here, I know that for a fact. But where I'm s'posed to go now?

I ain't looking to up and leave Cal here with Greg by hisself. And I know Cal wouldn't wanna be alone here neither. But everybody else looking out for theyself. Time I started doing that too.

I'm still dragging my ass 'round one in the afternoon

when Patrick come downstairs with his old-ass basketball, like, "C'mon, Ty. We supposed to be working out today."

Shit. I forgot 'bout him. Trying to get Patrick in shape ain't been easy for him, but it's damn near killing me.

But I gotta say, after we done playing, I'm glad he came down to get me 'cause working up a sweat felt good. Patrick can't play for shit, but them other guys that was playing out there today wasn't no good neither so it worked out alright.

I had to leave anyway 'cause we got a agency visit at 5:30 and I gotta be there this time.

"You lookin' tired," my pops say to me the second I walk into the visiting room. "You not getting no sleep?"

"Nah." I shake my head. This the first time I'm seeing him since he came by Cal apartment acting like a fucking asshole, and now he trying to act like he wanna know how I'm doing. Like he care. But if he wanna know what's going on, I'ma tell him. "A couple dudes was kicking at our door in the middle of the night. Shit getting crazy. I don't know how long I'ma be able to stay over there."

I wait for him to say something, but all he do is look at the time on his cell and go, "When that lady bringing Troy? I can't be waiting all night."

I sit down on one of the chairs 'cross from my moms. In her lap she got a big bag from Target. "You buy something for Troy?" I ask.

"Yeah, your father wanted to get him some stuff for school." She look over at my pops. "We still need a lot for the apartment, but . . ."

"I'ma get him a backpack, so don't get that."

"Too late," she say. "Your father got it already. And new sneakers. What you think is in this bag?"

Fuck. What I'm s'posed to get him to go back to school? Underwear and socks? And the thing that get me is the way she saying everything. Like my pops beat me in a competition or something. The look on her face is like she happy her man won.

I'm too tired for all of this. Okay, they wanna buy everything for Troy. Cool. He know who been there for him through all this, and it wasn't them. Definitely not my pops. So what I got to worry 'bout?

Through the whole visit, I sit there while Troy act all excited 'bout the backpack they got him even though I can tell it ain't exactly the one he wanted. He having fun though, and I'm trying not to let nothing my moms and pops do get in the way of that. 'Specially 'cause by the end of the visit he gonna start crying again and we gonna hafta deal with that too.

When he do, I gotta watch the whole thing play out again. I'm fucking tired of this and it ain't over, 'cause my pops set up a meeting with Ms. Thomas after Troy leave to find out what they gotta do to get Troy back.

All three of us squeeze into her piece of office and my

pops get right to the point. "I'm back now and I'm trying to get my family right. What I gotta do to make that happen?"

Ms. Thomas look like she wanted to go home a while ago and she woulda if it wasn't for us. She turn to my moms and say, "You're doing real well with the parenting classes. I got a report that you haven't missed any and that you're asking questions and getting involved in the discussions. That's good." Then she turn to my pops. "Have you been looking for a job? The judge is going to want to know that you're able to support your family."

"I'm a DJ. I know I'm not supposed to throw my own parties because in the past they got outta hand, so what I'm trying to do now is find a club that needs a new house DJ. I been talking to some people and there's a spot out in Staten Island that wanna hire me. I'm waiting now."

I don't know what he talking 'bout, but I know it's bullshit.

"What's the name of the club?" Ms. Thomas ask. "I'll put it down in my notes."

"It's a small club near that college they got out there. You should come check it out sometime." He smile at her like she the hottest woman he ever seen. Like my moms ain't even in the room. "When I start working there, I'ma get you free passes."

Ms. Thomas shake her head, but for the first time she got a little bit of a smile on her face. "Wish I could," she say. "But I never have time anymore. I used to."

"Soon as I get the job, I'ma bring you them passes. You gonna have fun." He still working her, looking her in the eyes and shit.

It don't take long before she say, "Well, since you're all doing everything you're supposed to, I'm going to come by the new apartment and check it out. Then, if the home is safe and everything looks good, I'll let Troy come for a short visit." She don't even see that my pops got her to forget 'bout the name of the club.

After the meeting over, my moms gotta stay there for her parenting class. Me and my pops go down in the same elevator. When we get outside, I'm 'bout to walk to the train when he turn to me and go, "I need you to come by the apartment and help me get Troy room set up before that bitch come by tomorrow."

"I'm s'posed to help you after the way you came to my place the other day and broke my shit? How that helping me?"

"You want Troy to stay where he at?"

Me and him just stare at each other for what seem like a long time. I know what he doing, using Troy to get me to do what he want. It piss me off, but if Ms. Thomas come to the apartment tomorrow and say it ain't good enough for Troy to visit there, I'ma feel like shit. I sigh. "I'ma give you a hour. That's it."

My pops go, "A hour. That's all I need." And we walk down the block to his van.

THIRTY-FOUR

Setting up Troy room ain't all that hard and don't take that long. All I'm thinking 'bout is that I'm doing this for Troy. The foster mother he with now is fucking crazy and I can't take him being with her no more. If this apartment pass the inspection and the visits go good between Troy and my moms and pops, then maybe they could let him come home faster than we thought.

The room come out looking real nice when we through. I know he gonna like it.

I'm thinking we done and I can bounce, when my pops go, "We gotta make your room look like you live here."

"My room?"

My pops stare at me like I'm dumb. "The room with your shit in it."

"A'ight," I say. Might as well get this over with so I can get the fuck outta here already.

Fixing up that room ain't too hard neither. All we do is move all the furniture 'round, put the bed together, and fix the knobs on the dresser that got broke when the marshals moved everything. Weird thing is, me and my pops ain't hardly talking, except when we hafta, like when he tell me to give him the screwdriver, or when I ask him where they put the pillows. I wanna make the room look like I really stay here, so Ms. Thomas could believe it and tell the judge the family together. That the only one missing is Troy.

After I put the sheets and blanket on the bed and everything look alright, I go in the living room where my pops is, sitting on the couch smoking weed. Chillin'. "We done?" I ask him. "'Cause I'ma go now."

"I ordered a pizza," he go, not even looking at me. "You ain't hungry?"

I stand there for a second, not knowing what he want. He trying to get me to stay or something? "I could eat," I say. "I could always eat."

I don't know how it happen, but a hour later both me and him is fucked up, eating the pizza and watching the Yankees, who getting beat 4–1 in the third inning. And we actually talking 'bout shit and laughing. To me, this the way it used to be with him. He always used to be the kinda pops I could chill with and tell stuff to. I'm just trying to figure out if that pops is back for good or what?

"How you and Novisha?" my pops ask, cracking open another can of beer. He on his third can already. I'm still on my first. "Y'all still together?"

"Nah," I say. "We broke up, like, in January."

"Damn. The way you was talking about her, I thought you was gonna be with her forever like me and your moms."

"Yeah, I know. I thought that too, but, I don't know." I think the weed starting to take over more.

"Why y'all split up?" he ask.

I shake my head. "She was lying to me, telling me what I wanted to hear."

"She cheated on you?"

I nod. "Yeah, something like that."

"Shit." My pops take another bite outta his pizza. "You did the right thing, cutting her loose, then. You can't be with a girl like that, that you can't trust."

I lean back against the couch and try to get my high to settle down, but talking 'bout Novisha ain't helping. It just remind me that we through, that she moved on and got another man, and I still don't got nobody. Matter of fact, I still ain't heard from Jasmine, so I don't know what's going on with her neither. Damn, why I get high? Only thing it's doing is making me feel depressed.

My pops light up a cigarette. "You know, Ty, the whole time I was away, your moms came to visit me every week or every other week, but you, you ain't come to see your pops one time in the whole year."

He ain't really asking no question. All he doing is stating a fact. So I don't say nothing.

"How you think that make me feel?" he ask. "My own kid don't make the time to come and see me."

"How you think it make me feel that my own father can't stay home where he s'posed to be? You ever think 'bout that?"

My pops just shake his head.

But I ain't through yet. "You ever think 'bout what it's like for us when you sitting in that jail? Us, living in a motel that got crazy roaches and shit. Us, not having no money 'cause all the money we had went to trying to keep you outta jail. You think 'bout us when you was locked up?"

"Every day," he say. "I thought about y'all every day."

"Truth is, you thinking 'bout us, that ain't help us eat."

Me and him don't say nothing for a while. I wanna up and go, but the weed really messing with me now. I close my eyes for a minute. Then my pops go, "You think I don't know what y'all was going through? You think I wanted to be there?"

I open my eyes and look at him, but he looking down. "I know you ain't wanna be there, but every time you get out, you keep doing the same shit, what got you locked up in the first place. So how that s'posed to look to us, to me? Why you can't just stop?"

"Stop and do what?"

"Something else. I don't know. You figure it out."

He turn to look at me and I stare at him back. "When you get to be a man, you gonna see that sometimes you gotta do shit you don't wanna do just to provide for —"

"I am a man," I say, and think 'bout standing up, but my head so fucked up I don't know if I can right now. I just need him to know that I'm serious.

"Like I was sayin'," he go, "a man gotta do things he don't always wanna do, if he got good reasons. I ain't saying I never made no mistakes. I did. But I made them mistakes for your moms. For you and Troy."

I hear him and I know he believe that shit, but it don't make me feel no better. He act like he don't got no other choice 'cept to do what he doing, but he could just do something different. "If you ain't keep making them mistakes, me and Troy would be home with you. But Troy living with this fucking bitch that don't even want me to see him, and I'm living with a bunch of dealers that ain't even watching each other back. 'Cause of you, 'cause I don't got no father helping me, you know what I had to do? I had to get in they business. I had to risk my own freedom."

I don't know why I'm telling him this, but I'm pissed off now. He ain't the only one that made mistakes, but all of mines was 'cause of him. At the same time, I know what he gonna do now. He gonna say I gotta come home, that staying with Cal and them is too dangerous or something.

"The difference between me and you, Ty," he say, "is I don't complain about my situation. I handle it."

Damn, where that come from? I jump up off the couch. "What I'm complaining 'bout?"

He stand up too and we facing each other eye to eye. "Every time I see you, you telling me about how bad it is at Cal place. Sound to me like you wanna come home."

"I don't."

"Good, 'cause you told me you don't need no father no more. Ain't that what you told me the other day? Or was you just running your mouth?"

"I don't need you. How long I been on my own now? You see me needing you?"

He get a little smile on his face, like he laughing at me or something. "I'm saying, if you don't like it at Cal place no more, you got a room right here. It's all set up for you. You could be laying in that bed tonight. But you ain't moving back in here 'less you ask me if you could. That way, both of us is gonna know the reason you back living with me is 'cause you wasn't man enough to make it on your own."

I don't get this guy. He losing it for real.

"There's only gonna be one man in this house, Ty. And that man ain't you."

"It's like that," I say, shaking my head. I must be the stupidest nigga out here. How I ain't seen what he was doing all this time? He testing me. He all 'bout trying to make me a child again when both us know I ain't. I'm my own man, and he need to recognize that.

THIRTY-FIVE

I get back to Bronxwood kinda late and, straight up, Cal looking mad scared outside by hisself. He leaning up against the building trying to look hard, but I been knowing Cal too long. Something 'bout the way he standing all stiff, with his eyes all wide and shit, give it away. Dude look like he 'bout to piss hisself.

This the first night since he went back to work that I wasn't out here with him the whole time, keeping a eye on him. I don't know if he could do it by hisself no more, not if this the way he gonna look.

Without saying nothing, I drop my backpack on the ground and lean against the building on the other side of the door. Cal look over at me. "You a'ight?"

"Yeah," I say.

"You look fucked up."

"I am."

"You gonna stay out here?"

"Yeah." I hafta. Anybody walking by could tell Cal can't handle hisself.

For a while I stand there watching him work and try and act like I'm just chillin', not trying to protect him or nothing. I can tell he happy I'm out there 'cause he ain't looking like no damn statue no more. Even still, I'm hoping nothing go down tonight 'cause this high don't seem to be wearing off no time soon.

Keith moms make him come home by midnight, so after he leave, Cal on his own and gotta keep his own stash. He still don't actually hold no drugs on him though. He keep most of it in a plastic bag that he stuff in a drainpipe on the side of the building 'bout two feet from where he standing. Then he keep a little in the grass right next to him. So now I'm not only watching out for Cal, but I'm trying to help him keep a eye on his weed too.

And trying to keep my eyes from crossing.

I ain't been this high for a while.

"You talk to Greg?" I ask him.

He shake his head. "Got nothing to say to him. He doing his thing, I'm doing mines."

"Brothers, man," I say. "Y'all s'posed to be tight."

"S'posed to be."

"Only one doing what they s'posed to do is you."

He shrug. This conversation look like it's starting to get to him. So I start telling him 'bout my pops and what he told me. "He think I'ma get on my knees and beg him to come home, but he don't know me. I don't even wanna live with them no more."

"You don't gotta go nowhere," Cal say. "Fuck your father."

I laugh 'cause he right. Why my pops think I wanna leave outta Bronxwood for? How I'ma go from being on my own to being with them again. For what?

Anyway, I can tell Cal don't want me to leave. If I was him, I wouldn't want me to go neither. I'm the only friend he got. Even his own brothers don't look out for him the way I do.

I hang out with him as long as I can, but that musta been the craziest weed I ever smoked 'cause I'm getting higher and more tired every minute that go by. Really, what I need is to get in my bed, but this weed making me dumb hungry too. "What time the Chinese place close?"

"I don't know," Cal say.

"I'ma go see." I start walking and turn 'round and see that look on Cal face again. Damn, I'm just going 'round the corner and he already scared. I don't know how he gonna do this job no more, not this way.

When I get back with my food, I tell Cal I'ma go upstairs to eat and go to sleep. I can't hardly stand up no more.

"You know what," he say, "my ribs is starting to hurt. I'ma go up with you."

I wait for him while he get all the weed together. I know it ain't been easy for him, standing out here all night with two broke ribs and shit, but me and him know it's way too early for him to be going upstairs. This the time he usually start getting most his business. Late.

Every night this week he been going upstairs earlier than he s'posed to, saying he in pain or something. But now it's just past midnight. I don't know, but something tell me Andre gonna have a problem with this.

THIRTY-SIX

I'm hardly awake when I hear Andre banging on Cal door and telling him to get his ass up. Fuck. We need to change the locks up in here. For real.

Not only is Andre knocking and making all that noise but Bin Laden is barking his brains out too. It's after ten in the morning, but after me and Cal came upstairs last night, we stood up late watching a karate movie on cable and eating them chicken wings and pork fried rice. Shit had me blasting all night, lighting this room up. Still funky in here.

I need to go to the bathroom, but I try to hold it 'til Andre leave. Fucking asshole. After the shit he put me through in Brooklyn, I ain't trying to run into him and hear him tell me how I should work for him again and how I ain't doing nothing to help them out. I'm trying to stay outta his way for a little while more.

Andre must go in Cal room 'cause I don't hear him knocking no more. So I open my door and see that Cal door is closed. I can hear talking but no yelling or nothing, so I go to the bathroom and, no lie, I'm in there a long time. Real long. Fucking Chinese food.

I barely get out the bathroom when I hear Andre voice all loud and shit. What the fuck is his problem? The door to Cal room is open now and Andre standing there, half in and half out. "I don't wanna hear none of this shit no more," he tell Cal. "How long you gonna say you in pain? Two months? A year?"

Damn. Andre acting like he ain't even human no more. I mean, Cal ain't just some guy that work for him. Cal his brother. What, he forgot that?

"This is a business," Andre say. "You can't decide to come upstairs when you feel like it. Why you don't get that?"

That's all he think 'bout. Money.

"I'm getting word that folks around here is starting to get they shit from dudes over by Baychester. Why? 'Cause my brother don't like working long hours no more. 'Cause my brother thinking more about his ribs than the family business. 'Cause my brother think he the only one that ever been in pain before." I hear Cal start to say something, but Andre still talking, or rather screaming, "I got shot, motherfucker. Shot! And did you see me pussying out like you doing?"

I come down the hallway and stand close to Cal bedroom door. Cal standing there, looking down like he got something to be ashamed 'bout. "Andre," I say. "Cal still hurt, man. He working as hard as he could."

The way Andre look at me, it's like he wanna kill me right here and now. "Ty, you the one who telling him he can do what he want? You the one telling him he don't gotta think about the rest of his family?"

"It ain't 'bout the family, Andre. It's 'bout Cal."

"It's always about the family!" He full out screaming now. "With us, it's always about family. Cal my little brother, Ty. I'm trying to teach him how to be a man, a man that know how to take care of his responsibilities. He need to learn how to work hard because that's what a man do."

"The dude got broken ribs, man," I say, raising my voice my own self. "How you 'spect him to —"

"I expect him to be a working part of this family!" Andre yell.

"You don't even know what the fuck going on in your family right in fronta your face," I say, looking him dead in the eye. "You need to talk to Greg 'bout —"

Cal grab my arm. "Ty, c'mon, man. Don't do this."

"Yeah," Andre say to me. "You always going, 'I ain't in this. I ain't in this.' If you ain't in it, then stay your punk ass the fuck outta it, then."

"A'ight," I say 'cause now it's like both of them is ganging up on me and I'm the one here trying to help, trying to calm the situation down.

I walk past them to my bedroom and that's when Andre say it. "Ty, you gotta get up outta here. Before you got here, Cal knew his priorities and knew who to listen to. Now he got you filling his head with shit and I can't be having this no more."

I turn 'round. "Andre, I ain't —"

"You through here, Ty. Get the fuck out. Next time I stop by, you better not be here."

Now it's Cal turn to try and talk to him. "Ty don't got nothing to do with this. It's my ribs, not Ty, making me leave work early."

Andre ain't hearing it. "Tell your friend to pack his shit and leave. I ain't saying it again. He better not be here when I come back around."

"When you coming back?" Cal ask. "Least give him time to find another place to stay."

"I'm coming back when I get here," Andre say. "That's all you need to know."

I go in my room and sit on the bed listening to them two arguing for a while. Andre just being Andre, but it piss me off that Cal ain't even trying to get him to change his mind. Yeah, he asking for more time, but that ain't the point. Andre throwing me out and I don't got no place to go.

After Andre leave and after I'm dressed, I go in my room, close the door, and call the only person I know I can call when I need something.

Regg pick up on the third ring. "Ty?" He sound kinda busy or something. "You okay?"

"Yeah, I'm . . . I mean, I'm a'ight."

"I'm in the middle of something. Let me call you back later."

Damn, he rushing me off the phone, not even letting me get a word out. "A'ight, but, Regg. Can I ask you something?" I don't know why, but I can't stand having to ask nobody for anything. Make me look weak when I ain't.

"What you need?" he ask.

"Um, a place to stay for a couple days or a couple weeks, I don't know. I gotta get up outta here and —"

"Ty, look, you know I would help you if I could, but I don't want your pops thinking I'm trying to step in where he don't want me to be. He your pops, you know."

"I know, but —"

"He my friend, Ty, and the other day me and him got into it. He outright told me to back up off you, that you his son. And I gotta respect that. He trying to get his family back together and —"

"All he want back is Troy, not me. He told me that last night." Regg don't say nothing so I go, "All I need is to stay with you a couple nights."

"Look, Ty. It ain't safe for you at my place. That little weed business Andre running ain't shit compared to what I got going on, and I don't want you getting mixed up in it."

I sit there holding the cell, trying not to hear what Regg telling me.

"Call your pops," Regg say. "Call him and tell him you

wanna come home. Y'all need to find a way to live together again. Y'all used to get along good, the two of you, and not all that long ago neither. Call him, Ty, and go home."

I just wanna get off this phone. "Talk to you later, Regg," I say.

I hang up before I hafta listen to any more of his bullshit.

Ms. Thomas said she was gonna stop by my moms and pops apartment 'round six o'clock, so I go by there a couple minutes early so she would think I live there. My moms is at the agency for her parenting class, so it's just me and my pops again. He put the TV on and we sit there watching the news. I ain't sure what the point of this is, really. How long I'm s'posed to act like I live here? Just 'til they get Troy back?

My pops kinda in a good mood though, and I'm thinking 'bout what Regg said 'bout talking to him 'bout me coming home for real, but the way he was talking last night, I don't know. Is that the way he really feel, or is that just the way he feel when he high?

I wanna talk to Jasmine, tell her 'bout all the shit going on at Cal and them apartment, and find out what she think I should do. But since I stopped by her job on Monday, I texted her twice and I still ain't heard back from her.

And I ain't gonna lie. Since I got with her last week, I been thinkin' 'bout her a lot, 'specially at night. But still, I don't wanna be chasing her down like some chump that can't get no other females. Jasmine know my cell number. She could call me too.

The whole thing is frustrating as hell.

The caseworker finally get there 'bout ten minutes late. My pops start right in on her. "I like the way you got your hair," he say. "It wasn't like that yesterday, was it?"

She smile. "It's a little different," she say. "You notice everything."

My pops nod. "Everything." He look at her for another couple seconds, then go, "Let me show you the apartment."

I follow them as they go from one room to the other. I can tell my pops smooth act getting to her 'cause she smiling more than I ever seen her smile before. Matter of fact, Ms. Thomas ain't really a smiling kinda person, you ask me.

But she don't let my pops keep her from doing her job. She check all the window guards in the apartment, like Troy stupid enough to fall out a open window, and she make sure all the fire detectors work. Then she check the refrigerator and the cabinets to see that we got food in the apartment. The whole thing don't take all that long, and when she done, she say, "Everything looks really wonderful, Mr. Green."

"Wonderful enough that Troy could visit us?"

"Well." She still smiling. "I'll recommend a short visit this Saturday. How does nine until noon work for you? Will you and your wife be home then?"

"They gonna be here," I say for him. And, yeah, I'm probably smiling now my own self. I ain't think she was gonna let Troy come visit this fast.

My pops tell her they gonna be home, and she say she gonna bring Troy herself on Saturday. "He's going to be so happy," she say.

"Yes, he is," my pops say. "Especially when he see his new room."

Since I got Ms. Thomas right there, and since everybody in such a good mood, I'm like, this my chance to bring up the problem with Troy new foster mother. So before she leave, I say, "Ms. Thomas, can I ask you a question?"

She stop by the door and say, "Sure, anything, Tyrell."

"I wanted to find out, like, if there was a way you could do something to change the home where Troy at. 'Cause he ain't happy there and now Ms. Woods, she wanna take Troy out his school, and he was getting mainstreamed, or whatever they call it, out of the special ed classes, and now I don't know if that's gonna keep happening at the new school, and he don't got no friends there." I spit all that out at one time 'cause I want her to get it, that she gotta do something for Troy. That this is serious.

Ms. Thomas look kinda surprised. "I didn't know anything about that. Let me look into it and see if there's anything I can do."

My pops clear his throat. "Ty, don't bother Ms. Thomas with all this right now. She a busy woman."

But I ignore him. What Ms. Thomas so busy doing? This her job. "You remember Troy first foster mother, Ms. Reed? I been trying to call her to see if she could take him back now that summer almost over. 'Cause she treated him real good and Ms. Woods ain't all that nice to him."

"You shouldn't call the foster parents, Tyrell. It's not the way we do things."

"I know, but she didn't mind when I called her when Troy was living with her. And if he could go back with her, he could stay in his school."

"Like I said, I'll see what I can do. No promises though."

My pops walk her out to the elevator, and I stay inside trying to figure out if she really gonna try and help Troy or not. I hope she do 'cause Troy could use a break. Least he gonna get to come and visit us this week. That's a good thing.

My pops come back inside and slam the door behind him. Hard. I look up at him. "What?"

The words is hardly out my mouth when my pops push me against the wall and get in my face. "Did I ask you to talk to that bitch 'bout Troy foster mother? Who told you you had to do that?"

I'm looking at him, and his eyes is locked on mines and he so mad. Like he just went from zero to sixty in a second. "What you . . . ? I'm trying to help Troy," I say and try and get away from him, but he so close to me with his arm holding me in place, that I can't move.

"Who Troy father, me or you?"

"You," I say.

"Then let me take care of his situation. You seen how I had that bitch right where I wanted her, then you had to fuck everything up."

"I —"

"Stay the fuck outta it, Ty. I got this." He let me go.

I grab my backpack up off the couch and head straight for the door. I got nothing more to say to this man. I swear.

I open the door and he go, "Tomorrow. I'll pick you up at nine."

Shit. I forgot 'bout his stupid party.

The door close behind me and I'm in the hall waiting for the elevator, pissed. What the fuck is wrong with him? Ever since he got out, something real off 'bout the man. Damn, and I was thinkin' 'bout asking him if I could come stay with them for a while. That woulda been so stupid if I did that. Crazy stupid.

I wish I coulda just told him to go fuck hisself 'bout the party, but I need the cash. 'Cause after tomorrow, I'ma hafta find another place to live.

THIRTY-SEVEN

It's been a long fucking day, and I ain't feeling like standing outside with Cal again tonight, 'specially not after the way he only half had my back with Andre this morning. But still, I stand there with him for a while.

"What's up with you?" Cal ask.

"Just pissed off," I tell him. "And tired."

"Me and you both."

I must just wanna talk, 'cause in between customers I tell Cal 'bout how my pops just turned on me and how crazy he was acting. "He think that just 'cause he ready to start actin' like a father again, I'm s'posed to stop looking out for Troy. When I was more a father to that kid for the last year than he was. Why I gotta be the one to step aside for?"

"You don't," Cal say.

"Damn straight, I don't." Talking 'bout this make me more mad. "And you know what's gonna happen, right? The second I let him start actin' like a father again, and Troy start thinking his pops is back, his ass gonna get locked up. How I'm s'posed to let Troy go through that again?"

Cal quiet.

My brain just keep going though, thinking 'bout how close I got to asking him if I could move in with them for real. "I don't know what I'ma do," I tell Cal, walking back and forth in front of the lobby door, which ain't really doing nothing to calm me down none. "I know Andre said the next time he come 'round, he don't wanna see me, but . . . where I'm s'posed to go?"

Cal just shake his head, like maybe he don't care or something.

"Why you being like that?" I ask him.

"Like what?"

"I don't know, like —"

"You just paranoid, Ty. You high again?"

"I ain't high and I ain't paranoid. I'm tired of everybody fucking with me. And now you too?"

Cal stare at me like I'm being stupid. And it's pissing me off more than everything else.

"Cal, I ain't standing out here with you so you can . . . I'm hanging with you, right? I'm being your boy. But you —"

"Ty," Cal say, and his voice come out real tired. Tired and old. "Go home. Just go home."

First Andre, then Regg, then my pops, and now Cal turning on me too. Shit is fucked up. "What you saying?"

"I'm saying go home. You got a place to go. You got a moms and a pops. You don't gotta —"

"A'ight," I say. "Be like that."

Cal sigh. "You being stupid, Ty. You know that."

"I'm stupid?"

"Why you here, Ty? You don't need to put up with none of this shit. I gotta be here. I gotta do this. You don't."

Fuck. Cal actually throwing me out.

"Look, Ty. I know your pops kinda hard and shit, but —"

"He ain't hard, he outta control."

"Okay, a'ight, I get that, Ty. But he right. And you know that. He the one s'posed to be looking out for Troy now that he back. You don't gotta do that no more, not like you used to. You gotta let all that go now."

I shake my head. I can't believe the shit coming out Cal mouth.

"Ty, you acting like Andre, man. Like you own Troy or something just 'cause he your little brother. It ain't right when Andre do that shit to me and it ain't right when you do it to Troy. You know that."

I'm tired of listening to him. Here I am, talking to my friend, telling him 'bout shit that's getting to me, and he gotta turn it 'round and make it 'bout him. That's some fucked-up shit. I'm standing out here, trying to look out for his ass and what he doing? Telling me I'm like fuckin' Andre.

I pick up my backpack off the ground and tell Cal I'ma go to sleep. "Last time I'ma stand here with you," I tell him.

"I'm helping my pops at his party tomorrow night, and after that, I don't know, man. I'ma hafta find some other place to stay or something."

Cal lean against the pillar and kinda nod and go, "Okay."

"A'ight," I say back, and that's it. The seven months we been living together like brothers is through. Time for me to move on.

Even though I'm pissed at Cal right 'bout now, I can't lie, I'm still feeling like shit for leaving him out here by hisself when his ribs is still broke and he still walking 'round all fucked up and shit. But he gonna hafta get used to working alone again.

No matter what he say, I got my own brother to look out for now. My real brother.

THIRTY-EIGHT

I don't wake up 'til after eleven, and even then I'm still tired. I go out to the kitchen to grab something to eat and I don't see Cal 'round. He probably still 'sleep. But it's good I don't hafta deal with him right now. I still can't believe the way he was acting last night. He don't know shit 'bout what's going on between me and my pops. How he gonna tell me what to do?

I'm still sitting there eating and thinking 'bout my pops party tonight, which I don't even feel like playing, when Cal come out his room. He musta been up a while 'cause he dressed already. He don't come into the kitchen or nothing, but he stand in the hall by the door and I'm like, what? He want me to talk to him or something? But he don't. He just say to me, "I'ma go out. I need to get something over on Willis Avenue."

This the first time he leaving Bronxwood since he got beat up. I don't know why he gotta go so far when he still in pain and still taking them pills, but what I'm s'posed to do 'bout it?

"You gonna be here later?" he ask me.

I don't get why he even trying to talk to me. "Nah." I don't even look up when I say this. I ain't one to let shit go easy.

"Okay." He stand there a second, like he waiting for me to say something, which I don't, so he just leave out the apartment.

He gone 'bout fifteen, twenty minutes when my cell ring. It's Jasmine.

"Ty," she say. "I stood home from work today. Emiliano's at work. Come over." She talking all fast and shit.

I ain't gonna lie. This girl confusing the hell outta me. One day she ignore me and then don't call me for the rest of the week. Now she sound like she desperate for me or something.

"I'ma be over there," I tell her.

And I don't waste no time getting my ass in the shower.

I get off the train on Grand Concourse, and while I'm walking to Jasmine building, I'm feeling real good that she called me and wanted me to come over. I missed her, talking to her, being with her. The closer I get to her building, the more I wanna see her and the more I know she my girl.

The second I get upstairs in Jasmine apartment and see her in a tank top and these little shorts that only just hardly cover her ass, it's all I can do to hold myself back. I put my arms 'round her waist and don't give her a chance to say nothing. I just start kissing her, my tongue all deep in her mouth, and I could probably do this for a while, just kiss her and know me and her is connected. It's like I'm finally feeling it with her, for the first time. This ain't just 'bout getting sex from her. It's 'bout knowing she mines. And she is.

We don't even make it to her bedroom. We standing right in the living room, taking each other clothes off and kissing and laughing. This girl so hot, damn, why wasn't I with her all this time? Next thing I know, me and her is on the floor and I'm getting them light blue panties off her. My jeans is on the floor halfway under us and I'm going through the pockets real fast, trying to find the condoms I stuck in there before I left my place. I need this girl now.

When I get inside her, I ain't gonna lie, it's just as good as the first time. Nah, it's better, 'cause now I'm feeling the same for her that she feel for me.

"I love you," Jasmine whisper. "I love you."

"I love you too," I say. And it's true. I do. This is the best feeling I ever had, the first time I'm ever doing this with a girl I love. And who love me back. The last girl I loved was Novisha and she never gave it up to me. Now that I'm with

Jasmine, I ain't sure Novisha really loved me the way I loved her.

Me and Jasmine is connected one hundred percent. That's how tight we are. This what I been looking for.

Like a hour later, me and her is eating Bagel Bites at the kitchen table. I got my jeans back on, but all Jasmine wearing is her T-shirt and panties and she look so pretty and sexy. Even though I'm wore out from her, I can't even keep my hands to myself 'round her.

I put one hand on the side of her face and the other on her thigh and tell her, "What I said, you know, 'bout loving you. I was serious. I don't say nothing like that 'less I mean it. You?"

She look me in the eye. "Me too."

We kiss. "I been thinkin' 'bout you a lot," I say. "'Bout us. And what we got going here. You think me and you —?"

"I want us to be together, Ty. You want that too?"

"Yeah. For real." I lean over and kiss her again, and when I pull my lips away, she smiling. Damn, she beautiful.

I get up and take her hand and walk her to her room. Now that we official, I wanna get with her again. And we gonna need to be on a bed for what I'ma do to her.

THIRTY-NINE

"You think everything is gonna be different now, because we together?" Jasmine ask me.

It's almost five o'clock, and me and her is laying in bed, still naked. "Yeah. I hope everything gonna be better," I say.

Jasmine laying on her side, facing me, looking so goddamn beautiful, I can't stop touching her, running my hand up and down the side of her body, her waist and her hips and her legs. All of this is mines.

"I mean, we were friends for a long time, Ty. I don't want to mess that up."

"No matter what happen, me and you always gonna be friends. Don't worry 'bout that." I lean over and kiss her.

"You decide what you gonna do? I mean, about school?"

I ain't thought 'bout it, but right now, knowing me and her is gonna be together and I'ma get to see her every day, maybe I will go back. "Yeah," I say. "I'ma be there."

She smile. "Good."

We kiss again. Then I ask Jasmine if she really liked her Sweet Sixteen party.

"I loved it!" she say. "Everything came out perfect, especially your music. Everybody had so much fun dancing!" She laugh. "The only thing that bothered me was Reyna. I don't get why she just came and then left so fast. She didn't even dance to one song. And she loves to dance."

"You know what happened," I tell her. "While you was opening your presents, her and Emiliano started talking."

"They did?"

"Yeah. Then they went in that little room, but only for, like, a couple minutes, like, three, four minutes. Then, after that, she left real fast."

"I didn't even see that. I can't even think of anything they had to talk about."

I shrug. The whole thing was kinda weird, but Jasmine don't need to spend no more time worrying 'bout Reyna when it should be the other way 'round. "C'mon, Jasmine. Don't start stressing 'bout this." I pull her closer to me and wrap my arms 'round her. I ain't gonna lie. I ain't looking for this day to end.

But it gotta. I know Emiliano gonna be home from work soon, and I gotta get back to Bronxwood to get ready for my pops party tonight.

"What's the matter?" Jasmine ask me. "The muscles in your arm just got tight. What you thinking about?"

"Nah, it's nothing."

She sit up and look at me. "Talk to me, Ty. I'm always telling you my problems, but you never —"

"It's not a problem."

"*Dios mio!* This is about your father, right? It's always about him, but you never really talk about him. Tell me."

I don't say nothing.

"*Digame*, Ty."

She ain't gonna stop, so I go and tell her 'bout how me and my pops ain't been getting along too good, and 'bout Andre telling me I gotta leave outta the apartment and I don't know where I'ma go next. "I'ma help my pops DJ one of his parties tonight. I don't wanna be there with him, but he gonna pay me good, and I need to find a place to stay."

"Why don't you go home?"

Now she sounding like Regg. And Cal.

"C'mon, Ty. You lucky that you got a mother and father. Just go home and deal with it, you know, 'til you finish high school and —"

"You don't know. My pops be going off on me all the time and . . ." I shake my head. "Forget it. Point is, me and him can't live together no more. Two men in one house don't work."

"Why don't you talk to him? Try. Promise me you gonna talk to him. I don't want you out on the street."

Still can't say no to her. I take a deep breath. "A'ight," I say. "I'ma talk to him tonight. After the party. If he in a good mood. But I don't think it's gonna work."

Even saying it make me feel mad, like I can't make it on my own. But maybe Jasmine and Cal is right. Maybe I could stay with my moms and pops for a while, just deal with it 'til I can find my own place. But I don't know though. It ain't gonna be easy no matter what.

I gotta change the subject fast. Thinking 'bout talking to my pops after the party is fucking my brain up. So I ask Jasmine what she doing tomorrow night. "'Cause me and you could go out," I say. "I could take you to the movies or something."

That's when she get kinda quiet. "I can't. Emiliano wants to go back to Connecticut again, for a whole week this time. He's on vacation, and they got a pool there and everything. We're leaving tomorrow, early in the morning." She point to the corner of her room where she got this big suitcase open and clothes inside in a pile. I ain't even notice that before. "I'm supposed to be packing."

"A week?"

She nod, but she get that look in her eyes again, like I seen at the restaurant the other day.

"You don't wanna go?" I ask her. "'Cause, why you don't just tell Emiliano you wanna stay here? Then me and you could —"

"I can't," she say, looking down. And everything 'bout her change. Then she start crying, and now I get it. Damn.

"He fucked you, didn't he?" I'm asking the question, but

I don't even need her to answer me 'cause I know what happened. Everything make sense.

Jasmine nod, and I sit up and wrap my arms 'round her tight and we stay like that for a long time, me holding her while she cry and talk. "He told me that sixteen was old enough to decide, that I should know if I wanna be with him — if I love him, because I was going to be sixteen. But I didn't know." She crying hard now on my shoulder.

"That was why you wanted to find Reyna," I say.

"I thought — I wanted her to, you know, take me with her, but . . ."

"She look messed up, Jasmine. You seen her, right? She look bad."

"I know. The way she looked, that's why I made a decision, for me. For my life. I don't wanna end up like her, out there, doing whatever she does, like, stripping or whatever. I don't wanna be like that, and I know, I know what girls that look like me could end up doing. I don't want that. So I told Emiliano I decided to be with him and when we went to Connecticut after the party, me and him —"

She stop talking so she could cry some more, and I'm so fucking pissed I can't even breathe hardly. "He hurt you?"

"No, he loves me. He waited for me. I'm old enough now." She wipe her eyes. "It's okay. I'm okay."

She stop talking and I keep holding her. It ain't easy dealing with none of this. Ever since I knew that Emiliano liked her, I knew he was just waiting for her, and I knew one day he was gonna get what he wanted. And even though I knew it was gonna happen, that don't stop me from being pissed.

At the same time, there's something I gotta know for my own self. "What happened between me and you, Jasmine, in my room, what was that 'bout?" I ask her. "I mean, if you knew you was gonna let him in, why you get with me then?"

She look me in the eye. "Because I love you, what do you think? I wanted to be with you, especially before —"

"Then what 'bout him?" I can't even hardly say his name no more.

"I'm only gonna do it with him when I have to, and he's not gonna do it unless we in Connecticut because the law is different there."

"Jasmine, I can't —"

"I need you, Ty. I —"

"I can't do it, Jasmine." I pull myself away from her and get up outta the bed. I find my underwear on the floor and start getting dressed. I'm mad. Only I'm not really sure if I'm mad at her or just everything, the situation. It's all fucked up. Everything, this whole day I spent with Jasmine, it's over and so is me and her. Over. I can't be with no girl if they just using me. That ain't what I want.

"Ty, don't go. I can't get through this without —"

"It don't work that way, Jasmine. Not for me, it don't. If me and you is together, we together. I ain't gonna share you with nobody, definitely not him."

Jasmine still sitting there on the bed, crying. But I gotta go. I need to get outta there.

I'm in the lobby when I see him. Emiliano. Home early. He don't see me at first. He getting his mail out the box and there's two ladies down there, going through the door. I just stand there, 'cause I don't know what I'm s'posed to do. Run and hide so Jasmine don't get in no trouble for having a guy upstairs with her. Or run up on this dude and kick his fuckin' ass hard enough for him to remember to keep his hands off her.

But before I can do any of them things, Emiliano look up and see me. And me and him is just looking at each other from one side of the lobby to the other. "You have to say to me something?" he go.

Fuck him. I got a lot of shit to say to him. But there's too much going on in my head and I don't know what to say. So all I go is, "You hurt her and I'ma fuck you up. You understand me?"

Emiliano practically laugh. "You fuck up me?"

Yeah, alright, he do work out every day, lift weights and shit. And yeah, his arm the size of my leg. But he don't understand how I fight when someone mess with a friend of mines. 'Specially Jasmine. After everything I been through with that girl.

I walk closer to him, not sure what I'ma do, but he hold up his hand like he want me to stop. "I love her," he say. "I no hurt her. I want to take care of her. Who she got now? Nobody. No mother, no father, no Reyna."

"That ain't the point," I say.

"The point? The point is, I work hard, buy for her nice things. For her birthday, I make a big party. Now, for school, I buy for her clothes and shoes and books. I tell her, no more working at the restaurant. I give to her money. She study hard, do good grades."

"She sixteen," I say, but ain't no getting through to this guy.

"I love her," he say. "I no let her go."

I can't decide if I should punch him or not. Yeah, he could take me, but I could get a couple good punches in before that. Might make me feel better.

But it ain't. "You gonna bring her back from Connecticut?"

He look kinda surprised, like he ain't think I knew what he was up to. "She stay there. The schools good there. I'm looking for a nice apartment, for me and for her. I treat her very good."

I try to control myself, but it ain't easy. Emiliano gonna take Jasmine away, and ain't nothing I say gonna change that. Truth is, I can't do nothing to make Jasmine situation better.

A hour ago me and her was as close as two people could get. Now everything is fucked up. And I'm losing her for real.

FORTY

It's after two in the morning and I been helping my pops DJ his party all night. He probably got three-hundred-something people here in the basement of a out-of-business lumber store, and course, just like all the rest of my pops parties, all kinds of illegal shit is going on all 'round me.

Regg over by the door taking money and making sure nothing too wild go down. When we all first got here, I ain't say a word to him, not after the way he treated me yesterday. He always telling me to call him if I need something, then the first time I do that, he tell me he can't do shit for me. Cool. Least I know for a fact now that the only person that's gonna look out for me is me.

While my pops do the DJing, I'm helping him with the records, which ain't enough work to keep my mind here where I'm at. Matter of fact, it's like I ain't even here. My mind pulling me in all different directions, and I'm just going through the motions behind this DJ table. Straight up, I'm fucking depressed, thinking 'bout everything that happened with Jasmine and Cal and Andre. And I'm trying to figure out what I'ma do next, where I'm s'posed to move to. 'Cause Andre come by the apartment on Saturdays a lot, and I ain't looking to get into nothing with him. Soon as this party over, I need to get back to Bronxwood and pack some shit and go. Just don't know where I'ma go to.

Before he let me do my own DJing, my pops get on the mic and go, "I'm gonna let my son take over for a while so I can come out there and dance with some of you beautiful ladies."

A lot of the ladies smile and cheer, 'specially the fugly ones that ain't come with no man.

My pops smile. "I know Tyrell gonna turn this party out, but just remember, I taught him everything he know." He laugh and step away from the table.

I think 'bout getting on the mic after him and telling these people the truth, that, yeah, he taught me a lot, but I know a whole lot more than that now. That he can't even keep up with my skills now. But nah, I don't say nothing. A man don't gotta always tell people everything. He just gotta show them. So that's what I do. Not only show them, but show my pops that I'm good enough to do this for real now.

Playing music work for a while to take my mind off my problems. The music take over everything. I'm in it. The party turning out so good, my pops and some of his friends go into one of the back rooms and I don't see him for a while. But it's okay 'cause I'm holding it down while he do his thing.

I'm up there 'bout a hour 'til my pops come back and dance with some of the females. And another hour 'til he take back over at the table. By then it's after four and the party starting to slow down. Some folks is leaving, but a lot still trying to keep partying.

Me, now that I'm back to just helping my pops again, my mind fast-forwarding to what I'ma do next. Yeah, I could do what everybody want me to do and ask my pops if I could come and stay with them for a while. I mean, I'ma be over there in a couple hours anyway for Troy visit.

But I don't know. My pops changed so much since he went away that I'm standing, like, a foot away from the man, but I ain't trying to ask him nothing. Why would I? So he could tell me I'm a child that can't make it on my own? That I need his ass to save me from the streets?

Shit, I don't need to hear none of that.

Thinking 'bout everything make me wanna leave outta here right now, but I gotta wait 'til it's over, 'til when my pops pay everybody. I don't know what he gonna give me, but it should be alright, 'specially since I just played for two hours while he went and had fun. He need to remember that when he start handing out the cash.

My pops get on the mic and start talking over the music. He laughing and pointing out females in the crowd and talking 'bout how good they look in whatever they wearing. And that just get them all excited and they trying to get his attention so he could talk 'bout they outfit. "Short mama in the red skirt," my pops say, still laughing. "You killin' me, girl."

He in a mad good mood since he came back to the table. He all happy and shit. While a song is playing, he take off his headphones and lean over to me and go, "The girl in the black skirt and silver top, young girl, standing over there, she been checking you out all night."

I look to where his eyes is and just like he say, a girl that's 'bout twenty, twenty-one or something, looking right at me. She cute and everything but, I don't know. "She too old," I tell my pops.

He laugh. "Older women is where it's at. Go dance with her."

I shake my head. I ain't thinkin' 'bout no other female other than Jasmine. So I tell my pops, "I was with a girl all day. I don't got nothing left."

He bust out laughing and I laugh with him. "You making sure there ain't gonna be no little Tyrell juniors running around the Bronx, right?"

"Course."

He slap me on the back. "Alright, then."

He still smiling, and I'm thinking, maybe this is a good time to ask him, as good as any other time. But how I'ma do it? And what he gonna say?

But before I can figure out a way to ask him anything, I see Dante coming 'cross the room, coming right in our direction. I can't believe this shit. Why he gonna come now, when the party almost over?

Dante don't just come over to the table, he come behind it like he working this party with us. Him and my pops do a guy hug and Dante say over the music, "Sorry I'm late, man. I was with a woman. . . ." He shake his head. "The lonely ones, they don't never let you leave." They both laugh.

"Hang around," my pops go. "We gonna go to the Black Rock."

My pops put his headphones on and get on the mic to tell everybody that this the last song. He start playing "Before I Let Go."

While he doing that, Dante come up to me and go, "Your moms, man. She didn't want me to leave, you know." He flash me this crooked-ass smile. "She don't like being there all alone in that big, new apartment."

I stare him down for a second. I don't believe him, but at the same time, I can't have this nigga talkin' 'bout my moms like that and getting away with it. I move closer to him and just 'cause I can, I trip his ass, and on his way down, he hit up against the DJ table and the music just stop. I don't care though. I'm 'bout to jump on him and punch him in the face, but before I could, my pops pull me away, saying, "What you doing, Ty? What's going on?"

I get away from my pops and kick Dante down there on the floor. Can't help myself if I wanted to, that's how pissed I am. Then Regg come over, grab me, and hold me back like it's nothing, and I watch my pops help Dante up and look back over at me like I'm the one he don't get, like I'm the one that did something wrong.

The room kinda quiet now and everybody standing 'round watching us. My pops start walking away with Dante, like he making sure he okay or something, but I can't take it no more. "You think he your friend, but he ain't," I yell to my pops. "You don't know what —"

"Don't say no more," Regg say to me, looking me in my eyes, warning me. "Don't say nothing, Ty. Don't say it."

But my heart is pumping hard and even though I hear him, it's hard to stop myself. I wanna tell my pops how stupid he looking right now. How he getting played by that asshole who claim to be his friend.

"Ty, listen to me, man," Regg say, leaning in closer to me. "You tell your pops and he gonna kill that man and where that gonna leave your moms and Troy, Ty? You listening to me?"

I nod, but still, I can't calm myself down. I can't.

Regg grab up my backpack and hand it to me. "Leave," he say. "Just go."

He put his arm 'round my back and get me to walk a couple steps with him toward the door. But I break away from him. I ain't done yet.

I go back to the table and search through the deck for the songs I got loaded on there. I look right at my pops on the other side of the room, standing there with Dante, looking at me, pissed.

Fuck him.

I get on the mic and go, "This one for you." I start playing "Papa'z Song" by Tupac and over the music I say, "So you know the truth."

As I walk to the door with Regg, I hear the song start playing:

"Daddy's home. Heh, so?
You say that like it means somethin' to me
You've been gone a mighty long muthafuckin' time
For you to be comin' home talkin' that 'Daddy's home' shit
We been getting along fine just without you
Me, my brother, and my mother
So if you don't mind, you can step the fuck off, Pops,
Fuck you!"

I don't wait 'round for the part where Wycked talk 'bout how his moms had to have all kinds of men in and outta they house just to help out with the rent and shit, but my pops know the song and I know he gonna put together what the lyrics is telling him, and he gonna find out what that dude he think is his friend been up to with his wife while he was gone.

And when he do, Dante gonna be worse off than what I was gonna do to him.

Good.

FORTY-ONE

When I leave the party, I'm so pissed off and pumped up that I walk, like, fifteen blocks before getting on the train. By the time I get back to Bronxwood, it's probably something after six in the morning and the sun is just starting to come out. I walk 'round the corner and before I even get close to my building I see a bunch of people out in front of it, standing 'round. And there's two cop cars with flashing lights, and I can tell something went down and I know it got something to do with Cal and them. I can feel it.

I stop walking and stand there on the sidewalk for a minute just watching. All these people from my building is standing 'round talking, shaking they head. I feel the breath leave outta my body. Something musta happened to Cal again. Somebody musta hurt him worse this time. Somebody musta —

"Ty." Keith come 'cross the street on his scooter. What

the fuck he doing out here this time of the morning? "You wasn't home?"

"Nah," I tell him. "What's going on? Is Cal —?"

"You missed a lot," he say.

"C'mon, Keith. What the fuck happened?" Can't believe I'm looking for answers from a thirteen-year-old on a scooter.

"Cal got arrested," he say. "He shot some dude that I think was trying to rob him or something."

"Shot?" Nothing making sense no more. "Cal don't got no —"

Gun.

Shit. That's why he left outta Bronxwood, to go to Willis Avenue by hisself. That's what he had to go get. I wasn't even hardly paying no attention to him.

I look through the whole crowd and I'm like, what these people still standing 'round for? "The guy he shot, he alive?"

Keith shrug. "I seen an ambulance come and take him away, but I don't know."

"And Cal was *arrested*?" I can't believe this.

Keith nod. "About two hours ago, I think."

Cops is still walking 'round outside the building and in the lobby, like they trying to find something. They got yellow tape up 'round the front door and there's a female cop standing there, looking like she making sure nobody get underneath that tape.

I look 'round to see who I know out here, somebody that could give me more information. Only one I kinda know is this guy Evan that live on my floor. He tell me that the dude Cal shot ain't dead, but they don't think he gonna make it. "They investigating it like a homicide," he say, shaking his head.

Homicide. Cal mighta *killed* somebody. He musta been scared out his mind to do something like that. "Damn," I say. "Damn."

"You can't go upstairs, Ty. The cops is in y'all's apartment now."

"You know if Greg there?"

"Yeah, he there. Cal went up there after he shot the guy and that's where the cops found him. Now they searching the place with a warrant."

I stand there for another couple minutes knowing they gonna arrest Greg soon as they find what he got up there. Least Cal ain't the only one going down for the shit his brothers got him into. Wouldn't mind seeing the cops drag Greg ass outta there. But, nah. I ain't gonna give Greg the chance to try and drag me into they shit.

All my stuff is upstairs, all my clothes and my equipment. Everything. All I got is the clothes on my back, my backpack, and the money I got left over from what Emiliano paid me last week.

Everything going on is fucked up and it kill me what Cal probably going through right now. But I knew something like this was gonna go down one day. I'm just lucky I wasn't 'round when it did.

So I tell Evan I'ma see him 'round, and I turn and walk back down the block, back toward the train station. I don't know where I'm going, but I leave outta Bronxwood and don't look back.

FORTY-TWO

'Cause I'm tired and 'cause I don't got nowhere else to go,
I take the train to Jerome Avenue, and walk down Mosholu
to my moms and pops apartment. I was gonna end up
there anyway for Troy visit, but the real truth is, I don't got
no other choice. I'ma hafta ask my pops if I could stay
there for a while, least 'til I get my equipment outta Cal
and them apartment, play some parties, and save up enough
money for my own place.

Then I'ma be on my own for real. 'Cause what I was
doing at Cal apartment all this time wasn't being no man.
All I was doing was playing.

It's Saturday morning and people is starting to come out
already. I don't even know what time it is. As I walk, I dig
'round at the bottom of my backpack and find my cell. I
turned it off before my pops party and forgot 'bout it. I put
it on and it's 7:40. And I got four texts. The first two is
from Cal. The first one say: call me

Then the next one just say: 911

The other two is from Patrick trying to find out where I am, and if I was home when everything went down with Cal.

Thinking 'bout Cal texting me after everything that happened and me not calling him back, that hurt. He shot that guy and ain't know what to do, and where was I? And why he ain't even tell me he was gonna get that gun? Me and him used to talk 'bout everything.

Now he going through something nobody should hafta. And his freedom is gone. He through.

I'm 'bout to put the cell in my pocket when I see I got a voicemail too. It's Troy first foster mom. "I'm still out of town, Tyrell," she say, "but Ms. Thomas called and said Troy wants to come back and stay with me. And that's fine by me. That little boy wasn't a problem at all." She say more, 'bout how she coming back from vacation after Labor Day, but I don't need to know all that. I'm just glad that Troy gonna be somewhere where he happy. 'Til they let him come back home for real.

Knowing that make it easy to go back home and deal with my pops. Nothing he tell me could fuck this feeling up for me.

When I get upstairs to they floor, I knock, but nobody answer. I know my pops was gonna go to the Black Rock, but where my moms at? She s'posed to be home waiting for

Troy to get here. I don't got no key, but I try turning the knob and it's open. I'm like, what's up? Why the door ain't locked?

When I go inside, I see my pops sitting in the kitchen. He drinking a beer this early in the morning and he look so pissed, I don't even think he see me come in.

That's when I hear crying coming from the back of the apartment and I know what's up already. Damn. Fuck.

I run down the hall to my moms and pops room, but she ain't in there. She in the bathroom, on the floor, and I can't believe what I'm seeing. My pops fucked her up real bad this time. For a second, I just stand there in the door looking at her 'cause I don't know what to do.

My moms ain't wearing nothing but her panties, and she curled up in a ball on the floor between the sink and the tub, like she hiding. Her mouth is bleeding and I can see that one of her front teeth is knocked out. And there's blood all over her face and her hair and her neck. It's crazy.

But the crying is the thing that get me. She look and sound like a little girl. I get down on the floor next to her and try to help her up, but she ain't moving. She shake her head and say, "I can't. I can't."

"You need a ambulance?" I ask her. "You want me to —"

"No, no, no," she say. "No, don't call nobody. I don't want —"

"You hurt," I say. I snatch a towel off the rack and start to wipe her face with it. I wanna see how bad he beat her. But every time I touch her face with the towel, she let out

322

a high-pitched cry, 'specially when I get to the left side of her forehead. She got a cut that's real deep, like maybe where my pops ring dug into her. "Stop, Ty. Stop, I'm okay. I'm —"

"You need stitches," I tell her. "And you need to go see a dentist or something."

"I can't. I can't. They gonna arrest him and then what I'm gonna do? What can I —?"

"You can leave his ass," I tell her, but watching her sitting there, shaking her head, I know it ain't gonna happen. Never did before, no matter how bad he beat her. Ain't gonna happen now.

While I clean her up the best I can with warm water on a towel, I listen while she talk on and on 'bout why did she wait for him to get outta prison when she coulda found somebody else to be with, and why she gotta live like this, and why, why, why? This ain't the first time I'm hearing her say shit like this. It's what she do.

But what she say next is new. "We was trying to have another baby, you know, your pops and me. We wanted to have us one more baby, maybe a little girl this time. We was trying to give Troy a little sister."

I close my eyes for a second. Damn. That's what they was up to. Trying to make another baby that would end up in foster care too the next time my pops get locked up. What the fuck is wrong with them?

It take a while to get my moms up off the floor, but I don't let her see herself in the mirror 'cause she look that bad. She scary-looking. Not one, but two teeth is knocked out and they still on the bathroom floor, and the cut over her forehead still gushing blood. The washcloth I gave her to hold against it is already soaked.

It's hard, trying to get her to walk too, she in so much pain. But I get her back to her room, help her put on a T-shirt, and get her to lay down in bed. Then I leave outta there, even though she still crying, still talking to herself 'bout how she deserve to be treated better than this.

This whole thing my fault.

My pops still sitting in the kitchen. Nigga ain't even move to help his wife, ain't even see if she alright. "What the fuck you had to do that for? Why you —"

"You know I'm all about respect, Ty." My pops voice is calm, like he ain't just wild out on my moms a little while ago. "I can't have nobody disrespecting me like that, not even my wife."

"But she —"

"You gotta demand respect from people!" He look at me hard. He mad at me. "I taught you that, Ty."

"I know. Didn't you say you taught me everything I know?" I stare back at him now.

"I did!" Now he outright yelling at me.

"You wrong. Only thing you did was teach me everything *you* know. What, you don't think I learned nothing else all this time you was locked up?"

He stand up. "What you learned? You a man now?"

I move closer to him and we standing, like, two inches away from each other. "I am."

He try and do that thing again where he grab me by the throat, but I don't let it happen. I been letting him do that shit to me all this time but not no more. Never again.

This time I push him back and, I don't know if he wasn't expecting it or what, but I catch him off guard and he fall back against the counter. Then without even thinking 'bout what I'm 'bout to do, I punch him in the face as hard as I can, just to make him feel some of the pain my moms felt.

Just like I knew he would, he come back at me and, next thing I know, we fighting. It don't last long, but this a first for me and him. It used to be just him hitting me, and me not doing nothing back, but not this time. This time we like two men fighting. For real.

By the time my moms make it out there and get us to stop, the kitchen is jacked up. Broken glass is all over the floor 'cause the table got knocked over and the vase and some glasses that was on it got smashed. My pops lip is bleeding and I got cut on the hand, but that's it. We done.

Before I leave, I go back down the hall to find my backpack in my moms and pops room. My pops wallet is on the dresser. I open it up fast and grab a handful of bills. I don't count it, but the way I feel, it's what he owe me for helping him DJ.

Then, before I leave, I look 'round and know for a fact, with the way the apartment look and how beat up my moms is, ain't no way Ms. Thomas gonna leave Troy there. He ain't coming home no time soon.

And I can't be here when Troy find that out. I can't take the look on that kid face.

I leave out the apartment and go down in the elevator, not knowing where to go or what to do. I walk outside and more people is out there now. It's a nice sunny morning, but everything in my life is so fucked up I can't even think straight.

My cell ring and I pull it out my pocket. It's Novisha. "Hello." I sound mad tired.

She sigh. "Oh, my God. I'm so glad to hear your voice. I thought . . . I was worried about —"

"I'm okay, Novisha."

"Good. When I heard about Cal, I prayed you weren't —"

"I wasn't home. I'm a'ight."

"Good," she say again. Then she stop talking and I keep walking, not knowing what to say to her neither. After everything that just happened with my moms and pops, and everything that happened between me and Novisha in the past, I don't know. It's hard to know what I'm s'posed to say to her no more.

Finally, she say, "Ty? You still there?"

"Yeah. I'm here." I get to Jerome and stand there waiting for the light to change.

"Ty, I know you were mad at me for what I did and I understand that. I know I messed up. But I'm always gonna want you to be okay. I'm always gonna want you to be happy, even if it's not with me."

What come out my mouth next surprise the shit outta me. But I'm too tired to lie to her. "It's the same with me, Novisha, you know what I'm saying? No matter who you with and who I'm with, you was the first girl I had feelings for, for real."

She quiet again.

"Me and you, Novisha, right now, we cool. We friends, a'ight?"

"Alright, Ty."

"I gotta go now, okay?"

"Okay. Bye."

We hang up and, I gotta be honest, that felt alright, 'specially after the shit that just went down. Yeah, Novisha disrespected me, but why I gotta stay mad at her for? I ain't my pops.

I cross the street, and it ain't 'til I'm on Grand Concourse that I even notice where I'm walking to. The cell is still in my hand and all I gotta do is go through my contacts real fast and hit the talk button.

"Tyrell?"

"You still sleeping?" I ask.

"No," Jasmine say. "I'm waiting for Emil to get back from the car wash place. We're leaving in a little while. What — what's going on?"

"I'll tell you everything when I see you." I start walking faster.

"Ty, I told you. I'm leaving."

"Tell me this. You wanna go or not?"

She sigh. "You know I don't, but —"

"Then come downstairs. And bring some stuff with you, what you think you gonna need."

"What, where are we —?"

"I don't know. But I wanna be with you. That's all I want."

"Me too," she say, "but —"

"Come with me, then."

Jasmine don't say nothing for a long time and I'm walking to her apartment, hoping she don't say no 'cause right now it feel like she all I got. "Jasmine, you with me or what? 'Cause I —"

"Then stop talking and get here already," she say. "And hurry up."

"A'ight." I smile. "I'ma be there in a minute."